CAPTIVE
SET FREE

OTHER BOOKS BY AL LACY

Angel of Mercy Series:
  A Promise for Breanna (Book One)
  Faithful Heart (Book Two)

Journeys of the Stranger series:
  Legacy (Book One)
  Silent Abduction (Book Two)
  Blizzard (Book Three)
  Tears of the Sun (Book Four)

Battles of Destiny (Civil War series):
  Beloved Enemy (Battle of First Bull Run)
  A Heart Divided (Battle of Mobile Bay)
  A Promise Unbroken (Battle of Rich Mountain)
  Shadowed Memories (Battle of Shiloh)
  Joy From Ashes (Battle of Fredericksburg)
  Season of Valor (Battle of Gettysburg)

CAPTIVE SET FREE

BOOK THREE

AL LACY

MULTNOMAH BOOKS

CAPTIVE SET FREE
published by Multnomah Publishers, Inc.

© 1996 by ALJO Productions, Inc.

Edited by Rodney L. Morris
and Deena Davis
Cover design by David Carlson
Cover illustration by Ed Martinez

International Standard Book Number: 0-88070-872-7

Printed in the United States of America.

For information:
Multnomah Publishers, Inc.
Post Office Box 1720
Sisters, Oregon 97759

Library of Congress Cataloging-in-Publication Data
Lacy, Al.
    Captive set free/Al Lacy.
      p. cm.--(the Angel of mercy series: bk. 3)
    ISBN 0-88070-872-7 (alk. paper)
    I. Title. II. Series: Lacy, Al. Angel of mercy series: 3.
PS3562.A256C37   1996   96-6248
813'.54--dc20   CIP

00 01 02 03 — 8 7 6 5 4

In loving memory of my sweet sister,
Barbie Swisher
who departed this life in January 1992 and is now
in the presence of Jesus.

I miss her very much,
but soon I will see her again
in that bright land of the saints where
"God shall wipe away all tears from their eyes;
and there shall be no more death,
neither sorrow, nor crying."
REVELATION 21:4

1

EARLY MORNING SUNLIGHT crept across the rippling, windswept waters of San Francisco Bay, throwing long shadows over the streets of the city.

At Union Station, Certified Medical Nurse Breanna Baylor noted the low hissing of the big engine as it built up steam, then she turned back to her sister and niece and nephew. Their faces mirrored her own reluctance to leave.

Suddenly the engine's whistle blew three short blasts and the conductor shouted, "All abo-o-oard! All abo-o-ard!"

Eight-year-old James Harper wrapped his arms around Breanna and said tearfully, "I love you, Aunt Breanna."

"I love you, too, James," she said, holding him close and kissing his forehead.

"Will you come back and see us?"

"Someday...of course I will."

James stepped back, wiping tears, and his little sister embraced her aunt. Breanna hugged her back and said, "I love you, sweetheart."

"I love you, too," Molly Kate said. "Promise? You *will* come back and see us?"

"Just as soon as I can," Breanna said, and kissed her cheek.

Breanna was about to embrace her sister when she saw Dr.

Matthew Carroll hurrying along the platform. She grinned and said, "Look who's coming, Dottie."

Dottie's face lit up when she caught sight of the tall, handsome doctor.

He rushed up out of breath, pulled the children close, and said, "I'm glad I made it before the train pulled out, Miss Breanna. I just wanted you to know I'll take good care of Dottie and these kids. Don't worry about them."

"I won't, Doctor," Breanna said.

"Could . . . could a prospective brother-in-law hug you good-bye?" he asked.

Breanna winked at Dottie. "I think that would be appropriate."

When Matthew released Breanna, the sisters hugged each other tightly one last time, tears streaming down their faces.

"All abo-o-ard!"

"I want to hear from you when you set the wedding date," Breanna whispered in Dottie's ear. "You deserve some happiness."

"You'll hear from me," Dottie whispered back. "I love you."

"I love you, too," said Breanna, picking up her overnight bag. "Bye-bye."

Breanna backed toward the platform of car number 3, etching her family's faces into her memory, trying not to think about how long it might be before she saw them again.

Passengers waved to friends and loved ones through the coach windows, and the conductor urged Breanna, "Better hurry and step aboard, ma'am. The train's about to pull out."

Breanna nodded. Just as she took hold of the rail and moved onto the first step, the whistle blew, the big engine ejected a blast of steam, and the train lurched forward. Breanna stayed where she was as the engine chugged forward, funneling black smoke into the sky. She continued to wave until the train curved out of the station and her loved ones passed from view.

Breanna steadied herself by leaning against the door. She pulled a hanky from her sleeve and dabbed at her eyes then picked up her overnight bag and stepped through the door of the swaying coach. It was about two-thirds full and she headed for an unoccupied seat on the right-hand side.

Jubal Brassfield was looking out the window and barely noticed Breanna move past him. When she stopped at an empty seat, the car rocked, causing her to sway off balance. The train continued on a long curve and she decided to wait for it to straighten out before hoisting her bag onto the rack. While she stood there, she caught Brassfield's eye. He glanced at her, looked away, then quickly looked back again.

He left his seat and moved toward Breanna, who stood with one hand gripping the edge of the seat and the other holding the handle of her overnight bag.

"Pardon me, ma'am," Brassfield said. "May I place the bag in the rack for you?"

She lifted her chin and smiled. "Why, thank you, sir. I appreciate that very much."

"Be my pleasure, ma'am," he said.

Breanna knew from his accent that he had to be from somewhere south of the Mason-Dixon line. Just as she let go of the bag, a female voice called from further ahead in the coach.

"Breanna!"

Breanna looked around and saw an older woman smiling and waving at her. It was Myrtle Henderson from Denver.

"Breanna, dear," called Myrtle, "come up here and sit with me!"

Breanna nodded with a warm smile. "The lady is a friend of mine. I had no idea she was on the train. I'll go sit with her. Thank you so much."

"Well, allow me to carry your bag up there, ma'am," he said softly.

"Thank you," she said, and headed up the aisle.

Myrtle scooted next to the window as Breanna approached and patted the seat, saying, "Sit down, dear. It's so nice to see you."

"It's nice to see you, too, Myrtle."

Brassfield placed the overnight bag in the rack, bent over Breanna, and said, "The bag is directly above you, Miss Breanna. It is *Miss* Breanna, isn't it? I don't see a ring on your left hand." His hair was thick and straw-colored, and had a slight natural wave. An unruly whorl fell across his forehead, and eagerness gleamed out of his pale blue eyes.

For an instant, Breanna wondered how the man knew her name, then she remembered that Myrtle had called it out. His boldness, however, made her feel a bit uncomfortable, but she shrugged it off and said, "Yes, I'm Miss Breanna Baylor. And thank you for your kindness, Mr.—?"

"Brassfield, ma'am," he drawled. "Jubal Brassfield."

"All right. Well, thank you for taking care of the bag for me, Mr. Brassfield."

Breanna's words held a tone of dismissal. She then turned to her friend and asked, "What brought you to California, Myrtle?"

Before the older woman could reply, Brassfield bent a little lower and said, "I was a captain in the Confederate Army during the War, ma'am. Fought under Generals Jackson and Beauregard. I come from a cotton-producing family in southern Alabama."

"That's interesting, Mr. Brassfield," Breanna said, then turned back to her friend.

"Perhaps you've heard of the Brassfield plantations, Miss Breanna," Brassfield said. "My three brothers each own a plantation, and I own one, too. All in the Dothan area in southeastern Alabama. My daddy, Aldrich Brassfield, still owns the largest plantation of the five. We're quite well-to-do."

"That's real nice, Mr. Brassfield," said Breanna, finding it harder to smile at the man.

"Where are *you* from, Miss Breanna Baylor?" pressed Brassfield.

Two young black men whose seat faced the interior of the coach had been watching the interchange. Like some of the other passengers, they were perturbed at Brassfield's lack of courtesy.

Breanna forced another smile and said, "I was born and raised in Kansas, Mr. Brassfield. I'm a visiting nurse. Right now, I make my home in Denver."

"Kansas, you say?"

"Yes."

"Kansas was split in the Civil War, ma'am. Which side did your family take?"

"By the time the War started, I had almost no family left. But personally, I took a stand against slavery."

Breanna's bold words caused Brassfield's head to bob, and the distaste he felt at her reply darkened his face. Bitterness twisted his lips, then he threw off the emotion for the sake of gaining her favor.

"I'm returning home from a business trip, Miss Breanna. Been in San Francisco over a month."

"I'm sure your wife will be glad to have you home again, Mr. Brassfield."

"Oh, I don't have a wife, ma'am. But I'm in the market for one. I'm just looking for the right young woman—someone like you, perhaps. Since you wear no ring, I thought—"

"I'm not wearing a ring, Mr. Brassfield, but I *am* spoken for."

Brassfield started to speak again, but Breanna cut him off. "Thank you, Mr. Brassfield, for putting my bag in the rack. Now, if you'll excuse me, I would like to talk to my friend."

The two black men at the front of the coach studied Brassfield with contempt, but they remained silent.

Myrtle Henderson finally told Breanna what had brought her to California—she had been visiting her oldest son and his family in San Jose. While Myrtle described her visit, Jubal Brassfield stood beside Breanna, staring at her. At last, with the two black men watching him warily, he wheeled and returned to his seat.

Four men sat across the aisle from Breanna and Myrtle. They glowered at Brassfield and muttered uneasily among themselves.

Breanna and Myrtle had known each other for quite some time. Myrtle was a patient of Dr. Lyle Goodwin, who was Breanna's sponsoring physician for her work as a visiting nurse. Whenever Breanna was home in Denver between assignments, she worked in Dr. Goodwin's office. This happened often enough that many of Goodwin's patients became well acquainted with the pleasant young nurse.

Myrtle was also a Christian and a member of the same church in Denver as Breanna. They chatted about the church for a few minutes, then Myrtle asked, "Honey, was it your nursing work that brought you to California?"

"In a roundabout way, yes. I was working in South Pass, Wyoming. The town's physician had died, and I was filling in for him until the town's new doctor could get there from back east. A wagon train came through on its way to California at the same time the new doctor arrived. One of the members of the wagon train—a woman—had become quite ill, and her wealthy husband hired me to ride the wagon train with them and care for her. It's a long story, but the poor woman died along the way. So when they arrived in Placerville, I was no longer needed. I figured since I was that close to San Francisco, I would take a little time and visit my sister and her family."

"Oh, yes. Dottie. That's her name, isn't it?"

"Yes."

"You've mentioned her a time or two when we've talked at church. I imagine Dottie was plenty glad to see you."

"Yes, she was. She…"

The train suddenly slowed, then veered onto a sidetrack and chugged to a halt.

Jubal Brassfield rose to his feet and said, "I'll go see what's happening, folks." With that, he was out the rear door of the car.

The passengers peered out the windows and saw that the caboose had been unhooked. Two additional cars were attached to the train. One was a regular coach, which had passengers inside, and the other was painted bright green and had fancy curtains at the windows.

Jubal Brassfield returned. "Folks, the conductor says he will come and explain the reason for this slight delay once the train is underway."

The train chugged backwards after taking on the additional cars and once more linked up with the caboose. There was a brief pause, then the big engine lurched forward and soon the train was back on the main track, picking up speed and heading northeast toward the towering Sierra Nevada mountains.

Breanna and Myrtle settled back, and Myrtle prompted, "You were telling me about Dottie…"

"Yes. Well, do you recall that I told you she was married to a Civil War veteran?"

"Yes. I can't recall his first name, but the last name was Harper."

13

"Jerrod."

"Oh, yes. Jerrod. A farmer, right?"

"Yes. Well, Jerrod had been wounded in the War, and—"

"Excuse me, Miss Breanna," Jubal Brassfield said.

Breanna looked up to see Brassfield standing over her once again. "Yes?"

"Are you going back to Denver, or is your work taking you elsewhere?"

"Why do you ask?"

"Well, I know this train goes directly to Denver. I'm changing trains at Cheyenne City, and I thought that if by some remote chance you were changing trains at Cheyenne City and heading east too, maybe we could…ah…have a meal together."

Breanna spun around on the seat and rose to her feet. "Mr. Brassfield, I'm trying to be nice to you, but you're making it very difficult. I told you that I'm spoken for, which means I'm very much in love with a wonderful man who is very much in love with me. I am not seeing other men in any way, shape, form, or fashion. Not even over a dinner table. Now, I thank you once more for being so kind as to help me with my overnight bag. It was nice of you to do that, and I appreciate it. But—"

"Well, you could show your appreciation by being a little friendlier," he said.

Breanna's mouth fell open. Her cheeks tinted brightly as she stared at the man, not knowing what to say next.

The black men who had watched the interplay between Breanna and Brassfield left their seats and approached Brassfield. "It's apparent, mister," one of them said, "that the lady is not interested in your company. Now, the best thing for you to do is find your seat and sit in it."

The four men across the aisle grew tense with anticipation.

"You stay out of it, blackie!" Brassfield said. "Nobody asked you to butt in!"

"Nobody *had* to ask! This nice lady didn't ask for you to be annoyin' her neither, but you insist on doin' it anyway. Now, like I said, you find your seat and make use of it."

Brassfield squared himself. "I suppose you're man enough to *make* me sit down, blackie!"

Breanna stepped between the two men, facing Brassfield. "Please, Mr. Brassfield, there's nothing to be gained by violence. The episode is over. Just take your seat as the man has advised."

"Hah! I want to see this big-mouth *make* me sit down! C'mon, blackie, try it! I'm gonna throw you off the train!"

The black man looked at Breanna and said, "I'm sorry for the way this man has pestered you, ma'am, but one way or the other, he ain't gonna trouble you no more." Then to Brassfield, he said, "Let's just see you throw me off this train, mister!"

2

"HOLD IT!" One of the men across the aisle sprang up and planted himself between Brassfield and the black man.

His friends followed, closing in on the would-be combatants. The other black man had kept Breanna from falling when Brassfield elbowed her out of his way, and he now stood beside her protectively.

"This is none of your affair, mister!" Brassfield said.

"I'm making it my affair, and so are these men with me. This has gone far enough. Now, back off or else."

"Or else *what?*"

At that moment the conductor appeared. "What's going on here?"

"This man is botherin' the nice lady, Mister Wonderly," the bigger of the two black men said. "I simply told him to go back to his seat and sit down. She don't want him botherin' her."

Wonderly eyed Brassfield, then turned to Breanna. "What about it, ma'am? He bothering you?"

"He was nice to me at first, Conductor. Then he began to make a pest of himself. No harm done. I just want him to leave me alone." She gestured toward the black man. "This gentleman saw that Mr. Brassfield was annoying me and told him to go back to his seat."

Wonderly nodded. To Brassfield, he said, "I assume you know, sir, that if you cause any more trouble, you will be put off the train."

Brassfield nodded slightly.

"All right," said the conductor. "Let this be the end of it. You men may all return to your seats. You first, Mr. Brassfield."

The Southerner glared at the black man and then walked to his seat as if oblivious of the passengers' stares. The conductor excused himself to Breanna and followed Brassfield. He bent over the Southerner and spoke in low tones.

Breanna turned to the six men who had come to her rescue and said, "Thank you, gentlemen. I appreciate what you've done."

The four white men introduced themselves as Carl Lynch, Del Ashmore, Wally Wyman, and Paul Jennings. They told Breanna they had hired on with the railroad to lay track in Colorado and New Mexico.

As they sat down, Breanna thanked the other two men for helping her. Addressing the bigger man, she asked, "What's your name?"

"My name's Moses Crowder, Miss Breanna." He smiled, showing a mouthful of pearly white teeth. "And this is my baby brother, Malachi. We've hired on with the railroad to lay track, too. We're originally from Mississippi, but we've been workin' in San Francisco for the past two years. Work run out, so we hired on with the railroad. That green coach you saw hooked on to the train…"

"Yes?"

"That's Mister Floyd Metz's coach. He's a vice-president of Union Pacific Railroad. He's the one who hired us and these other men, here."

"I see. Well, I'm glad you and Malachi were able to get jobs with the railroad."

"Us too, ma'am," Malachi said.

The conductor returned to the front of the coach and said to Breanna and the Crowder brothers, "If you folks will take your seats, I'll address all the passengers.

"Ladies and gentlemen," said the conductor, lifting his voice above the clatter of the wheels, "since your journey was delayed when we stopped and took on two more cars outside of San Francisco, I feel you are due an explanation. No doubt you noticed that one of the additional coaches was a regular one, and the other was painted bright green. The regular coach is carrying thirty-three Chinese men who, like the Crowder brothers and their four friends over here on my left, have been hired by the railroad to work on a track-laying crew. Union Pacific has been granted permission by the government to run a line from Denver all the way south to Santa Fe, New Mexico. How many of you folks are San Francisco residents?"

A small number of hands went up.

"You know that over the past few years, thousands of Chinese people have immigrated to San Francisco to look for work. Things are so bad in China that multitudes are starving. Because of San Francisco's rapid growth, there have been jobs aplenty for the Chinese men up until the past three or four months. Now there are just too many Chinese and not enough jobs. Many are heading south for Los Angeles, and others are trying to find work in other cities around San Francisco.

"The Union Pacific sent one of our vice-presidents from Denver to hire at least thirty Chinese men to lay track. His name is Floyd Metz, and the green car you saw is his private coach. Mr. Metz was able to hire thirty-three men, as I said, and would have hired more if they had accepted his offer. But few of the married Chinese men were willing to leave their families for that long.

"Since this is the first week of October, the railroad wants to get the track-laying started as soon as possible before winter sets in along the eastern range of the Rockies. Because of this, your trip was delayed a short time. I hope you all understand."

As he spoke the final words, Ralph Wonderly let his eyes roam over the passengers' faces. They seemed to have no questions, so he thanked them for their patience and left the car.

Moses Crowder caught Jubal Brassfield staring at him with hate-filled eyes. He met Brassfield's stare head-on until the wealthy plantation owner finally looked away.

Myrtle Anderson turned to Breanna and said, "Now, honey, you were telling me that your brother-in-law had been wounded in the War. I want to hear about that, but first I want to know about this man you're in love with. This is so exciting."

Breanna eased back on the seat, got a dreamy look in her eyes, and said, "Myrtle, he's the most wonderful man God ever made."

The older woman smiled. "You mean, next to my dear departed husband."

"I would expect you to feel that way!" Breanna said with a laugh.

She started at the beginning and told Myrtle how John Stranger had seemingly come out of nowhere and saved her life during a cattle stampede on the Kansas plains. She went on to explain that John was a Christian, and even, sometimes, a preacher, and that they had fallen deeply in love. Circumstances kept them apart until a few weeks ago when they met again in Wyoming. They planned to marry when it was God's time. Until then, they would both pursue the work the Lord had given them to do.

Breanna then told Myrtle about Jerrod Harper's mental illness. Dr. Matthew Carroll, San Francisco's leading psychiatrist, had treated Jerrod and tried to help him, but Jerrod finally had to be admitted to the insane asylum. When an earthquake toppled the walls of the asylum, Jerrod escaped.

Completely out of his mind, he went to the Harper home to kill Dottie for committing him to the asylum. He did not know that Breanna was staying with the Harper children, and he went after her, thinking she was Dottie. During the struggle, a lantern was knocked over and the house caught fire. Jerrod died in the fire.

"Dr. Carroll is a widower, Myrtle," Breanna said. "He fell in love with Dottie and has proposed marriage. I feel sure the Lord got them together and that Dottie will accept his proposal. The children adore him, and I'm so happy about it. Not only is he an excellent physician and psychiatrist, he's also a devoted Christian."

"It's marvelous how things have turned out for Dottie and the children, Breanna. I just wish you and John could marry as well."

"We will, in God's time. I miss John so much and want to be his wife as soon as the Lord allows it, but at least I know I have his undying love and the satisfaction that he knows he has mine."

"That's wonderful, honey," said Myrtle. "I'm sure the Lord will let you two marry soon."

The railroad had printed a schedule of the San Francisco-Denver journey and left one in a small rack beside each seat. Myrtle picked one up and said, "I assume you've never taken this trip by train between San Francisco and Denver before."

"No."

"Well, let's see where we'll be stopping before we get to Denver."

Breanna learned that their first stop would be Reno, Nevada, after they crossed the High Sierras and dropped down on the east side. From there, the train would continue on a northeasterly route to Winnemucca, then Elko, Nevada, and on to Promontory Point, Utah, where the first transcontinental railroad track opened in 1869 to join both coasts by rail.

From Promontory Point, the train would head southeast to Ogden, Utah, and on to Evanston, Wyoming. After stopping at Evanston, they would run past Fort Bridger, briefly stopping at points in between before stopping at Cheyenne City. There, passengers going east would change to another train, and the one Breanna and Myrtle were on would head due south to Denver.

The brochure advised that the trip from San Francisco to Denver would cover 1,494 miles, averaging 30 miles per hour, with ten stops. The train would be en route for 50 hours.

Breanna squeezed Myrtle's arm. "I'm sure glad we happened to be in the same car. Your company will make this long trip more enjoyable."

The older woman patted Breanna's hand. "I'm glad too, honey. It'll give us a chance to get to know each other better."

Breanna and her friend noticed the conductor enter through the coach's front door and ask Moses Crowder, "Everything all right?"

"Yes, sir."

"He hasn't shown any more signs of giving you trouble?"

"Not exactly, sir."

"What do you mean, not exactly?"

"He stared at me pretty hard for a while, but I stared back, and he finally looked away."

"Well, you let me know if he makes another move toward you."

"Yes, sir."

Carl Lynch rose from his seat and stepped close to the conductor. "Excuse me, Mr. Wonderly."

"Yes?"

"My friends and I were just discussing the Chinese men we'll be working with. None of us have ever been around Chinese people before. Do you have any idea how they are to work with?"

"Well, it just so happens I do."

Ashmore, Wyman, and Jennings left their seats and joined Lynch, curiosity showing in their eyes. Moses and Malachi Crowder moved closer too. At the other end of the car, Jubal Brassfield watched the gathering, wondering what they were talking about.

"I've worked around Chinese quite a bit," Wonderly said. "They're humble people. I've always found them to be very polite, easy to work with, and willing to work hard. You'll find them enjoyable work companions."

While the men asked the conductor more questions, Breanna's ears picked up the cry of a baby from the rear of the car. It was more than a normal cry; the little thing was in pain.

When the crying did not let up after several minutes, Breanna turned to see where the baby was. Her eyes met Jubal Brassfield's momentarily, then she saw the mother two rows behind him. The woman looked frustrated and worried and had the child wrapped in a blanket and pressed to her shoulder, patting its back. A man across the aisle scowled at them.

"I'm going to see if there's anything I can do to help that baby," Breanna whispered to Myrtle.

"Poor little tyke," Myrtle said. "I hope you can."

Just as Breanna was about to rise from her seat, a young man approached the conductor from the rear of the coach.

"Mr. Wonderly, my name is Clint Byers. I'd like to know if the railroad is still hiring men for the track-laying crew."

"I'm not sure. I would think so. The best thing would be for you to talk to Mr. Metz in his private car."

"All right. Do I just go and knock on his door?"

"No. You'll be received more warmly if I take you to him. We can go right now. You say your name is Byers?"

"Yes, sir. Clint Byers."

The baby was still crying. When the men saw Breanna stand up, they cleared a path so she could get past them.

"Thank you, gentlemen," she said, smiling.

Suddenly the coach lurched to one side, and Breanna stumbled against Byers. He grabbed her arms and kept her from falling into the lap of another passenger.

"Thank you, Mr. Byers. If you hadn't caught me, I'm afraid I would've taken a tumble. That would be rather embarrassing for a lady."

"You're welcome, ma'am—Miss Breanna, isn't it? I heard the lady you were sitting with call you Breanna."

"Yes. Breanna Baylor. I'm a visiting nurse. I work out of Dr. Lyle Goodwin's office in Denver. I heard you ask Mr. Wonderly about a job laying track."

"Yes, ma'am."

"Is Denver your home, Mr. Byers?"

"You can call me Clint, ma'am."

"All right. Is Denver your home, Clint?"

"No, ma'am. San Francisco is my home, but some things happened there that made me want to pack up and move elsewhere. I'm heading for Denver. When I left, I figured Denver might be a good place to find a job. I didn't know about the railroad hiring until Mr. Wonderly told us about it."

"Well, if Mr. Metz doesn't hire you, please let me know. I might be able to help."

"Oh?"

"I'm acquainted with many of the leading businessmen in

Denver. Dr. Goodwin is their physician, and when I'm home between assignments, I help treat them and their families. If this railroad job doesn't work out, I'll try to help you find employment when we get to Denver."

"Well, ma'am, I really appreciate that. Thank you. I'll let you know after I've seen Mr. Metz."

"Ready to go?" asked Wonderly.

"Yes, sir."

Breanna proceeded down the aisle ahead of them, heading for the mother with the crying baby.

Above the child's wailing, Breanna said, "Ma'am, my name is Breanna Baylor. I'm a certified medical nurse. I wondered if I might be of help to you?"

"Oh, of course. I'd appreciate that."

Jubal Brassfield had tried to catch Breanna's eye as she passed him, but she purposely avoided him. He half-turned in his seat to watch her as she talked to the worried young mother, who made room for Breanna to sit down. Breanna looked at the tiny, twisted face of the infant and asked, "What's her name?"

"Susannah."

"Oh, I love that name. May I examine her?"

The mother handed the wailing infant to Breanna, who laid the baby in her lap. She removed the blanket and bared the infant's belly. She gently felt the little girl's middle, then asked, "Has she been constipated?"

"No."

"Diarrhea?"

"No."

Breanna continued pressing with experienced fingers. After a few minutes, she said, "It appears to be a severe case of colic. I have a medical kit in my overnight bag up ahead. I'll mix some powders with water and give them to her. I think she'll feel better in no time." She wrapped Susannah with the blanket again and handed her back to her mother, then quickly hurried up the aisle. She was reaching for the overnight bag when Moses Crowder stood up and said, "Here, Miss Breanna, let me get that bag for you."

Brassfield had followed Breanna and now scowled at Crowder. "I'll get it for her, blackie! She's a white woman. You stay away from her!"

Breanna turned on him. "You insolent, contemptible cad! The color of Moses' skin does not keep him from being a gentleman. The Civil War is over, Mr. Brassfield! The slaves have been set free. If you were one-tenth the gentleman Moses Crowder is, you'd have something to brag about, but as far as I can see, you haven't got an ounce of gentleman in your whole body. I am happy to let Moses get my bag for me. As for you, you are excused!"

Jubal Brassfield just stood there, trying to think how to answer her, when the four men across the aisle rose from their seats. "The lady said you're excused, mister," Carl Lynch said. "Would you like me to help you find your seat?"

Brassfield shot Moses a hateful look, gave Breanna a piece of it, then swore under his breath and headed for his seat.

Moses grasped the overnight bag and handed it to Breanna, giving her a broad smile. "There you are, Miss Breanna. With my compliments."

"Thank you, Moses. You're very kind."

"It's a pleasure to serve you, ma'am."

Moses and the other men sat down as Breanna walked back down the aisle and sat beside mother and baby.

"That Brassfield is an obnoxious character, isn't he?" the mother said in a half whisper.

"That's putting it mildly. Now, let's take care of little Susannah here."

Breanna pulled her medical kit from the overnight bag and found the envelopes containing powders. She mixed certain powders with water and began spoon-feeding the mixture to the child.

3

FLOYD METZ SAT COMFORTABLY in an overstuffed horsehair chair inside his private coach, watching the tawny fields and rounded hills of northern California roll by. He took a puff on his Havana cigar and drained the whiskey from his glass. He smacked his lips and walked across plush carpet to the bar lined with liquor bottles.

As he reached for the whiskey bottle, he caught a glimpse of his image in the mirror above the bar. His face was so round that when he smiled, it almost squeezed his eyes shut. He had only a fringe of graying hair above his protruding ears, but he wore heavy muttonchop sideburns all the way to his rounded jawbones.

Metz lifted the glass to his thick lips and gulped a generous swig. He gazed at his reflection with admiration and chuckled aloud. "Well, Floyd, ol' boy, you did good in San Francisco. Thirty-nine new men. Morgan's gonna be pleased. Maybe when he learns what an excellent job you did, you'll finally get to meet him in person."

He tossed the rest of the whiskey down and belched as he set the glass on the bar. *Tap-tap-tap.* Now, who could be at the door? He didn't feel like talking to anyone at the moment.

"Yes?"

"It's Ralph Wonderly, Mr. Metz," came the muffled reply.

"What is it, Ralph?"

"I have a young man here who wants to talk to you about joining the track-laying crew, sir."

Metz hurried across the carpet, eased his portly body into a chair and called, "Come in!"

The door opened, letting the loud rattle of wheels invade the relative quiet of the well-insulated coach.

"Mr. Metz, this is Clint Byers," Wonderly said. "He's on his way to Denver to find employment. He wants to talk to you about laying track."

"All right." Metz nodded, his double chin wobbling. "You can go back to your job. I'll talk to him."

When Wonderly was gone, Metz said, "Come closer, boy."

There was another overstuffed chair, but Metz did not ask Byers to sit down. Metz took a puff of his cigar, blew smoke out of the side of his mouth, and asked, "You ever lay track before, boy?"

"No, sir. But I can learn."

"What was your name again?"

"Clint Byers, sir."

Floyd Metz liked being called sir. "Where's home?"

"It has been San Francisco, sir, but something happened there that made me want to leave."

"And what was that?"

Byers's face tinted with embarrassment. "Well, sir, I was engaged to be married to a young woman there, but...she broke off the engagement to marry another man."

"Mmm. Kind of tough, huh?"

"Not only that, sir, but my parents were killed in the earthquake that hit the city a few weeks ago. I have no siblings, nor any other family there. So there's really no reason to stay. I decided to go to Denver. I hear it's a growing town, and I figured I could find a job and start a new life. When Mr. Wonderly told us about the men you'd hired, I thought maybe Union Pacific could use a few more. I asked him about it, and he said I should talk to you."

"How old are you?"

"Twenty-three, sir."

"You're not real beefy, but you look strong and healthy."

"Yes, sir."

"What kind of work were you doing in San Francisco?"

"Construction, sir. Heavy work. I can handle laying track, I assure you."

"Well, the pay's good. Two dollars a day, plus a railroad car to sleep in and meals provided by the company. Sound okay?"

"Sure does, sir!"

"Then you're hired."

"Thank you, sir!"

"This particular job, Byers, is laying track between Denver and Santa Fe. You are aware of that."

"Yes, sir."

"It'll take anywhere from a year-and-a-half to two years to complete the job, depending on the weather and how many men we have in the crew. You'll be paid even on the days the weather prohibits track-laying."

"Thank you, sir."

Metz leaned forward and spoke around the cigar. "Do a good job, Byers, and we'll use you on the next track-laying project. Okay?"

"Yes, sir!"

Clint shook Metz's hand and left the plush coach, then entered car number 5, which carried the Chinese men. Many of

31

them smiled at him as they had when he passed through earlier. He smiled back and stepped onto the platform leading into the next car.

In car number 3, Breanna Baylor finished giving the medicine to little Susannah. Already the baby's crying had subsided.

Her mother held the tiny bundle close to her and smiled at Breanna. "Thank you so much, Miss Baylor," she said, reaching for her purse. "How much do I owe you?"

"Absolutely nothing."

"But that's not right. You make your living as a nurse."

"I do fine. There's no need for you to pay me."

"But…even if you donate your services, the medicine costs you."

"What little I used for Susannah won't be missed," Breanna said, rising to her feet and picking up the overnight bag. "The dose I gave her will probably do it, but if she needs more, it'll be on the house, too."

"God bless you."

"He does, ma'am. He blesses me by letting me meet people like you and little Susannah. Call me if you need me."

With that, Breanna moved up the aisle. When the Crowder brothers saw Breanna coming, Malachi jumped up first, telling Moses it was his turn to be a gentleman. He took the overnight bag and placed it in the rack overhead. Breanna could see that Myrtle was fast asleep, so she turned to the Crowder brothers. "I need some fresh air. Think I'll step outside for a while."

"You want one of us to go with you, Miss Breanna?"

"That's nice of you, Moses, but I'll be fine. Thank you."

When Breanna pulled the front door of the coach open, she found two men in conversation and decided to go to the other end. As she passed through the car, she avoided Brassfield's eyes.

The air was fresh and sweet, coming off the fields of grass.

Breanna held onto the rail and drew in deep breaths.

Brassfield waited four or five minutes then rose to his feet. At the other end of the coach, Moses saw him pass through the door and said to his brother, "He's followin' her outside."

"I see that. What are you gonna do?"

"I oughtta go out there and make sure he ain't botherin' her."

"Maybe you oughtta just find the conductor and tell him about it."

"Yeah. Maybe."

When another minute had passed, Moses said, "If I ain't back in five minutes, you find Mister Wonderly and bring him." Even as he spoke, Moses Crowder headed down the aisle.

Breanna was enjoying the fresh air and the beautiful view. The wind toyed with her hair as she watched a flock of ducks pass overhead. She thought of John Stranger and wondered how things were going for him in Arizona. Chief U.S. Marshal Solomon Duvall in Denver had asked him to ride to Apache Junction, Arizona, and help the town marshal, who was facing some kind of trouble.

Breanna's eyes took in the golden sun on distant hills as she whispered endearing words to the man she loved. The door opened behind her, and she turned to see who had come out. Jubal Brassfield grinned at her.

"I just wanted to make sure you were all right," he said.

"I'm fine, and I would like to have a few minutes alone, please."

"Look, Miss Breanna, I think you'd like me if you got to know me."

"I really don't need to get to know you, Mr. Brassfield. You're looking for a wife, and I'm not available. And even if I were available, you wouldn't interest me. What's the point then? As I just told you, I'd like to be alone."

Brassfield sighed a quick gust of irritation. "Wouldn't be interested in me, huh? Well, just what is it about me that your highness doesn't like?"

"Don't get me started, it would take too long. I want some peace and quiet, Mr. Brassfield. Would you please leave me alone?"

Clint Byers came out of the next car just as Brassfield said, "You don't own this coach, Miss high and mighty! I have as much right to stand on this platform as you do!"

"Then stand on the other side!"

"Hey, what is this?" Byers asked, stepping to the platform from the other car.

"None of your business!" Brassfield said. "On your way!"

"The lady doesn't want anything to do with you, mister! Can't you see that? Now, you leave her be! Have you forgotten that Southern men are supposed to be gentlemen?"

"Maybe you're man enough to *make* me leave her be!" Brassfield said.

"It wouldn't take much of a man to handle you, smart-mouth!"

Breanna flattened herself against the coach as Byers ducked Brassfield's hissing fist and threw his shoulder into Brassfield's chest, knocking him off balance. Brassfield tried to unleash another punch, but Byers threw a neck-hold on him.

Suddenly it turned into a wrestling match. Both men were dangerously close to the edge of the platform.

Byers grabbed his wrist with his free hand and compressed Brassfield's neck in the crook of his arm with all the strength he could muster. The two of them whirled round and round, slamming against the iron railing.

Breanna stayed flattened against the wall of the coach, biting her lips and praying that Clint Byers would not get hurt.

Suddenly Brassfield used his weight advantage to bend Byers over the rail.

"Stop it! You'll kill him!" Breanna yelled.

Breanna leaped on Brassfield's back and dug her fingernails into his eyes, screaming for him to stop. The Southerner let out a roar, shaking his head in an attempt to free himself from her.

The door burst open and Moses Crowder rushed through. For a brief instant, Brassfield let go of Byers with one hand and grabbed Breanna's wrist, breaking her hold. He elbowed her violently, and the blow knocked Breanna backward. She staggered toward the edge of the platform, where Moses caught her and helped her stand once again with her back against the wall.

"Stay here!" he shouted, and wheeled to attack Brassfield.

Breanna screamed as she saw Brassfield throw Byers's flailing body off the platform. He hit the ground and passed from view.

Brassfield turned and swung at Moses. The punch missed, and Moses landed a hard right that sent Brassfield reeling off the platform.

The train had left the grassy area where Clint Byers had fallen and now threaded its way among rocks and boulders. Brassfield landed on a large rock, his body tumbling over and over.

The conductor and Malachi Crowder opened the door in time to see Moses knock Brassfield off the platform. The conductor dashed back inside and pulled the emergency brake cord. Immediately the wheels locked and shot sparks as steel scraped on steel in a shrill, high-pitched squeal.

The train finally came to a stop. Breanna rushed past the Crowder brothers and bounded down the platform steps. Moses, Malachi, and the conductor were right behind her. As she ran, Breanna saw Clint Byers get to his feet and wave as he staggered toward the train.

The three men caught up with Breanna, and Wonderly took hold of her arm, slowing her to a walk. "Don't push yourself too hard, Miss Baylor," he said, gasping for breath. "Let Moses and Malachi get to Brassfield first."

The two brothers went on ahead, and Breanna cupped her hands around her mouth and shouted, "Moses! If he's alive, don't move him! I want to examine him first!"

Moses waved an acknowledgment, and soon Breanna saw him and Malachi kneel down. Brassfield was lying face-up with watermelon-sized rocks around and underneath him.

Moses looked up as Breanna and the conductor drew near. "He's alive, Miss Breanna, but he's in pretty bad shape. His head's bleedin'."

While Breanna examined Brassfield, the engineer, brakeman, and fireman arrived, along with a waddling, cigar-puffing Floyd Metz. Moses and the conductor explained what had happened as Byers approached the group on shaky legs. Breanna looked up from where she bent over Brassfield and asked Byers if he had any broken bones. He assured her he didn't. Breanna told him to sit down for a moment and catch his breath.

"What do you think, Miss Baylor?" asked the conductor.

She shook her head and said, "Mr. Brassfield has a bad head injury. He's losing some blood. I'm sure his left arm is broken, and I think his collarbone is too. We need to get him on the train. If you can have a couple of people move elsewhere, I'd like to put Mr. Brassfield on one of the seats."

"I'll take care of it, ma'am."

When the train was once again in motion, Myrtle Henderson helped Breanna wash the blood from the unconscious man's head in preparation for bandaging. The details of the incident had spread through the train, and people were talking about it in hushed tones.

Moses hovered over nurse and patient, telling Breanna how bad he felt that Brassfield was hurt so seriously. He had not meant to knock him off the platform. Breanna assured Moses that she understood, as did the railroad officials on the train.

By noon the train was climbing the steep slopes into the Sierra Nevada mountains, winding among sheer rock canyon walls and rocky clefts heavily fringed with timber.

By midafternoon, Brassfield had not yet regained consciousness. Moses watched as the two women joined hands and bowed their heads. When the prayer was finished, Myrtle quietly returned to her seat, leaving Breanna alone with Brassfield. Moses crossed the aisle, bent over Breanna, and asked, "What do you think, Miss Breanna?"

"I'm afraid he's going to die, Moses. It's hard for me to tell just how bad he's hurt. I can't see inside his head."

"I didn't mean for him to die, Miss Breanna. All I wanted to do was keep him from hurtin' you."

"I know that, Moses," she said, patting his shoulder. "You simply did what you had to do. You're not guilty of anything but doing what was right at the moment."

"Thank you, ma'am. Miss Breanna…I saw you and the other lady prayin'. Are you a born-again type Christian?"

"I sure am, Moses. Jesus lives in my heart because I asked Him to come in many years ago. How about you? Are you a child of God too?"

"Yes'm. I sure am. I took Jesus into my heart when I was twelve. Malachi is a Christian, too."

"That's wonderful, Moses. That makes you and Malachi my brothers in the family of God."

"Oh, yes, ma'am. And you're our sister, too!"

Breanna kept a vigil at Jubal Brassfield's side as the train reached the top of the pass and headed down the east side of the mountains toward Reno, Nevada. The conductor came by from time to time to check on Brassfield's condition.

They had been over the pass about an hour when Breanna covered Brassfield's face with a towel. Myrtle rose to her feet and moved to Breanna.

"Is he…?"

"Yes. He just died."

Moses heard Breanna's words and stepped across the aisle with Malachi on his heels. "I didn't mean to kill him, Miss Breanna!"

"We all know that, Moses," she said soothingly. "So does the Lord. Don't punish yourself. Like I said, you did what you had to do at the time. You saw him almost knock me off the platform, and you saw him throw Clint off. You only reacted as a real man would. I'm sorry about this tragedy, too, but Mr. Brassfield's death was his own fault."

Moses nodded slowly. "Yes'm."

Malachi found the conductor and told him of Brassfield's death. As the conductor talked with Breanna, he said he would have the body carried to the baggage coach, which was just behind the coal car. When they reached Reno, he would turn the body over to the authorities, who would try to contact Brassfield's family in Alabama.

The Crowder brothers, along with Carl Lynch and Wally Wyman, volunteered to carry the body to the baggage coach. When they had gone, Clint Byers told Breanna he was having pain in his back and between his shoulder blades. She sat him down and worked her fingers across his back, telling him that he had no doubt strained some muscles.

"Sometimes this kind of injury doesn't show up until several hours after it happens," she said.

"Sort of delayed reaction, huh?"

"Yes. I'll give you some belladonna. I have some in my medical kit."

"What's that?"

Breanna smiled. "It's a perennial European herb. It relieves pain and also checks nerve spasms. That's what you're experiencing right now. You'll feel a lot better within a half hour after I give it to you."

"Sounds good to me."

Breanna took belladonna powders from her medical bag and mixed them in a cup of water. "How did it go with Mr. Metz?" she asked.

"Oh, real good. He hired me. Said if I do a good job, he'll put me on more track-laying jobs when this one's finished."

"Well, I'm glad."

"But I want to thank you for offering to help me find work if this hadn't panned out. It was awfully nice of you."

"You're welcome. I just care about people."

"That's evident, ma'am. You'd have to care about people to be a nurse."

"Can't argue with that."

Clint Byers was also hurting in his heart. Finding Breanna to be compassionate and understanding, he decided to talk to her about getting jilted. After downing the belladonna mixture, he told his story. Breanna listened quietly, then told him she had once been jilted but had since fallen in love with a wonderful man named John Stranger.

"Clint, I know Someone who can take the hurt from your heart," Breanna said.

"Pardon me, ma'am?"

"His name is Jesus Christ."

"Oh. Yes. God's Son."

"That's right. You believe Jesus is the Son of God?"

"Yes, ma'am. My grandmother used to talk to me about Him, and read to me from the Bible."

"Did Grandma explain that you must open your heart to Jesus in repentance of your sin and ask Him to save you?"

Clint cleared his throat nervously. "Yes, ma'am."

"You know if you don't let Jesus save you, you can't go to heaven, don't you?"

"Grandma told me that, yes."

"Well, Grandma was right, Clint. You need to take care of that matter. It isn't something to put off. What if you'd landed on rocks like Jubal Brassfield? You could be dead now. You'd be in hell. Do you understand that?"

Clint gritted his teeth against the pain in his back and shoulders and stood to his feet. "I won't bother you any longer, Miss Breanna. I'll head back to my seat, now."

Breanna touched his arm and said, "I'm serious, Clint. Don't put Jesus off."

"I appreciate your concern, Miss Breanna. I...ah...I need some more time to think about it. Thank you for the belladonna."

Don't give him any rest, Lord, till he opens his heart to You, Breanna prayed.

The train stopped in Reno as the sun was going down. Jubal Brassfield's body was delivered to the town marshal, and then the train headed northeast toward Winnemucca.

Darkness had fallen when the conductor entered car number 3 from the rear door. Breanna was asleep with her head on Myrtle's shoulder.

Myrtle looked up as Wonderly stopped and said, "I'm sorry, ma'am, but I'm going to have to wake her. I need her services."

"I'm sure she won't mind," Myrtle said. She squeezed Breanna's hand and said, "Honey, Mr. Wonderly needs to talk to you."

Breanna stirred and opened her eyes, blinking. "Hmm?"

"Miss Baylor, I need your help."

Breanna sat up straight, rubbed her face, and said, "Of course. What is it?"

"I've got a problem in car number 5, ma'am. One of the Chinese men is ill."

"All right," she nodded, standing up. "I'll get my medical kit."

Breanna followed the conductor and found the sick man laid on a seat. He had a high fever and his face was blotched with red marks.

The other Asian men watched with concern as the nurse examined the man by lantern light. A few of the Chinese men knew English, and through one of them interpreting, the sick man told her he had a very sore throat. Breanna's face turned grim when she looked inside his mouth. She opened his shirt and checked his chest, finding red blotches there, also.

As she buttoned the man's shirt, she looked up at the conductor and said, "Mr. Wonderly, this is not good. He has scarlet fever."

"Scarlet fever! That's highly contagious!"

"Very much so, and very serious." She turned to the man who had been interpreting for her. "What is your name?"

"Chung Ho, Missy." He smiled, bowing his head slightly.

"My name is Breanna Baylor, Chung Ho. Will you ask the men if any of them are not feeling well?"

Breanna waited while Chung Ho spoke to the others in Chinese. Most of them shook their heads no, but two of them pointed to their throats and spoke words Breanna did not understand.

Chung Ho said, "Missy Breanna Baylor, these two say they have sore throats and headaches."

"These symptoms are early signs of scarlet fever, Mr. Wonderly. We must isolate all three men immediately."

"We can put them in the baggage coach, ma'am," he said. "There's room in there to lay down. Or we could put them in the caboose. Of course, if we do that, the brakeman will have to vacate it."

"The baggage coach will do fine," said Breanna. "I'll need you to stop the train so we can take them there without passing through the other cars. I don't want to expose anyone else."

When the train stopped, the three sick men stumbled their way to the baggage coach by the light of the conductor's lantern. Wonderly slid the large side door open, and Breanna helped them climb inside. Wonderly found spare blankets for the men to lie on.

Breanna hung the lantern on a hook and looked down at Wonderly, who was about to close the door from the outside. "When we get to Winnemucca, I must find the town's doctor and pharmacist, no matter what time of night. I've got to have sage leaves to make tea and water bottles to give them cold enemas. Without them, these men could die. I'll also need a barrel of water brought to this coach. These men must have plenty of fluids."

"I'll see that you get everything you need, ma'am."

Breanna was supplied with sage leaves and three water bottles in Winnemucca, though it was the middle of the night. When the train resumed its journey, Breanna heard the rear door of the baggage coach open and looked up to see Myrtle Henderson.

"Don't come in here!"

"It's okay, honey. I've had scarlet fever. Mr. Wonderly told us what was going on, and a few people spoke up, saying they had had scarlet fever and offering to help you. Mr. Wonderly decided to let me come and help because he knew we are friends."

✦

In his private coach, Floyd Metz swore a blue streak as he paced the floor. Why did this have to happen? What if more of the Chinese men came down with scarlet fever? Morgan would be furious if he didn't get the workers Metz had promised him.

In the baggage coach, fever soon showed up in the other two men. Under Breanna's directions, Myrtle helped her administer cold water enemas and bathe the bodies of the inflicted men to bring down the fever, then give them hot blue sage tea. The tea would bring out more rash and help them reach the illness's crisis point sooner.

While the two women worked to save the men's lives, Myrtle told Breanna of her bout with scarlet fever some thirty years previously. When she had told the story, she asked, "What about you, honey? Have you had it?"

"No." Breanna was bent over the man she was caring for and did not look up.

Myrtle's face paled. "Breanna! It'll be a miracle if you don't come down with it."

THE GRAY SKY LOOKED FLAT and hard as Mae Trotter stepped out the back door of her house. It was early morning on the Colorado plains, and a raw gust of October wind hit her in the face.

Mae was a thin woman in her late forties, but she looked older. The lines in her face gave silent evidence of the hard life she had lived on the plains with her husband and three sons.

The Trotter ranch, the *Bar T,* was located some fifteen miles due east of Denver, and they had experienced almost as many bad years as good in raising cattle and producing the grass and hay to feed them. Hard winters had left some of their cattle frozen to death, and dry years had reduced the production of the fields.

The Trotters had grown bitter over their problems and carried a grudge against God and the weather. They also carried a grudge against their neighbors, who seemed to handle the hard times better. Their bitterness had grown even deeper six weeks earlier over the loss of their oldest son, Willie.

Mae's graying hair was pulled into a matronly bun, but the wind found some loose strands and whipped them into her eyes. She brushed them back and stepped off the porch. Every day since they had planted Willie's body in the unfeeling ground, she had visited the grave at sunrise and at sunset. It was a vigil she planned to maintain until they planted her in the same sod.

She looked toward the simple wooden grave marker beneath the willows. The grave mound had settled since Willie was buried in late August and now was almost level with the ground. Her throat tightened and her hands balled into fists as she stood there. The memory of her last look at Willie's face fused itself into her consciousness like a brand seared into flesh.

Deputy Sheriff Curt Langan had brought Willie's body home, draped over the back of his own horse. Harley and their two other sons, Chad and Cy, were in the yard at the time. They had laid Willie's lifeless body on the front porch and called Mae from the kitchen. When she stepped out on the porch, she saw the colorless features of her oldest son frozen in death.

Langan, who was in his late twenties, had been deputy to Denver County Sheriff Brad Yates for seven years. He stood that day with a solemn look on his face and told the Trotters that three hours earlier, Sheriff Yates had been summoned to the Lone Pine Saloon in Denver to break up a fight between Willie and a gambler named Dick Castin.

When the sheriff entered the saloon, he found Willie holding a gun on the gambler, hammer cocked, cursing him for cheating in the poker game they had been playing. Yates was trying to talk Willie Trotter out of shooting Castin when Willie suddenly turned and shot the sheriff, killing him on the spot. At the same instant, Langan bolted through the batwing doors, gun drawn, and told Willie to drop his weapon. Willie cocked the hammer and swung his gun on the deputy. Langan fired first, his bullet exploding Willie's heart.

The Trotters railed against Langan, telling him he could have shot Willie to wound him. Langan declared he had no choice but to shoot to kill, and two dozen witnesses agreed. The

Trotters were welcome to question each one, which they did. But they had never given in to the facts. As far as they were concerned, Langan—who succeeded Yates as sheriff—had murdered Willie.

The smoldering anger Mae carried deep inside thickened her voice as she stood over the grave. "You were a good boy, Willie. You never deserved to die like you did. Langan could have spared you if he'd wanted to. Sheriff Yates should've let you kill Castin for cheatin' you, anyway. He had it comin'. And now your poor mother will never lay eyes on you again. I'll never hear your laughter or those compliments you always gave me about my cookin'. And it's all that no-good Curt Langan's fault.

"If I hadn't talked turkey to your pa and your brothers, they'd have gone after Langan and shot him down like a mangy cur. But I told 'em it wasn't worth it. The law would just come after 'em and hang 'em for it, then I'd have nobody. You just rest in peace, son. Ma's not gonna forget you. I'll...I'll be back this evenin' and talk to you again."

Chad, at twenty-four, was the Trotters' second son. He stood at his bedroom window on the second floor and watched his mother step off the back porch and head for Willie's grave.

Chad's father and younger brother had left two days earlier to hunt big game in the mountains west of Denver. They had asked him to go, but Chad didn't think it wise to leave his mother, since she was still grieving so hard over Willie.

Chad let his hatred for Sheriff Langan boil over as he watched his mother beating a path to the grave, bending her body against the wind. *Langan had to die.* Chad couldn't bring Willie back, but the only thing that was going to give some peace and satisfaction to his mother was seeing Langan dead.

When Mae entered the kitchen a quarter of an hour later, the smell of hot coffee filled the room. She stepped to the stove and moved the steaming coffeepot to a cool spot and glanced at the setting for two on the kitchen table. Past time for breakfast; where was that son of hers? She moved along the narrow hall toward the front of the house, passing her sewing room and Cy's bedroom and moved to the bottom of the stairs at the edge of the parlor.

"Chad! You about ready? It's time for breakfast!"

When there was no answer, she called again, "Chad! Breakfast!"

Dead silence. Mae lifted her skirt and stomped up the stairs. The door to Chad's bedroom stood wide open. "Chad!" She moved inside the room, eyes flitting from side to side. His bed was made up, and his gunbelt was not on the bedpost where he always hung it.

Mae wheeled and ran the length of the hall and down the stairs. She bolted out the back door toward the barn.

Chad's chestnut mare was not in the corral, and his saddle was not in the barn. She darted to the front of the house and stopped when she saw Chad astride the mare, turning onto the road a half mile to the west. There was no use calling to him. Chad would never hear her above the howl of the wind. She stared after the diminishing figure of horse and rider.

Mae turned back toward the house and tried to convince herself that her son was going to town for some kind of business deal he hadn't mentioned to her. Chad was always picking up extra money to help the family's finances by doing different kinds of work that he never explained. He was a good boy.

Time passed slowly for Mae Trotter. She cleaned the kitchen for about an hour, then settled down in her sewing room to make

Chad a new shirt. She thought of all the shirts she had made for Willie and wept as she realized she would never make him another one. Willie was buried in a shirt Mae had made for him—one she had just finished and he had never worn before. She wasn't going to let him be buried in that shirt with the bullet hole and blood on it. Langan could have taken Willie alive if he'd wanted to. All lawmen were killers at heart. Used their badges to murder and get away with it.

It rained lightly for a while. Mae looked out the window of her sewing room and told herself the raindrops were almost snowflakes. It wouldn't be long till the snow would fly again. She glanced toward the pasture and let her eyes take in the *Bar T* cattle. They were bunched up along the fence, tails turned toward the wind.

About noon the rain stopped and the clouds began to break up. By two o'clock the sun was shining and the air smelled fresh and clean. The wind had become a slight breeze.

Mae returned to the kitchen, stoked up the fire in the cookstove, and began kneading dough to make bread. Harley and Cy would be home late this evening or tomorrow morning. They would be hungry. Chad...Chad would be home before sundown. He'd be hungry for sure.

When the bread was in the oven, Mae looked up at the old clock on the kitchen wall. Three o'clock. Since the wind had died down, she would go out and sweep the leaves off both porches. When she had finished the back porch, she rounded the house to the front. She had just begun to sweep when movement caught the corner of her eye.

Mae looked up to see two horses turning toward the house where the lane met the road. Only one horse had a rider. Mae's breath hitched in her chest.

She tried to bring the horses and rider into focus. Was that lead horse Sheriff Langan's? Too far away to tell yet, but the rider was tall in the saddle and broad-shouldered like Langan.

That familiar cold stone settled in Mae's stomach again as the horses drew closer. It was Curt Langan, all right. And the horse he was leading was definitely Chad's mare.

Then she saw it—a man draped over the saddle of Chad's horse. She gripped the broom handle, sucked in a painful breath, and moaned, "No! No!"

Sheriff Langan dreaded the confrontation with Harley and Mae Trotter and their remaining son, Cy. His deputy, young Steve Ridgway, had volunteered to return the body to the *Bar T* and break the news to the Trotters, but Langan had told him it was his responsibility since he had killed Chad. Steve had pressed the sheriff to let him go along. Harley and Cy might just decide to try to gun him down.

Langan told Ridgway he was needed in town in case of trouble. The sheriff would have to take his chances with Harley and Cy Trotter.

Curt Langan saw Mae standing on the porch like a statue. Her eyes stared in disbelief, her face rigid. As he drew up to the porch, Langan touched his hatbrim and said, "Mrs. Trotter, I'm sorry about this, but Chad gave me no choice."

The sheriff let his eyes flick toward the front door of the house, expecting to see Harley or Cy any second.

For a moment, Mae was unable to speak as her eyes stayed riveted on the body of her dead son.

Langan's eyes darted from one side of the house to the other. Where were Harley and Cy? Looking back at Mae, he threw his leg over the horse's back and swung to the ground. "Are Harley and Cy here, ma'am?"

Suddenly the woman's eyes drilled into Langan. "You murderer! You killed him, didn't you? You cold-blooded murderer!"

Mae bounded off the porch and rushed to her dead son. She clawed at his body and screamed, "Chad, you can't be dead! I can't stand to lose another son! Chad, please! Don't be dead!"

Chad's mare nickered and danced away from Mae. Langan moved in swiftly and seized the bridle. Mae went from clawing at Chad's lifeless form to clinging to his head, which hung low, arms dangling. Piteous sobs and wails filled the air as she vented her sorrow.

Langan steadied the mare, allowing the grieving mother to cry it out. At the same time, he maintained a wary eye for the Trotter men.

Chad's body abruptly slipped from the mare's back and crumpled to the ground. Mae's wailing became louder as she fell to her knees and laid her head on the dead man's chest. Sheriff Langan waited until the agonized sobs lessened to sniffling and whimpering.

Bending low, he said in a soft tone, "Mrs. Trotter, I need to talk to Harley. Is he here?"

Mae shook her head without looking up.

"Cy?"

This time, she raised her head and looked at him through hate-filled eyes. "No, they're not here! They're in the mountains, hunting! Trying to kill some deer and elk so we don't have to butcher our cattle for food!"

"When will they be back?"

"This evening or in the morning. And I'll tell you what— they'll come gunnin' for you, too!"

"Ma'am, I know Harley and Cy will want to bury Chad beside Willie. I'll carry the body in the house for you."

Mae leaped to her feet, wild-eyed. Saliva spewed from her mouth as she said, "Don't you touch him, you animal!"

Langan kept his voice steady. "Mrs. Trotter, I'm going to tell you the truth. There are plenty of people in town who can back up my story. Chad came into town this morning and put some liquor under his belt at the Gunbarrel Saloon. He boasted that he was going to brace me and make me draw against him. I happened to be on the street when he came out of the Gunbarrel. He wasn't drunk, but he had put down enough whiskey to raise his courage."

"Liar! My Chad didn't need whiskey to give him courage! He had plenty enough on his own!"

"Ma'am, Chad squared off with me in the street and challenged me to go for my gun, saying he was going to dance on my grave. I told him to get on his horse and go home. He swore at me, saying he was going to give his mother some peace by gunning me down. At least a hundred people were there, Mrs. Trotter. They will tell you that I did my best to keep from having to kill Chad. I talked to him as calmly as I could, telling him he was no match for me with a gun...that if he went for his weapon, I'd have no choice but to take him down. He swore again and went for his gun. I shouted a warning, but I could wait no longer. I had to defend myself."

"Harley and Cy will come after you, murderer—and *I'll* dance on your grave!"

"It would be a bad mistake for Harley and Cy to come after me, Mrs. Trotter. Even if I didn't get them, the law would. They'd hang. Now, I didn't have to come out here. I could have let you and your husband wonder why Chad didn't come home and go into town to find out. I brought Chad's body home, even as I did Willie's, as a gesture of kindness. This time, as well as the other, I wanted to tell you people the truth about what happened."

"Truth? The truth is that you're a cold-blooded killer! You're gonna pay, you are! Harley and Cy will see to it!"

"Mrs. Trotter, you tell your husband and son it will be a serious mistake if they come gunning for me. There's been enough killing. You make them see that."

Langan stared at her a few seconds, then turned and mounted his horse. From the saddle, he said, "Don't let them come after me, ma'am. I don't want to kill any more Trotters."

At midmorning the next day, Deputy Sheriff Steve Ridgway was sitting at the desk in the sheriff's office when a well-dressed man in his late thirties walked through the door.

Ridgway smiled and said, "Good morning. What can I do for you, sir?"

The man smiled back, noting that the badge on Ridgway's chest identified him as a deputy. "My name is Harold Bateman, Deputy. I recently moved to Denver from St. Louis. I'm a reporter. I was with the *St. Louis Dispatch* for several years, and now I'm with the *Denver Sentinel.* Is Sheriff Langan in?"

"No, sir. He's out of town at the moment, but I expect him back at about noon. He has an appointment at one o'clock with Marshal Duvall. Anything I can help you with?"

"No doubt you could shed some light on these mysterious disappearances, Deputy, but Archie Sellers, my editor-in-chief, told me specifically to get an interview with Sheriff Curt Langan."

"The *Sentinel* did a couple of stories on the disappearances back when they first started happening ten weeks ago, Mr. Bateman."

"Yes. By reporter Dale Pitts. I'm replacing Mr. Pitts, and Mr. Sellers wanted an update on the story. People are wondering what's being done about the disappearances, according to Mr. Sellers."

"Well, sir," Ridgway said, "it so happens that the sheriff is out trying to find some clue as to what's happening to these men and who's doing it."

"I see. So you say he'll be back around noon?"

"That's what he said before he rode out."

"You think if I come back at noon he'll have time to answer some questions before his meeting with Duvall?"

"Might. You just be here, and we'll see."

At precisely 12:08, Sheriff Langan entered the office. Harold Bateman was there and Ridgway introduced him to Langan, explaining what he wanted. Langan told him he could have twenty minutes.

As the sheriff eased onto his chair, he said, "I assume you've read Dale Pitts's articles."

"Yes."

"Well, we don't know any more than we did then...except that another eighteen men have disappeared."

Bateman wrote on a pad he had taken from a small briefcase. "What's the total number of disappearances to this date?"

"Twenty-four."

"Mr. Pitts's article said the men were ranchers, laborers, and travelers."

"That's right. There could be more than twenty-four now, however. The travelers who've been abducted, that we know of, were moving through with their families when they were reported missing. In each case, it was when the man had gone to a stream to get water or had left the wagons for some other reason. I've investigated every case. In about half of them, I've found physical evidence—markings on the ground—of the abductions. Some of them were taken away on horseback and others in wagons. But they always ended up reaching a well-traveled road, and at that point, I lost the trail."

"You speak of travelers that you *know* of. You mean there

could be men traveling alone who've been kidnapped, but you would not know it?"

"That's right."

"So there could be more than twenty-four men abducted."

"Yes."

"When you say *laborers,* what do you mean?"

"Farm and ranch workers."

"And by ranchers, you mean men who are ranch *owners?*"

"Yes. So far, every man who's disappeared has been between twenty and fifty years old. No one younger, no one older."

"And always men. No females?"

"No females, thank God."

Bateman finished writing a line, then asked, "And what do you think is happening to them?"

"I have no idea. If they're being killed, it's after they're taken somewhere else. I've found no blood or any other evidence they're being killed at the spot of abduction."

"If they're being murdered, we must have some psychopathic killers banded together, wouldn't you say, Sheriff?"

"Have to be something like that."

"But let's say that's not the case. Let's say these men are still alive. What do you think is being done with them?"

Langan leaned forward. "I have no idea, Mr. Bateman. My predecessor, Sheriff Yates, didn't either. The thing had him as baffled I am."

"And you, personally, are scouring the area, looking for some kind of clue?"

"That's right."

"Big job for one man. Can't you get help somewhere?"

"I've had some townsmen work with me like a posse, but they can't give a lot of time to it. They have jobs and businesses to run."

"But can't you get help from the authorities?"

"I've tried. Went to the army. They've got so much Indian trouble right now, they can't spare any men. U.S. Marshal Duvall has given me men to help when he's had them to spare, but this is wild country, Mr. Bateman. It's not civilized like St. Louis. Bad men roam this country like vultures after spoiled meat. Marshals are run ragged trying to track down all the outlaws and killers."

"I see."

"In fact, my appointment in a few minutes with Chief Duvall is about this very matter. He asked me to meet with him. I think he may have some help to give me."

Harold Bateman glanced at the clock on the wall and said, "Sheriff, you've been very kind to give me this time, which I see is just about up. Thank you."

Langan smiled, showing a set of white, even teeth.

Just as Bateman was rising from his chair, Deputy Ridgway came running through the door, panting for breath.

"Sheriff! We've got trouble!"

"What is it?"

"It's the Trotters! Harley and Cy are over at the Bullhorn Saloon, bragging that they are going to come over here and gun you down!"

Langan sighed. "I was afraid they wouldn't be able to keep their cool about Chad. I better try to intercept them before they leave the saloon. Half the town must be out there on the street."

"I'll go with you."

"You'll stay here," Langan said.

"But, Sheriff, there are two of them!"

"I know. But I'm going to try to take them peacefully. If they see you come in with me, they might start shooting. You get a cell ready. I can lock them up for publicly declaring they're going to go after a lawman. Maybe a few days in the hoosegow will cool their heels."

"I'd like to go with you, Sheriff," Bateman said.

"Not too close, my friend. I don't want you shot. Don't come near that saloon door. Get your story from a safe distance so you'll be alive to see it in print."

Tremont Street—where the sheriff's office was located—had seven saloons in a four-block section. The Bullhorn was in the same block, at the opposite end.

Curt Langan was running toward the Bullhorn when he saw the Trotters emerge from the saloon and step into the dusty, sun-washed street. They saw him and exchanged quick words. Cy nodded and kept pace with his tall, lanky father as Harley led him to the middle of the street. People cleared the street quickly and inquisitive faces began to appear from inside the stores.

Harley and Cy stopped and let the sheriff come to them. When he was some forty feet away, Langan hauled up, tilted his hat back, and said, "It's just like I told your wife, Harley. Chad wouldn't listen. Plenty of people on the street saw it. They can testify that I did everything in my power to keep from killing him."

"You're a stinkin', acid-mouthed liar!" Harley yelled. "You didn't need to kill either one of my boys! You're just a trigger-happy tin star who enjoys usin' that badge to murder decent men and call it legal. You oughtta hang!"

Both Trotters dangled their hands loosely over their holstered guns. Langan was ready to draw and shoot if they forced him to, but he would take them alive if possible. "I'm arresting both of you for coming to town bent on killing an officer of the law. Now move real slow and drop your gunbelts."

"We ain't goin' to no jail!" Harley said.

"It's jail or the grave, Harley."

"You think you can take both of us?" Cy said.

"Yep. But even if I can't, I'll get one of you for sure. Maybe it'll be you, Cy. That what you want, Harley? Want to lose another son?"

Harley licked his lips nervously.

"I didn't think so," Langan said. "All right, Harley, tell your son to drop his gunbelt, and you do the same."

"Pa," Cy said from the side of his mouth. "Don't let him buffalo you!"

"Shut up. I'm thinkin'."

"Neither Willie nor Chad gave me a choice, fellas. Now, don't make me kill any more Trotters. Do like I said, and drop those gunbelts."

Harley wiped sweat from his brow while keeping his gun hand close to the butt of his revolver.

"Let's take him, Pa! He killed my brothers!"

Harley blinked, drew in a deep breath, and said, "He'll get one of us, son. It ain't worth it. I can't take the chance of losin' you, too."

"But, Pa!"

"Do as the man says, Cy. Drop your gunbelt."

Harley bent over, untied the rawhide thong holding the holster to his leg, then unbuckled the gunbelt and let it fall to the dust. Cy reluctantly followed suit.

There were heavy sighs of relief along the street. No blood would be shed on Tremont Street this time.

"All right, Harley...Cy, let's go," Langan said. "We've got a nice comfortable cell waiting for you."

Deputy Ridgway had followed and stood near a wagon a few steps behind his boss. He moved up beside him and said, "Sheriff, I'll take them in for you."

Langan nodded. "You boys cool off for a while. I've got an

appointment, and I'm late already. I'll be back in an hour or so, then we'll talk."

Several men and women gathered around Sheriff Langan to compliment him on the way he had handled the Trotters. Langan's eyes strayed past the circle of people and found a stunning young woman he had never seen before. She was standing between the porch roofs of two buildings where the sunlight seemed to form a halo around her. She was about his age, had long, shiny auburn hair, and was dressed in a split-skirt riding outfit with a flat-crowned hat and neck cord. The hat hung by the cord on her back, and the sun's rays danced on her hair, making it look like burnished copper.

Two of the men who offered their congratulations to Langan were ranchers Todd Blair and Lance Tracy. They chatted a moment, then said they needed to get home to their wives and children.

Tracy laid a hand on Langan's shoulder and said, "You know, Curt, it's time you worked on having a wife and kids to go home to."

Todd Blair chuckled, "He's right, Curt. When you going to quit baching it and get married?"

Langan stole another look at the redhead, then he grinned at his friends and said, "I'm just waiting for the right woman to come along, guys. When she does, I'll marry her, and we'll have a whole passel of kids!"

Both ranchers laughed, said they would see him later, and walked away.

Curt Langan's heart leaped to his throat when he saw the young woman headed straight for him, smiling warmly.

5

"SHERIFF LANGAN," THE YOUNG WOMAN SAID, "the way you handled those two troublemakers was magnificent. I detest violence, and you averted it in such a marvelous way. You certainly showed a great deal of courage."

Curt smiled, slightly out of breath, and said, "Well, thank you, ma'am. Have...ah...have we met before?"

"No," she said, taking a step closer. "My name is Sally Jayne. J-A-Y-N-E. I'm new in the area, but I heard about you almost as soon as I arrived. My father owns a ranch in the mountains a little over thirty miles west of Denver. I just moved here to live with him."

"I see. Do I know your father? What's the name of the ranch?"

"Daddy knows about you. He's the one who first mentioned you to me. We have neighbors who have mentioned you, too. Folks hereabouts have a lot of confidence in you, Sheriff."

"I'm glad to hear that."

"Anyway, Daddy's name is Wendell Jayne. And the ranch is the *Circle J.*"

"I don't think I've ever met your father, unless it's been here in town. I've covered a lot of territory in the mountains west of here, and no doubt have seen your father's spread, but I don't recall the name *Circle J.*"

"Depends on when you might have been in the area last," Sally said. "The *Circle J* is fairly new. Daddy came to Colorado from New Mexico just under two years ago. He bought the land, built the house and buildings, and established the *Circle J* at that time."

"Oh. That's probably why it's not familiar to me. I haven't been thirty miles west of here in probably three years…although I have been doing a lot of riding in the mountains of late. What part of New Mexico are your parents from?"

"Silver City area. That's where I've been since Daddy decided to move north to Colorado. I was doing office work for one of the silver mines there. Actually, it isn't both my parents who moved here. My mother died nineteen years ago, when I was six. Daddy's never even considered marrying again. He's still a young man…in his early fifties, but he recently fell ill. I came to the ranch to take care of him."

"Faithful, loving daughter," Curt said with a nod. "I admire you for it."

"Thank you. It's the least I can do for such a wonderful dad. You…ah…said you've been doing a lot of riding in the mountains of late. Something in connection with your job?"

"Yes. For nearly three months now we've had a rash of disappearances. Men just vanishing without a trace."

Sally's eyebrows arched. "You mean they're being kidnapped?"

"Apparently so. I've been riding everywhere, trying to find some trace, some clue. Has me baffled."

"No women? Just men?"

"Mm-hmm. Ranchers, laborers, and some men who were just passing through this area bound for somewhere else. They vanished into thin air."

"But you have no idea why they're being kidnapped?"

"None whatsoever."

"No ransom notes?"

"No."

"You don't think they're being tortured and killed by some maniacs, do you?"

"I sure hope not."

Sally shook her head. "If no one's demanding a ransom, what possible reason could there be for abducting these men?"

"Like I said, it's got me baffled. Tell me more about your father, Miss Jayne. What kind of illness does he have? Denver has three excellent doctors. I can recommend all three, especially Dr. Lyle Goodwin."

"Daddy has a severe stomach problem. Gives him a lot of trouble. Quite often keeps him awake at night. However, just recently we had new neighbors move onto a small ranch near us. The man is a retired physician, and he's been taking care of Daddy. Seems to have a pretty good supply of medicine and herbs. I don't really know what all he's been giving Daddy, but there is definite improvement. Tell you what, though. If Daddy doesn't get a whole lot better under this retired doctor's care, I'll sure look up this Dr.—"

"Goodwin. Lyle Goodwin."

"Yes. Him. I sure will."

"He's the best."

"I appreciate your telling me about him."

"Miss Jayne, did you ride into town by yourself?"

"Oh, no. Daddy would never stand for that. He's very protective of me."

"Good. This is rough country. Lots of outlaws and no-goods roaming about. A young lady like yourself isn't safe traveling alone."

"You sound just like Wendell Jayne, Sheriff," she said with a quick laugh. "Daddy sent two of his most trusted ranchhands with me. I had to do some business for Daddy at the Rocky Mountain Bank down the street. I just finished it when those two men started trouble with you on the street. Nick and Alf went over on Glenarm Street to the gun shop. They should be coming after me at any moment."

Sally smiled as she looked past the sheriff and said, "Well, speak of the devil! Or should I say devils? Here they come now."

Langan turned and saw two riders trotting their mounts around the corner. They were rugged-looking men, but well-groomed and clean. They were dressed like cowhands and sat their horses as if they were born to the saddle.

Sally waved to get their attention and called their names. They drew up and dismounted, and she introduced Nick Beal and Alf Spaulding to the sheriff.

"I've seen you two around town. Just didn't know who you were."

"Well, now you do," Spaulding said with a chuckle.

"Miss Sally, I don't mean to be an old woman about this, but we need to head back for the ranch. Your daddy'll be getting worried if we don't show up by three o'clock."

"Yes, of course, Nick," she said.

"Is your horse still over at the bank, Miss Sally?" Alf asked.

"Yes. We had some excitement in the street, and though I can't stand violence, like everybody else I have to see what's going on. When I heard there was a ruckus, I hurried down the street and left my mare where she was tied. You boys should've seen Sheriff Langan handle two men who were bent on gunning him down. He needled them into surrendering without a shot being fired. And he didn't even draw his gun. He's got them locked up over at the jail."

"Well, Miss Sally, we've been told some good things about Sheriff Langan," Beal said. "Guess we can add this to our collection."

Sally smiled up at Langan. "And I'll bet there's lots we haven't heard, too."

The sheriff blushed, marveling at the effect she had on him.

"I'll get your horse, Miss Sally," Alf said, and trotted his mount toward the bank.

Sally turned to the other ranchhand. "Nick, Sheriff Langan told me about a good doctor here in town who can help Daddy if Dr. Wiggins isn't able to make him lots better."

"Good."

"Sheriff, it's been a real pleasure meeting you," Sally said to Langan.

"The pleasure has been all mine, Miss Jayne," he replied, trying to breathe normally. "Are you planning to come to town again any time soon?"

"I'm sure I'll be back in a few days."

"Well, my search for the missing men keeps me out of town a lot, but I would love to see you if I'm here. How about just dropping by my office when you're in town? It's right up there."

"Yes, I saw the sign. And I'll be happy to stop by. If I don't catch you next time, I'll try again another time."

"Please do."

Alf trotted up with Sally's bay mare in tow.

Offering her hand, Sally said, "Good-bye until next time, Sheriff."

Langan took her small, delicate hand in his and wished he could hold it for a while. "Good-bye until next time," he said.

He watched her mount up ever so gracefully into the saddle. She warmed him with another smile and rode away between Beal and Spaulding. When she was about to pass from view, she turned in the saddle and looked at him. Langan waved, Sally waved back and was gone.

"Sorry I'm late, Chief," Curt Langan said as he entered the office of Chief U.S. Marshal Solomon Duvall. "Had a little ruckus on Tremont Street. Happened just before I was to head this way."

"No bloodshed?" the tall silver-haired man asked.

"No bloodshed."

"A miracle these days."

Two men with federal badges on their chests were seated in front of the chief's desk. They rose to their feet at Langan's entrance.

"Sheriff Curt Langan, meet Deputy U.S. Marshals Dennis Coulter and Bob Lowery. I've filled these deputies in on the disappearances around here. They're new under my command, and I'd like to break them in by having them help you search for the missing men and the kidnappers. I can let you have their services for a week."

"That would be wonderful, Marshal."

"I don't want them separated, you understand. So wherever you send one, the other will go, too."

"Fine, sir. Lately it's been only me, so this will double the areas that can be searched."

"I'll let you tell them what to look for, Sheriff," Duvall said. "And they'll report directly to you. If you send them so far they can't make it back to town, they have bedrolls and they know how to eat rations."

"I really appreciate this."

"Glad to help. These men will report to your office in the morning. What time?"

"Six o'clock?"

"Six o'clock, it is." Duvall nodded and rose from his chair.

Coulter and Lowery left the office, saying they would see Langan in the morning. Duvall laid a hand on the sheriff's shoulder as they moved slowly toward the door. "I sure hope this kidnapping thing can get cleared up. Bad business."

"Yes, sir. It's that, all right. I just wish..."

"Wish what?"

"Oh, I was thinking how good it would be if your friend John Stranger was here to help me. He's got such an uncanny way of solving mysteries."

"What the West needs is a hundred John Strangers, Curt. Or maybe I should say, a thousand. Right now, I've got him doing a job down in Arizona. Marshal of Apache Junction's dealing with a pack of no-goods who've been trying to take over the town. As you may know, Apache Junction's close to the Superstition Mountains where prospectors are finding a lot of gold. The outlaw gang means to cash in on the wealth."

"Well, if I know John Stranger, he'll put a stop to it in a hurry."

"That's what I'm counting on," Duvall said with conviction.

At the *T-Slash-B Ranch* some twelve miles east of Denver, a little boy stood on a front porch, looking westward with tears streaming down his cheeks.

Elaine Blair stepped onto the porch with her other children, eight-year-old Susie and five-year-old Todd Jr. She walked up to her oldest son and laid both hands on his shoulders. Ten-year-old Terry lifted his face and sniffled as he met her tender gaze.

His birthday party was over. The children and mothers who had attended had already gone home to their neighboring ranches.

"Honey, you know Papa wouldn't miss your birthday party unless something very important happened to detain him."

Terry's voice quivered as he said, "It just isn't like Papa to let anything keep him from my birthday party. Something bad has happened to him, Mama. I just know it."

"Now, Terry, nothing bad has happened to your father. He'll be here soon, and we'll understand what kept him when he explains it."

Elaine knew that her husband had gone to town with his neighbor and friend, Lance Tracy. Terry was right. It wasn't like Todd to miss something as important as his son's birthday party. Fear began as a tiny needling in her stomach and slowly worked its way upward.

"Terry," she said, "we're going to hitch up the team and drive over to the Tracy ranch. If your father and Lance aren't there, we're going into town and find them."

Donna Tracy was in the kitchen with her mother, who lived with her and Lance and their two small children. Clara Miller was setting the table while her daughter shelled peas at the cupboard.

"Now, honey, there's no reason to panic. I'm sure those two men found something to occupy them in town, and they've just let the time get away from them. Lance'll be riding in here any minute."

"Mother, I'm trying not to, but I keep thinking of all those men who've been kidnapped and have never been seen since." Her eyes filled with tears.

Clara took her daughter in her arms and hugged her tight. "Donna, just because Lance is a little late getting home doesn't mean—"

The sound of a wagon rattling into the yard broke off Clara's words. It moved past the side of the house and stopped at the back porch.

"It's Elaine, Mother. I'm sure of it. She's come looking for Todd."

Elaine Blair was climbing down from the wagon seat as the two women appeared on the back porch. One look at their faces and Elaine said, "They haven't been here, either?"

"No, and I'm as worried as you are. It's just not like Lance to be this late."

"You want to go with me to town?"

"Yes."

"You can leave the children with me, Elaine," Clara said. "I'll feed them supper."

Sheriff Langan and his deputy entered Lil's Café as darkness enfolded Denver for the night. Townspeople greeted them as they threaded their way among the tables and found an empty one in the corner. The waitress came to pour them coffee and told Langan she had heard about the Trotter incident. She congratulated him on a task well done.

"Sheriff," Deputy Ridgway said, "I'm mighty pleased Duvall is giving you those two deputies for a whole week. Maybe we can get somewhere with a little extra help."

"I sure hope so."

"Wish I could help you in the search."

"Somebody's got to stay and keep an eye on the town and the county."

Langan's back was to the door, but he heard it open and noted that his deputy's attention was drawn in that direction. "What is it, Steve?"

"Elaine Blair and Donna Tracy. They're coming our way, and from the looks on their faces, something's wrong."

Langan rose to his feet as the two women weaved their way among the tables. The eyes of nearly everyone in the place were fixed on the ranchers' wives.

"Sheriff," said Elaine, with a tremor in her voice, "Donna and I think our husbands have been kidnapped."

"How long have they been missing?"

"Maybe you can tell us," Donna said. "A couple of people said they had seen them talking to you right after you had a problem with Harley and Cy Trotter."

"Was that the last you saw them, Sheriff?" Elaine asked.

"Yes. That was…mmm…about twelve-thirty. Come to think of it, they both said they needed to get home."

"Todd did, for sure," Elaine said. "He was supposed to be there for Terry's birthday party. He never showed up, and Lance hasn't been home either. There aren't many people on the street right now, but we couldn't find anyone else who has seen them."

"With all these kidnappings the past several weeks, we're afraid the same thing has happened to them, Sheriff," Donna said.

Curt Langan felt his mouth go dry. "I hope that isn't the case, ladies, but since your husbands are the steady, dependable type, you just may be right."

"What should we do?"

"The best thing is to go on home to your children. Since it's dark, I'm going to escort you. If your husbands haven't shown up by the time we arrive, I'll go on a search early in the morning."

"Sheriff, we appreciate your willingness to escort us home, but you're about to eat your supper."

"I'll live if I miss a meal, Mrs. Tracy."

"Sheriff, let me escort them," Steve said. "You stay here and eat."

"Appreciate your offer, Steve, but I'll feel better if I go with them. Let's go, ladies."

Suddenly the door burst open and Mae Trotter stormed in, fiery eyes fixed on Langan. Mae had the attention of everyone in the café as she elbowed Elaine and Donna out of the way, stood before Langan, and bellowed, "Sheriff, I've been told you jailed Harley and Cy!"

"You were told right. As you well know, they came into town to gun me down for killing Chad."

"I told you they'd be on your tail!"

"Well, ma'am, you're fortunate they're both alive. One or both of them would be dead if they'd tried it. I was able to talk sense to Harley, and he saw the futility of making the attempt. Cy argued with him, but Harley won out. You'd have buried another son if Cy had gone for his gun."

"Then what're they locked up for?"

"Because they came into town to kill me. That's against the law. I told them when they cooled down I'd have a talk with them. So far, I haven't had time. I hope I can get to them tomorrow some time. Right now, I've got something more important on my mind."

"You gonna let 'em out tomorrow?"

"Can't say yet. Depends. If they're genuinely repentant for wanting to kill me, I'll consider it."

"I want to see 'em!"

"Can't. It's past visiting hours."

Mae had the look of a she-wolf about to devour him. "What time can I see 'em in the morning?"

"Anytime after nine. Unless my deputy is out of the office."

Mae wheeled around and swore vehemently, then stomped out the door.

71

✦

The next morning the eastern horizon was showing first light when Deputy U.S. Marshals Coulter and Lowery met Sheriff Langan at his office. Langan gave them a map of the Territory and marked the area they were to search for signs of the kidnapped men. He wanted them to talk to every resident they encountered. Men could not be hauled around in wagons or on horseback without somebody seeing them.

The search area would take the deputies two full days to cover. If they returned with no clues, he would assign another area.

When the federal men had ridden away, Langan mounted his horse and headed east. He wanted to follow the road Todd Blair and Lance Tracy would have ridden from Denver to their ranches.

Langan rode slowly, carefully studying the ground on both sides of the road. The sun peeked over the earth's eastern edge and soon detached itself from the horizon. By eight o'clock it was sitting in the crystal blue sky, slowly shortening the shadows.

Suddenly his eye spotted fresh wheel prints veering off the road into a meadow. The tracks headed for a cluster of cottonwood trees fringed with lilac bushes. He leaned from the saddle and saw another set of tracks a few feet further down the road where the wagon had returned. Heavy hoofprints gave evidence of which tracks led in and which ones led out.

He guided his mount toward the trees and scrutinized the sod. He could see there were five horses besides the wagon team going toward the trees and only three horses coming back to the road.

As he drew near the trees, horses nickered at him and his own horse nickered back. When he reached the small clearing where the two horses were tied, he recognized them as Lance Tracy's and Todd Blair's.

His heart sank. The only bit of encouragement was that there was no blood on the saddles nor any sign of a struggle on the ground. Sheriff Langan took the horses back to the wives of their owners and confirmed that Todd Blair and Lance Tracy had been kidnapped. He explained that the hoofprints and the wagon tracks were traceable until they reached the hard-packed, well-traveled road. Tracking them from that point was impossible. There was no way to tell which direction the kidnappers and their victims had gone.

Langan tried to encourage the women, explaining that he found no blood; their husbands had been taken away apparently unharmed.

At the Blair house, Elaine had sent the two younger children outside to play while she talked with the sheriff. Young Terry was allowed to stay.

"Sheriff, what can all of this mean?" Elaine asked. "Why would anyone do a horrible thing like this? What do they want with our husbands?"

"I don't have any answers. But I assure you, I'm going to give it everything I've got to bring them back safe and sound. I've got some help for the search this week."

"Oh?"

"Chief Duvall gave me two new deputies. Maybe they'll turn up something...or maybe I will. Certainly somebody somewhere has seen something. Don't you give up."

"I won't, Sheriff," Elaine said, struggling against the tears that were about to surface.

When Langan headed for the door, Terry moved up to him. "Sheriff..."

"Yes?"

"Since I'm ten years old now, could I ride with you as you search for Papa? I have my own horse."

Langan looked down at the boy's innocent eyes, put an arm around him, and said, "Terry, it's more important that you stay here with your mother. She needs you right now. Until your papa's back, you'll have to be the man of the house."

A slight smile curved Terry's lips. "I hadn't thought of it like that, Sheriff. You're right. I'll stay and take care of Mama. And my little brother and sister."

THE UNION PACIFIC TRAIN STEAMED out of Elko, Nevada, about an hour before dawn. Floyd Metz was wide awake. The brief stop in Elko did not disturb his sleep, for he had not slept at all since going to bed at eleven-thirty. Worry picked at his mind over the three sick Chinese men being cared for by Breanna Baylor and Myrtle Henderson in the baggage coach.

Metz turned on one side then another, trying to get comfortable, but nothing seemed to work. Finally, he lay on his back and stared into the dark. What if more of the men came down with scarlet fever? What if some of them died? Morgan would be furious. Metz decided to talk to the nurse. He had to know more about the fever and find out just how dangerous it was. How long would it take the sick men to get over it? How soon could a man work at hard labor after he was over it? Metz would have the nurse come to his coach this morning. He needed answers.

Metz tried to shove the scarlet fever threat aside and think positively. Enjoying the rhythmic rock and sway of the coach, he let his mind go back almost a week to the morning he left Denver for his trip to California. Metz and Duff Pasko, Morgan's front man, were standing on the platform at Denver's Union Station, waiting for George Matson to show up. It was twenty-five minutes before departure time.

"So there's a good supply of these little Chinese guys out of work in Frisco, eh?" said Pasko, an ex-convict who had done time at Colorado Territorial Prison in Canon City. Pasko was barrel-chested and muscular, and stood a head taller than Metz.

"That's right," Metz said. "I'm told that San Francisco is overrun with them, and they need jobs. I shouldn't have much trouble finding willing subjects."

"Let me repeat, Floyd. Mr. Morgan is gonna be real happy if you come back with at least thirty good men, no matter what color their skin is. Any less, and he'll be very *un*happy. And believe me, you don't want to make my boss unhappy. You'd be better off to have a Bengal tiger by the tail."

"I'll come back with at least thirty, even if I have to promise them the moon," Metz replied. "Say, am I ever gonna get a chance to meet Morgan? I like to get to know the people I'm working for."

Pasko gave him a sidelong glance. "Nope. Mr. Morgan prefers to do all his business through me. I guarantee you, he won't come to town. And it wouldn't be safe for you to show up at the mine. He's an extremely private person and has a wicked temper. Besides, if you and Morgan were seen together, this entire operation would be jeopardized. Take my advice, Floyd. Just go along with Morgan. Do everything his way and you'll make yourself a bundle. The salary you draw from Union Pacific will look like peanuts in comparison."

The two men entered the green luxury coach Metz would travel in, and he proudly showed it off to Morgan's front man. Pasko was impressed with the plush carpet, tapestries, delicate lace curtains, imported European furniture, and liquor cabinet.

Metz glanced at the Swiss clock that hung on the rear wall of the coach and said, "Little more than fifteen minutes before the train pulls out, Duff. If Matson doesn't show up in the next few minutes, there's going to be a problem."

Pasko started to reply, but was interrupted by a knock at the car's front door. "I'll wager that's him now."

Pasko went to the door and pulled it open. "Hello, George, I thought it might be you. Come on in."

George Matson was a tough-looking man. His clothes and hat were dirty, and his greasy hair hung down to his shoulders. His teeth were tobacco-stained, and he hadn't shaved in four or five days. Metz ventured a private guess of how long it had been since Matson had bathed.

"Sorry I'm late," Matson said. "Couple of my men tried to kill each other, and I had to help make peace."

Matson's eyes roamed over the interior of the coach. "Some rig, eh, Duff?"

"George Matson, meet Floyd Metz," Pasko said.

It was all Metz could do to touch Matson's hand, but he gave him a frail handshake and said, "Well, we'd better get right down to business." Metz sank into his fanciest horsehair chair and the other two found seats.

"I believe Duff has explained our operation to you." Metz said.

"Yeah. You supply Duff's boss with slave labor for his gold mine some twenty-five miles or so west of Denver."

"That's right. From what Duff tells me, Morgan works his slaves hard, even brutally. Every so often one tries to escape and has to be shot. Others die of exhaustion. So it keeps me busy supplying slaves. Morgan recently discovered a new vein and needs more slaves real soon. He's smart enough to know that this operation can't go on much longer without the authorities figuring it out and finding the mine. So he's gotta increase the number of slaves to get out as much gold as he can."

"I can see why it couldn't go on too long," Matson said. "Not when you're kidnappin' local men. I'd think the law would be hot on your trail."

"It is. Denver County's new sheriff has been snooping around the mountains a lot and has been seen a couple of times dangerously close to the mine. It's well hidden, but one of these days he's liable to stumble onto it."

"So how many men are you plannin' to bring from San Francisco?" Matson asked.

"At least thirty. Maybe as many as forty. You and your boys should bring along enough wagons to carry forty, just in case I'm fortunate enough to come back with that many."

"And you're gonna tell them they've been hired by the railroad to lay track between Denver and Santa Fe, is that right?"

"You've got it." Metz reached inside his coat and pulled out a folded map. "Let's go over here to the desk."

Metz moved to the desk and spread the map on its top. Pasko and Matson stood on each side of him. The map was one produced by the railroad, and it showed every track line west of the Missouri River.

Metz pointed to a red X on the track line just north of Denver. "This is where you and your boys are to wait for us. It's exactly ten miles north of the town limits. Two small creeks intersect about twenty yards west of the tracks right there, and where they meet, there's a patch of wild raspberry bushes. You can't miss it. Now, Union Pacific's Denver office is headed up by Jonathan Squires. I wrote his name in the corner of the map, see?"

"Yep."

"Squires is expecting me to wire him when the train stops in Cheyenne City. I'll advise him as to exactly how many hired men I have aboard the train. This'll give Squires time to make preparations for beginning the work on the new track once the new men have arrived in Denver."

"Oh? So you really are supposed to be hirin' men to lay that track from Denver to Santa Fe?"

"That's correct. On the surface, this whole thing is on the up-and-up. Now, the train's last stop before Denver is at Fort Collins, some forty-five miles south of Cheyenne City. When the train stops in Fort Collins, there will be a telegram waiting for me at the Union Pacific office in the depot. It'll supposedly be from Squires, but it will actually be from you, George."

"From me?"

"Exactly." He turned the map over and showed Matson a message he had written. "See this? It's the message you'll wire to me at Fort Collins. It simply says that Squires has decided to unload the men from the train ten miles north of Denver. They're to be placed in wagons and taken to a special camp nearby that has been set up for training them how to lay track."

"Okay."

"This is a bit unusual, but I'll comply by showing the telegram to the engineer and the conductor. In the message, here, I've specified the exact spot where the train is supposed to stop. The engineer and the conductor will think nothing of it when they see the wagons waiting alongside the track. The telegram will be explained to the hired men so they too will think everything is in order."

"Slick," Matson said.

"Now, look here," said Metz, running his finger westward from the X on the map. "You and your boys will take the hired men over here to a place I've marked with a red dot. See it?"

"Mm-hmm. What is it—'bout two-three miles?"

"About four. It's a tree-lined ravine. Duff and Morgan's men will be waiting there. When you pull the wagons into the ravine, Duff and the others will throw guns on the suckers and put them in chains. Duff and Morgan's boys will then lead you and your men to the mine so you can deliver the new slaves to Morgan. Understand?"

"Sure do. Pretty slick."

"When the slaves are secure in the mine, you and your boys will be paid in gold for your services, even as Duff has told you."

"Twenty thousand, right?"

"Right."

"Sounds good to me."

Metz adjusted his suspenders underneath his coat. "Then, of course, I'll ride the train on into Denver. I'll go directly to Squires's office and tell him I turned the hired men over to the men with wagons as he directed in his telegram." Metz laughed. "Ol' Squires will say, 'Floyd, I didn't send a telegram.' I'll act shocked and hand it to him. Tell him some underhanded culprit must've learned about the men on the train and decided to take them...probably for the same purpose that so many other men have been abducted around Denver."

"Duff told me you'd be on the train that arrives in Denver from San Francisco one week from today."

"Precisely. I'll be back one week from today. If the train is on schedule, it'll be at the pickup point north of town about ten o'clock that morning."

Matson shook his head and popped his hands together. "Boy, what a clever idea! Who came up with it?"

Metz grinned and said, "The idea was all mine."

The bell on the big engine began to clang, the whistle blew, and the conductor could be heard calling for all passengers to board.

"Well, George," Pasko said, "I guess we'd better get off."

Matson nodded, then said to Metz, "I do understand correctly that my boys and I get twenty thousand in gold no matter how many men you have on the train. Right?"

"That's right."

"Fair enough. Let's go, Duff. See you a week from today, Floyd."

Metz went to the liquor cabinet and poured himself a glass of whiskey. He carried it to his favorite easy chair, settled in and took a sip. "Floyd, ol' boy," he chuckled to himself, "not too many men around with your kind of brains. You're going to be one wealthy man before this venture with Morgan is over."

THE CLOCK ON THE WALL told Metz it was 7:25. The conductor would be there with hot water any minute.

Metz rolled out of bed and shouldered into his robe. Worry over the sick men still scratched at the back of his mind. He had to talk with Breanna Baylor as soon as possible. He padded to the mirror and ran a palm over his bald pate just as he heard the expected knock.

The conductor entered, carrying a pail of steaming water. "Here you are, sir," he said with a smile. "You get shaved and ready to face the day, and in about thirty minutes I'll be back with your breakfast."

"Fine," replied Metz, taking the pail. "And after I've eaten my breakfast, I want you to bring Nurse Baylor to me. I need to talk to her about this scarlet fever business."

"I'll tell her, sir."

The church was decorated with a variety of beautiful flowers, and the sun's bright rays slanted through stained-glass windows. Every pew was filled, and when the organist pumped extra hard and went into "Here Comes the Bride," the crowd came to its feet.

Breanna Baylor held Dr. Lyle Goodwin's arm as they walked down the aisle of her church in Denver. She felt elegant in a shimmering white gown and was honored that Dr. Goodwin would be the one to give her away.

Just ahead were the bridesmaids, followed by Breanna's sister, Dottie, her matron of honor. On the right side of the aisle stood Dottie's husband, Dr. Matthew Carroll. James and Molly Kate were beside him, smiling at their aunt.

Breanna felt a touch of sadness that her parents had not lived to see this day. The sadness faded, however, when her eyes fell on the tall, handsome groom who waited with the preacher and his groomsmen at the altar.

Finally, the day had come when John Stranger and Breanna Baylor would take their marriage vows and become one in the eyes of God. Breanna's heart was pounding with excitement. When she and John left the altar, they would be husband and wife.

"Breanna! Breanna!"

Suddenly she was aware of the click of steel wheels and the baggage coach's steady rock and sway. She felt a pang in her heart as she was pulled from sleep. It had been such a lovely dream.

Myrtle Henderson spoke again. "Breanna, dear, I'm sorry to disturb your sleep. I told Mr. Wonderly you had been awake all night with your patients, but he said Mr. Metz wants to see you right away in his private car."

Breanna covered her mouth and yawned. She rolled over on the blanket that lay between her and the hard wooden floor-boards of the coach and rose to her knees. She looked at her three patients as they slept. "How are they doing?"

"They haven't awakened since you lay down two hours ago."

"Good. The more they sleep, the better. Have you checked their temperatures?"

"Yes. The one who got sick first is definitely cooler. I'm sure the enema helped. The other two don't seem any hotter."

Breanna ran her fingers through her hair. "Wish there was a mirror in here."

Myrtle reached out and touched up the blond tresses. "There. You look fine."

"So, did Mr. Wonderly say what Mr. Metz wants to see me about?"

"No. He just said he would be back to escort you to Metz's coach in about ten minutes."

"All right. I guess because the man is a vice-president of this railroad, he can call for an interview with anybody any time he wants."

"Seems so." Myrtle paused, then said, "I don't know about you, honey, but there's something about Metz that bothers me."

"Well, to tell you the truth, I feel the same way. Can't put my finger on it, but I get these little sensations in the back of my neck when I look at him." Shrugging her shoulders, she said, "Oh, well."

Breanna experienced those same sensations the moment she stepped inside the green coach after being escorted there by the conductor, who excused himself and backed out the door.

Floyd Metz smiled as he guided Breanna to the chair next to his favorite overstuffed one. When she was seated, Metz asked how the sick men were doing.

"As well as can be expected. We're doing all we can for them—bathing them in cool water and giving them cool water enemas periodically. This, along with the sage tea, should pull them through all right. My main concern now is that other men in the coach will come down with it. Scarlet fever is highly contagious."

"This is what I wanted to discuss with you, Miss Baylor," said

Metz, worry evident in his eyes. "Tell me, how often do people die from scarlet fever?"

"It depends on how severe a case they have, Mr. Metz. A lot of it depends on how strong and healthy they were before they came down with it—how much strength their body has to fight it."

"I see."

"In the severest case, the victim will have paroxysms when the blood gushes from his nose, eyes, and ears."

"Ugh."

"Yes. Ugh. When it's that bad, the person usually dies, ninety-nine out of a hundred times." What is it about this man, anyway? His eyes? His mannerisms? His voice? She still couldn't put her finger on it. "When children get it, they often die, even without the profuse bleeding. Children also are usually nauseous the first day or two and vomit a lot."

"How do you tell scarlet fever from other types of fever?"

"It takes a trained eye. There are many types of fever, and some that remain unnamed, but scarlet fever's symptoms are easily recognizable once you've dealt with it."

"Such as?"

"The first symptoms are a sore throat and a headache. Many fevers start out that way, but with scarlet fever a red rash soon appears on the neck, in the armpits, in the groin area, and on the chest. It's this red rash from whence comes its name *scarlet* fever."

"I see."

"About the same time the rash starts to appear, the temperature begins to rise. When the fever reaches its high point, the face will be flushed and there'll be a ring of pallor around the mouth. By then the throat is inflamed and red spots appear on the palate. The tongue is coated a pink color, and the edges of the tongue will be deeply inflamed with a bright red.

"If the victim receives no medication, but his body is strong enough to begin fighting back, it usually takes four or five days for the rash to begin to subside and the coating on the tongue to disappear. The redness along the edges takes much longer to go away. The eruption and the fever last a week to ten days, and in about a third of the cases, there is a peeling on some areas of the skin. Most of the time the peeling will be on the scalp or on the palms of the hands."

"So if they receive no medication, and they are not strong of body to begin with, they will die?"

"Yes, sir."

"Do these Chinamen seem strong to you?"

"As best as I can tell, yes. And, of course, they are receiving medication and the cool water treatments."

"So you're optimistic they'll be all right?"

"Yes. With treatment, the healing process is much faster."

"The medication you're using is…what did you say? Sage tea?"

"Yes. The tea brewed from its leaves has a great deal of healing power. It forces the rash to mature quickly. When it's used, the healing process begins within three days. Then, of course, the use of cool water baths and enemas brings the fever under control much faster."

Metz smiled, making his eyes almost disappear in the thick flesh of his cheeks. "I see you know your stuff, Miss Baylor."

"Well, I'm supposed to, anyway."

"You know these men have been hired to lay track. How soon can a man work at hard labor once the symptoms have disappeared?"

"It depends on the man, Mr. Metz. But on the average, a healthy man should be able to resume heavy labor within ten days after the symptoms are gone."

Metz knew that Morgan was temperamental. Duff Pasko told him it got mighty unpleasant around the mine when Morgan threw a fit. But surely Morgan wouldn't get too upset about having to feed the three scarlet fever victims a few days before they started to work. And surely he wouldn't get upset with Floyd Metz. It wasn't his fault they caught the disease. The big problem would be if more of the men came down with it.

Metz adjusted his obese frame in the chair and asked, "What are the chances that the other men will come down with it, Miss Baylor?"

"There's no way, really, to conjecture on it, sir. All I can tell you is that every one of them was exposed when the first man's fever hit its highest point. It's the fever that makes it so contagious."

"How soon will a person come down with the fever after being exposed to it?"

"It varies. Usually within two to seven days after exposure, but it can go longer. I've seen people come down with it as late as three weeks after they were exposed. I can understand your anxiety, Mr. Metz, but even if all of them get the fever, they can be treated in Denver and won't be down too long."

"Yes. Of course. You're right about that. I want to thank you for coming to talk to me, Miss Baylor. You've helped me to understand what we're facing here."

When Breanna was gone, Floyd Metz stewed and muttered to himself while pacing the length of the coach. There was no way the men could be treated in Denver. He swore and swung a fist through the air. Why did things have to turn out this way?

As Breanna entered car 5 on her way back to the baggage coach, she saw Chung Ho standing with the other two men who could speak English. They had spoken only briefly to her when she passed through earlier, for she had quickly explained she was wanted immediately by Floyd Metz. She had mentioned that their three friends were doing as well as expected, which eased their minds.

All three bowed as she drew up, and Chung Ho said "Missy Breanna, we thank you to be so kind to our friends. They be well because of you."

"I'm doing my best," she said with a smile.

"Mr. Wonderly say you are angel of mercy. We agree."

"Thank you. Are any more of your friends showing signs of the fever?"

"No. We have been asking. So far, so good, as you Americans say."

"You will let me know if any of you begin to get a sore throat or a headache, won't you?"

"Yes, Missy Breanna. We will."

Breanna passed through to car 3 and saw Clint Byers standing with the other six men who had been hired to lay track. They were discussing their new job as Breanna walked up. All attention turned to Breanna as Moses Crowder asked about the sick men. Breanna said she was sure they would be fine in a week or so.

Breanna was about to enter car 2 when she heard Clint Byers call above the noise of the clattering wheels. He hurried toward her and closed the door behind him.

"I just want to thank you for talking to me about my being jilted. I've been in better shape ever since."

"I'm glad, but Clint...you'd be in even better shape if you'd let Jesus into your life. He can make such a difference. He gives joy and peace like this world can't give you. He has a way of bringing order out of chaos in a person's life that—" Breanna broke off speaking when she saw how uncomfortable Clint was.

"What is it about Jesus Christ that you don't like, Clint?"

"Why...nothing, Miss Breanna."

"Then why do you look like you just smelled a jar of dill pickles?"

"Well...it's just that...I mean—"

"It's your old sin nature, Clint—it's at enmity against God. You need to let Jesus save you so He can give you a new heart that's attune to His." Breanna looked at him tenderly. "I only tell you this because I care what happens to you, Clint, not to offend you."

Clint smiled weakly. "I know that, ma'am. I appreciate you talking straight to me. I've been thinking about it. Really I have. And what you just said helps me to understand what's going on inside me. I'll give it a lot more thought."

Breanna took hold of his upper arm. "Don't think on it too long. *Do* something about it. A lot of people intend to get saved someday, but 'someday' never comes."

Clint nodded. "I understand, Miss Breanna. "

As she moved through car 2, Breanna prayed, "Dear Lord, keep working on him. Break down his defenses. Help him to see his need for Jesus."

8

SHERIFF CURT LANGAN RODE INTO TOWN as the sun set over the jagged mountain peaks. He felt weary and discouraged. He had ridden the banks of the South Platte since early morning, searching for some sign where wagons or horses might have entered the river. Nothing. He wondered what, if anything, Deputies Coulter and Lowery had found in the mountains.

As the sheriff rode up the street toward his office, he thought of ten-year-old Terry Blair. He could still see those eyes looking up at him as Terry asked if he could ride along to help find his father. Langan's heart felt heavy for Terry and his mother and the two smaller children. Where *was* Todd Blair? And where was Lance Tracy? Who had taken them and why?

Langan spoke to people on the street as he rode along, then stopped at the hitch rail in front of his office. As he wrapped the reins, he could hear a loud female voice from inside the office.

No guess as to who the voice belonged to. With a shake of his head, he crossed the boardwalk and opened the door. Mae Trotter's voice assaulted his ears as she railed at Steve Ridgway. "What are you wearin' that badge for, anyhow? Doesn't it give you any authority at all? I demand—"

Mae looked over her shoulder when she heard the door open. She saw who had entered and stomped toward Langan.

"Whattaya got a deputy for if he can't do anything on his own?"

Langan looked past her to Ridgway. "Sheriff," Steve said, "she's been demanding that I let Harley and Cy out of jail. I told her I couldn't do it without a direct order from you."

"That's right," Langan said. "There are some things I have to keep absolutely under my control, Mrs. Trotter. And who goes from this jail is one of them. Deputy Ridgway was only acting under my explicit orders."

Mae set her jaw. "You were gonna have a talk with 'em and let 'em out. Why ain't you done it?"

"Because I've got more important matters on my hands, that's why. And I will have that talk, but it'll have to be tomorrow. I'm worn out. And you'd best understand that it depends on their attitude whether they get out or not."

"I want 'em out, Langan. And I want 'em out now! This little game of your'n is beginnin' to gall me!"

"Let me remind you, lady, that those two made plans to kill me. I want to make sure they've got that idea out of their heads *and* that they realize the error of their ways. They're not going to walk out of this jail till I'm fully convinced of that. Understand?"

Mae Trotter emitted a string of profanities as she stomped to the door, then stopped and looked back. "So you gonna have that talk tomorrow for sure?"

"In the morning."

She nodded stiffly and was gone, leaving the door open.

The early evening air had taken on a chill, and Langan strode to the door to close it. Suddenly a lovely face and figure appeared where Mae Trotter had been only seconds before.

"Hello." Sally Jayne smiled, changing the atmosphere in the office.

"Hello, yourself," Langan said.

As she stepped inside, Langan saw Alf Spaulding and Nick

92

Beal astride their horses at the hitching rail. Sally's horse stood between them. Langan smiled and nodded to both men.

Sally glanced over Curt's shoulder at Steve. "This is your deputy, I assume, Sheriff Langan."

"Oh! Yes. Steve Ridgway, this is Miss Sally Jayne."

Ridgway hurried around the desk. Touching his hatbrim, he said, "Glad to meet you, ma'am. Sally Jane what?"

The redhead giggled. "Jayne is my *last* name, Deputy Ridgway. J-A-Y-N-E."

"Oh. I'm sorry. I thought—"

"A lot of people make the same mistake," she said. "You're pardoned."

"Miss Jayne is new here, Steve," Langan said. "I met her the other day right after the Trotter incident—while you were bringing Harley and Cy to jail."

Steve cuffed his boss playfully on the shoulder. "See what you did to me by making me lock up the Trotters? If you'd have done it, *I* would have met Miss Jayne first!"

Curt grinned. "Life has its little sacrifices, my boy."

"Boy?"

"You're much too young for the likes of Miss Jayne. From something she told me the other day, I figured out she's twenty-five. You're only twenty."

"I'll be twenty-one in three months!"

"Well, I'll leave you two to argue," Sally said with a smile. "Nick and Alf want to get started back to the ranch. I just wanted to stop by and say hello, Sheriff."

"Glad you did."

"Anything new on the kidnappings?"

"Two more men are missing. Young ranchers...family men."

"That's awful. No clues yet as to what the kidnappings are about, I guess?"

"No. I've been working on it myself, and I've got two federal marshals scouring the mountain country for me. Sooner or later, somebody's going to see something that'll put me onto the kidnappers. Or the kidnappers will make a mistake. This thing's going to break open one of these days, and when it does, I'm coming down on the kidnappers like an avalanche."

Sally saw the black look in the sheriff's eyes. "I wouldn't want to be in their boots when you do, Sheriff. From what I hear, it's dangerous to get on your wrong side."

"Believe me, ma'am, you heard right," Ridgway said.

"Well, I've got to be going."

"Miss Sally…" Langan said.

"Mm-hmm?"

"Would…would it be all right if I come out to the *Circle J* sometime soon and meet your father?"

"Oh, I'd love to have you come. But it'll have to wait a while. Right now, Daddy is in such an ill frame of mind with his stomach problem, I'm afraid he'd embarrass me."

"Then, Miss Sally, may I be so bold as to ask if I can take you to dinner sometime soon?"

Deputy Ridgway grinned to himself and went back to the desk. He sat down and pretended to busy himself with some papers.

Sally smiled warmly, moved a step closer to Curt, and said, "That's awfully nice of you, Sheriff. I'd be delighted to have dinner with you. By dinner, I assume you mean an evening meal."

"Well, yes, if you can work it. Nick and Alf might not want to escort you all the way back to the ranch late at night, though."

"If we had dinner at seven, we'd still be able to head back by nine, wouldn't we?"

"Sure."

94

"Well, we'll just work it out. Next time I'm in town, we'll set the date, okay?"

"Yes, ma'am!"

"Good. See you soon."

Curt opened the door for Sally, who cast a glance at Steve and said, "Nice meeting you, Deputy."

"You, too, Miss Jayne."

Curt gazed after Sally for a long time as she rode away with her two escorts in the fading light.

Deputy Ridgway could hold it no longer. He snorted, laughed, and said, "Boss man, if I've ever seen one of the male species bitten by the love bug, it's you!"

Langan's features tinted with embarrassment. "What're you talking about? Miss Sally and I are simply becoming good friends."

Steve snickered. "I saw the look in her eyes, boss. And I saw the look in yours. Good friends, eh? Sure. Like Romeo and Juliet were good friends."

"You're crazy."

"I may be crazy, Sheriff, but I'm not blind."

Langan gave a mock scowl. "Haven't you got work to do?"

At dawn Deputy U.S. Marshals Coulter and Lowery rolled out of their blankets to start searching in a narrow ravine running east and west. While Lowery was rolling up his blankets, Coulter walked in a westerly direction, studying the thick carpet of pine needles that lay over smooth rocks.

"So what do you think, Denny?" Lowery asked.

Without taking his eyes off the pine needles, Coulter said, "Just as I thought. Looks to me like wagons and horses have trafficked through here. Last night it was too dark to see for sure, but now I do. Those wagon tracks we lost on that rocky area a half-mile north of here?"

"Yeah?"

"I've got a strong feeling we've found them again. There were saddle horses riding alongside the wagons back there, and they're here, too. Hard to see if you're not looking for them, but they're here."

Bob Lowery hurried to where his partner stood and studied the crushed and broken pine needles. He let his gaze follow the westward line of the ravine. "Denny. Look up there. In the shadows of those pines. See those horse droppings?"

"I hadn't till just now. No question about it, we're on to something. Let's eat breakfast and then follow those tracks."

The sun was just peeking over the mountaintops as the two federal men leaned from their saddles, studying the ground while slowly riding west. A pair of sharp-eyed hawks rode the air waves in wide circles overhead, studying the riders. Smaller birds chirped and sang in the treetops, flitting from limb to limb and tree to tree. Chipmunks darted across their path, disappearing as fast as they had appeared.

Soon they came to the bank of a shallow creek about twenty feet wide. Lowery glanced to the other side. "No tracks over there, pard. You know what that means."

"Yeah, it means they're using the creek to throw off anybody who's following them."

"Like us."

"If you weren't doing something wrong, you wouldn't need to cover your tracks, would you?"

"Nope."

"So now, it's left or right. Want to toss a coin?"

"Don't think so. I've got a strong hunch."

"Okay. Which way?"

"Right."

"North."

"Yep."

"Well, since my huncher isn't working today, let's go by yours."

The deputies scoured both sides of the gurgling creek, looking for signs where saddle horses and wagons had pulled out onto dry ground.

They had gone about two miles when Coulter pointed ahead. "Look! Up there."

Bob Lowery saw a spot about fifty feet ahead on the opposite side of the creek where the rocks had been disturbed. Though the drivers and riders had used rocky ground to pull out on, they had not only disturbed the rocks, they had scarred them with the iron wagon wheels.

The deputies followed the tracks and more horse droppings through dense forest, winding amid towering pines and white-barked aspen. The trail led them northwest. After about fifteen minutes, they heard the sound of a roaring waterfall.

"Lot of water going over that precipice, wherever it is," said Coulter. "That's more than a creek. There's got to be a river close by."

The sound of the waterfall grew louder as they followed the tracks. Suddenly both men saw a clearing ahead with an old unpainted barn and weatherworn sheds standing on the edge of it. The buildings were almost camouflaged by deep shadows from the surrounding pines. A split-rail fence formed a corral around three sides of the barn. The charred remains of a small cabin lay in a jumbled heap near the largest shed. The cabin's stone fireplace still stood, and by its weathered look, they knew it had been a long time since the cabin burned and the place was vacated.

Dennis Coulter drew rein, and as Bob Lowery came alongside him, he said, "What do you make of this, Bob?"

"Well, for sure it isn't where the kidnappers are keeping their captives."

Coulter swung from the saddle and Lowery did likewise.

"Looks like a path leading through the trees over there. But they couldn't have taken a wagon through. Too narrow."

Both men followed the narrow path for several yards. The roar of the waterfall became louder with every step. Soon they came to a stone ledge and saw a steep, winding trail leading into a canyon. The forest was so thick around it they could see ahead only about thirty yards before the path wound out of sight.

Lowery knelt down and pointed out hoofprints and bootprints. "They sure enough use this trail, Denny. I've got a funny feeling we've found the place where the kidnapped men are being taken…somewhere down in that canyon."

"But where are they stashing the wagons?"

Lowery looked back in the direction they had come. "Probably in that largest shed. It'd hold a couple of wagons."

"Before we follow the trail into the canyon, let's take a look in the shed. We'll have to ditch the horses, too. No sense taking them into the canyon."

The shed had a wide set of double doors on the front side, and a smaller door around the corner.

"Let's use the little door," Coulter told his partner.

Rusty hinges squeaked as the lawmen moved inside. Cracks in the walls let in sunshine, but the corners lay in deep shadow. One old wagon stood on the wavy wooden floor. The wagon's sideboards were warped and its metal rusty. It was covered with a layer of ancient dust. The bed of the rickety old wagon held about half a load of dust-covered rocks, ranging from watermelon size to cabbage size.

"Probably a thousand pounds of rocks in there, Denny. Wonder what they were going to do with those?"

"Your guess would be as good as mine," said Coulter, turning back toward the door. "Let's check the barn. I bet we'll find the wagons in there."

Lowery nodded and followed his partner outside. They both stopped short at exactly the same time. Three men with guns pointed blocked the path.

"Well, lookee what we've got here, boys," the one in the middle said. "Looks like we done caught us some trespassers!"

"Yeah, Ken," laughed the one to his left. "A couple of *badge-totin'* trespassers! You dudes reach for the sky!"

The deputies exchanged anxious looks and raised their hands.

"You men better think this thing through," Dennis Coulter said. "We're federal marshals. Anything happens to us, and you'll have more trouble than you can imagine."

The one on Ken's right sneered and said, "We'll put you in a place where nobody can find you, tin stars. We ain't worried about any trouble your kind can put on us."

"Just who are you, anyway?"

"Well, allow me to introduce us," the one called Ken said. "I'm Ken Botham. This here's Wayne Decker, and this is Merv Norden. Feel better, now, lawman?"

"Just what's your game?" Lowery said.

"No game," Botham said. "It's serious business."

"And that is?"

"You'll see."

"What about their horses, Ken?"

"We'll take 'em down with us."

Wayne Decker laughed. "Boy, is Morgan gonna be happy when he finds out we've done got him some federal lawmen who came to volunteer for work!"

99

The three men had a good laugh as they relieved the deputies of their guns and pushed them toward the narrow path they had found only moments before.

At the same time the two marshals were being escorted into the canyon, Sheriff Langan left his office and entered the cell block in the Denver County Jail. Harley Trotter and his youngest son were the only two prisoners at the moment. Both rose to their feet and moved to the cell door when they saw Langan come in.

"We gonna talk now, Sheriff?" Harley said.

"Yeah." Langan stepped close to the bars. "You two have had a couple days to think on what you did. Still want to kill me?"

Father and son eyed each other sheepishly, then Harley cleared his throat and said, "Sheriff, it ain't easy for a hardheaded old fella like me to admit he's been wrong."

"Even a fella that ain't so hardheaded or old like me," put in Cy.

Langan nodded. "I'm listening."

Harley scratched his head. "Well, Sheriff, I've been doin' a lotta thinkin', and Cy and me have been doin' a lot of talkin'. Seems we've come to the conclusion that Cy's older brothers were fools. Neither one of 'em should've gone up against you like they done. What you did was self-defense, pure and simple."

"We ain't got nothin' against you, Sheriff," Cy said. "We was just hot under the skin at you for killin' Willie and Chad. But Pa and I realize you were just savin' your own life and doin' your job. Same thing any good lawman would do in that situation. Ain't that right, Pa?"

"Sure is, son."

Langan studied their faces for a long moment. "Harley, you think you can cool your wife down? She's still got a deep grudge against me."

"I'll handle Mae. She's got a temper a whole lot like mine, Sheriff. I know how to bring her into line, and I'll do it."

Langan paused another long moment. "I want to let you out, Harley, but how do I know you aren't just saying all this now to get out, only to come after me again later?"

Harley looked at the floor. After several seconds, he met the sheriff's gaze again, and said, "Well, I realize all you have is our word for it. But believe me, Sheriff, we've learned our lesson. We don't want no more trouble with the law."

"That's good, Harley. But let me caution you—don't slip even once. If you so much as look cross-eyed at me, I'll run you in and lock you up. And next time, I'll throw away the key."

"We understand, Sheriff," Cy said. "From here on, Pa and I will walk a straight line."

"Well, speaking of walking straight lines, the two of you better swear off the liquor. If you don't, one day soon you'll get tanked up and forget this little talk of ours. You do, and you're going to look at the inside of this jail until it gets so old it collapses. Are you listening to me?"

"Sure are, Sheriff. Cy and me ain't gonna touch another drop."

Langan stared at them hard. "You really mean it?"

Harley raised his right hand. "On my poor mother's grave, Sheriff."

Langan sighed and took the cell door key from his pocket. "Okay, Harley, Cy. I'm going to give you a chance to prove it."

The sheriff turned the key, swung the door open, and said, "You're free to go."

"What about our guns?" asked Harley.

"I've got them locked in my desk. Let's go."

"What about our horses? Where are they?"

"I had my deputy put them at O'Hara's Stable. You'll have to pay to get them out."

Harley did not flinch. "Okay."

Langan opened the drawer and pulled out their gunbelts. As he handed them to father and son, he said, "I don't ever want you two in this jail again."

"And we don't want to be here either, Sheriff," Harley said.

Ten minutes later, the Trotters rode eastward out of Denver. When they had passed the city limits, Cy laughed heartily.

"What's so funny?" Harley asked.

"You."

"Me? What're you talkin' about?"

"Swearin' on Grandma Trotter's grave that you'd never touch another drop of liquor."

Harley laughed. "Well, is it my fault she burned to death and we had no body to bury? C'mon. Let's go home and celebrate our freedom with your ma over a few glasses of whiskey!"

"Okay!"

"And while we're drinkin', we'll figure out a foolproof way to murder that stinkin' sheriff."

Some thirty minutes later, father and son were about halfway home when six riders came thundering out of a nearby thicket, guns drawn.

"Hold it right there!" shouted the rider in the lead. "Throw those revolvers on the ground!"

Both Trotters quickly obeyed.

"What do you want from us?" Harley asked as he let his gun slip from his fingers.

"We want you to turn around and ride into those trees," came the leader's gruff voice.

Harley pressed them again, wanting to know what was going on as he and Cy were forced to ride into the thicket. No one answered. When they were well into the dense trees and bushes, father and son saw another man waiting on the seat of a wagon hitched to four horses.

"All right, off your mounts," growled the leader, waving his gun at them.

"Look, if it's money you want, we ain't got any," Harley said.

"Pa's tellin' you the truth," Cy said. "We're just poor ranchers."

"Shut up and get into the back of the wagon!"

"Where are you takin' us?"

The leader stepped close and brought his gun barrel down on Harley's head. Harley crumpled to the ground.

"What'd you do that for?" Cy wailed.

"You want the same thing, kid?"

"N-no."

"Then shut your mouth and do as you're told!"

While Cy obeyed, two members of the group picked Harley up and dumped him in the wagon bed. Quickly, the unconscious Harley and his frightened son were bound and gagged. Harley started to moan and come around. The leader waited till he was conscious, then said to both, "You two are gonna be covered with this big tarp while we make our little trip. You lie still and don't even think of making any sounds. We'll probably meet people along the way. You stay perfectly quiet, 'cause if you don't, we'll not only have to kill whoever hears you, we'll kill you, too. Got that?"

Both Trotters nodded, biting on their gags.

"All right," the leader said to the others, "we'll take their horses with us. Once we're in the mountains, we'll strip off the saddles and bridles and turn 'em loose. Where these boys are goin', they won't need no horses."

The procession moved out of the thicket and pulled onto the well-traveled road, the hooves of their horses and the wheels of the wagon blending in with other travelers' marks. On the road

west, they met mounted riders and people in horse-drawn ve-
hicles. The kidnappers greeted the travelers, none of whom sus-
pected there was anything wrong.

When they reached the Rockies, both the Trotters' horses
were unsaddled, unbridled, and turned loose to fend for themselves, and the procession headed for the high country.

FLOYD METZ STOOD IN THE ENGINE CAB as the engineer pulled on the throttle to slow down the train.

"Yep, there they are, Mr. Metz. Just like Mr. Squires ordered."

Four large wagons were parked on the right side of the tracks, and a half-dozen saddled horses were bunched together near the lead wagon.

The passengers had been informed that a Union Pacific executive had wired Floyd Metz in Fort Collins, giving orders that the men hired by the railroad should be taken off the train ten miles north of Denver.

In the baggage car, Breanna Baylor was examining the three Chinese men when someone knocked at the rear door.

"That will be Chung Ho, Myrtle," Breanna said. "Would you let him in, please?"

Chung Ho greeted Myrtle with a slight bow and said, "Mr. Wonderly say Missy Breanna want to talk to me."

"Yes, Chung Ho. Come in."

The Chinese man's eyes showed fear. "But—"

"It's all right, Chung Ho," said Breanna, rising to her feet. "Their fevers have all broken. They're not contagious now. I need you to talk to them."

"Yes, Missy?"

"These men are still very weak. I want you to explain to them that they should go on into Denver with me. I'll take care of them until they have completely recovered, then they can go to work for the railroad."

Chung Ho nodded and went to his friends. He squatted down beside them and explained what Breanna had just said. The conversation went on for several minutes.

Finally, Chung Ho turned to the nurse. "I explain what you say, Missy Breanna. They want to stay with us, even though they cannot work until they are stronger."

"Well, the choice is theirs, but it's against my better judgment. You sure they won't change their minds?"

"I am sure," Chung Ho said with a smile. "We are very stubborn people. My friends want you to know how very much they appreciate the care you give them, though."

"I'm glad I could do it," Breanna said.

The train halted with a squeal of brakes. Myrtle and Breanna left the baggage coach as several of the Chinese men helped their three friends to the ground and guided them to the wagons.

Floyd Metz was talking to George Matson as if they were strangers. Matson explained about the new training camp while his men guided the workers to the wagons.

As Breanna and Myrtle watched the men head for the wagons, Moses and Malachi Crowder and Clint Byers walked toward her followed by the other men who had come to her aid during Jubal Brassfield's harassment of her.

The Crowder brothers told Breanna good-bye and said they would be praying for God's blessings on her life, then they hurried to the wagons. George Matson called for the rest of the new track layers to hurry just as Clint Byers stepped up.

"Thank you for letting me share my heartaches with you, Miss Breanna," he said warmly.

"Hey! Let's go over there!" Matson shouted toward Byers.

"Clint, what about your soul?" Breanna asked.

"I've been thinking on it some more, ma'am."

"Don't put it off, Clint."

He smiled and then turned and ran to the wagons.

Breanna sighed. "Well, I can't push Jesus down his throat, Myrtle."

"Sometimes we wish we could, don't we, dear? Come on, let's get aboard."

When they stepped up on the train's platform, Breanna looked back at the wagons. Lord, please don't let Clint have any peace until he opens his heart to You.

She saw Floyd Metz say some final words to the man who headed up the wagon crew then move toward his private coach.

Inside car number 3, Breanna sagged onto the seat the two women had occupied before their stint in the baggage coach. "I'm really tired, Myrtle. I need to get some rest."

The older woman studied Breanna's face. "You look a little peaked, honey. Are you sure it's just fatigue?"

"It has to be. I'll be all right once I rest these tired bones."

George Matson and his nine hardcases moved the wagons west across the prairie toward the Rockies. Matson rode beside the lead wagon, which held Moses and Malachi Crowder, among others.

"You know, Moses," Malachi said, "we're gonna do real good workin' for the railroad. Time we get that track laid between Denver and Santa Fe, we're gonna be set!"

"Sounds good to me, little brother," Moses said with a laugh. "Sounds good to me!"

Matson and his men exchanged furtive glances, knowing

these men would either die from exhaustion or be murdered when the mine played out. For sure, not one of them would ever breathe free air again.

As the wagons headed due west, Matson let his horse drift back along the line. When he came near the wagon bearing Clint Byers, Clint said, "Say, Mr. Matson, how far is it to the training camp?"

"Only a few more miles. It's back in those foothills straight ahead of us."

The sun was just reaching its zenith when the wagons threaded through a narrow gap between two hogback foothills. On the other side they pulled into a grove of aspens beside a small creek. Six riders waited under the aspens' fluttering golden leaves.

Clint frowned and said to the other men in his wagon, "This doesn't look like a training camp to me." Then to Matson, "Where's the camp? And who are those men?"

Duff Pasko and Morgan's other men moved up, pulling their guns. Matson looked back at Byers and said, "You're right, pal. This ain't no trainin' camp. You dudes are now the prisoners of Mr. Duff Pasko and his boys. A certain Mr. Morgan's gonna give you employment instead of the Union Pacific."

"What are you talking about?"

"Yeah!" Moses Crowder yelled. "We didn't hire on to no Mr. Morgan, whoever he is. We hired on to lay track for the Union Pacific Railroad! What are these men doin' pointin' guns at us?"

Clint Byers stood in the wagon and set fiery eyes on George Matson. "I don't know what this is supposed to be, Matson, but it isn't going to work!"

"Sit down and shut up!"

"I'm not sitting down, and I am not shutting up! I want to know—"

Duff Pasko cocked the hammer of his revolver, pointed it at Byers's face, and said, "The man said to sit down and shut up, buster! Do as he says!"

Byers licked his lips and went to his knees.

All but three of the Chinese had no idea what was being said, but the way their eyes bulged indicated they knew they were in trouble. The three who spoke English signaled for the rest to remain still.

Pasko backed away a few steps so he could look at all the prisoners. "Now you boys listen up!" he bawled. "My name's Duff Pasko. I work for Mr. Morgan, as do these men with me. You all wanted employment, didn't you?"

The forty men just stared at him, unable to believe what was happening.

Pasko moved close to Moses Crowder and sneered, "Well, didn't you, black boy?"

"Yes, but—"

"Well, you've *got* employment! In fact, it'll last you the rest of your lives!"

Clint stiffened. "What do you mean by that?"

Pasko's harsh features split in a sadistic grin. "You'll find out when we get to where we're goin'."

"And where is that?" Clint said.

"Just keep your eyes open and you'll find out."

"Look, you! I don't know what's going on here, but what you're doing is known as kidnapping! There are laws against this kind of thing! I demand you let us go! We've been hired by the railroad to lay track, and that's what we mean to do!"

"Shut up!" yelled Emil Hadley, Pasko's right-hand man, as he rushed to the side of Clint's wagon.

Before Clint could dodge him, Hadley slammed his gun against Clint's head. Clint crumpled to the floor of the wagon.

Hadley leaned over the side and said, "Any more lip outta you, and next time I'll crack your skull!"

"Okay, Emil. Put 'em in the chains," Pasko said.

While two of Morgan's men held guns on the prisoners, the others clamped leg irons on each man, then chained the men in each wagon together. The faces of the Chinese men were frozen into masks of horror. The three English-speaking Chinese were afraid to tell them what was going on.

When the shackling was done, Pasko faced the prisoners and said loudly, "I want all of you to listen to me! If any of you give us trouble, you will pay for it in ways you won't like. And when we get to our destination, you had better be quiet and submissive, or Mr. Morgan will make you suffer. Believe me, you don't want to get my boss irritated."

Chung Ho lifted a hand timidly. "Mr. Pasko, most of my countrymen do not understand English. May I tell them what you just said and what is going on?"

"By all means. I want everybody to know exactly what I said."

After Chung Ho had explained the situation to his friends, the wagons moved out. Puzzlement and despair showed on forty faces as the wagons headed west, winding further into the Rockies. Clint Byers was nursing a throbbing headache, which pounded all the more each time the wagon hit a bump.

After three hours of slowly ascending rough terrain on a barely visible trail, they came over a sharp rise and broke out of the tall timber, heading down into a broad, sweeping valley.

Pasko and Matson rode side by side in front as the wagons moved along the north end of the valley for nearly five miles. Pasko then veered to the right at the top of a grassy knoll and led the procession into a narrow ravine that ran east and west between a stand of towering pines. The smooth, rocky floor of the ravine was carpeted with pine needles. Soon they came to the bank of a shallow creek some twenty feet wide. Pasko led them into the creek and followed it midstream northward for about two miles, then he led them out at a rocky spot on the west bank.

Again they were in dense forest as horses blew and wagons rattled. The drivers had to work hard to guide the wagons through a narrow opening between the trees. Pasko angled them a bit north, and after several minutes the sound of a waterfall met their ears.

Presently they approached the same clearing where the two U.S. marshals had been captured not long before. The chained men saw a deserted old barn and three weather-beaten sheds. The blackened remains of a small cabin lay in a heap, with grass growing amid the charred fragments and around the stone chimney that stood like a sentinel over the ruins.

Pasko reined in and dismounted. "You boys can leave your horses over there in the corral," he said to Matson and his men. "Pretty steep trail goin' down. We'll be leavin' the wagons in the barn."

Matson grinned and glanced at his men. Twenty thousand in gold would soon be theirs.

"Leave the prisoners chained together," Pasko said to Emil Hadley. "Even though it'll make it harder for 'em goin' down into the canyon, we won't have anybody tryin' to run for it."

Emil nodded and told Morgan's other men to get the prisoners out of the wagons.

Clint Byers exchanged glances with Moses Crowder, but they both knew better than to say anything. Somehow they would work together to escape at a later time.

When the wagons had been stashed in the barn and Matson's men had placed their horses in the corral, Pasko said, "Take 'em on down, Emil. I'll meet you down there after I make my report to Morgan."

Emil pointed to the path amid the trees and said, "Okay, boys, let's go!"

Pasko watched the prisoners follow Hadley single file, shuffling awkwardly in the chains and shackles. The rest of the men walked behind them, leading the horses, including Pasko's. The path was far too steep and treacherous to ride.

When the procession had passed from view, Pasko hurried to the largest of the three sheds, the one with a wide set of double doors on one side and a smaller door around the corner. He glanced around to make sure he was alone and entered the shed through the small door.

He walked straight to the darkest corner. Kneeling down, he carefully slipped his fingertips into what looked like naturally worn grooves in the floor. He gripped the edge of a trapdoor cleverly camouflaged and raised it, leaning it against the wall.

He slipped his feet into the dark shaft and found the sturdy ladder. Then he moved down a few rungs and reached up to close the trapdoor before continuing down.

Lanterns hung along the walls of the tunnel, giving off their dim light at every turn as he made his way through the bowels of the mountain. He stopped in front of a massive wooden door next to a storage space which held several boxes of dynamite and various other mining supplies.

Some seventy feet from where Pasko stood, a dark passageway funneled into the yawning mouth of Morgan's gold mine. He could see sunlight shining through the mouth of the mine, splashing the rocky walls.

Pasko knew how happy Morgan would be to learn that Floyd Metz had provided forty new slaves. He gripped the door handle and pulled on the heavy wooden door, eager to take the news to his boss.

✦

Emil Hadley and his men guided the prisoners and the Matson bunch down the steep, twisting trail. The men in chains moved with difficulty. Suddenly one of the Chinese men went down, and the men chained to him fell too, tumbling on top of each other. When they stopped rolling, Hadley swore at them, telling them to be more careful.

Wing Loo gained his feet and helped up the chained man beside him. "It would be much easier for us to descend this steep path, Mr. Hadley, if we were not chained together," he said.

"Well, that's just too bad, 'cause you're gonna stay just the way you are."

"How much farther do we have to go?"

"What difference does it make? All right, the rest of you! On your feet! We gotta keep movin'!"

The procession continued to descend, and the roar of the waterfall grew louder. Soon the waterfall came into view. The river was some fifty to sixty feet wide where the swirling white water cascaded over a rocky ledge and plunged about ninety feet before continuing its journey. A mist floated where the falling water struck bedrock, and a steady wind carried the mist upward. Water sprayed the group as Emil Hadley led them along a narrow ledge behind the waterfall.

Hadley marveled that all the gold had to come out of the canyon on the backs of pack mules via this arduous trail. Plenty of gold had come out already, and there would be plenty more, especially since they had found a new vein. And these poor unfortunates in chains were going to dig it out.

After they reached the other side of the waterfall, Morgan's men guided the group downward for about five hundred yards into a vast, shadowed canyon. At the bottom, they came to a large open area where the mouth of the mine was located. There was heavy brush in some spots, especially at the base of the massive rock walls.

A large bunkhouse had been built at the west end of the canyon, while at the opposite end, within twenty-five yards of the mine entrance—and socketed right into the mountainside—was a large log cabin with a porch. The ninety yards between the cabin and the bunkhouse were dotted with several small shacks, privies, and tool sheds, along with a crude barn butted up against the canyon wall. A split-rail fence formed a large corral next to the barn and held a good number of horses and mules.

Half as wide as it was long, the canyon's granite walls were over a hundred feet high, and the sun's rays penetrated to the bottom only a few hours a day. Heavily armed guards stood in the shadows, many of them barely visible to the newcomers as they filed into the open area in front of the large cabin, whose base and porch were ten feet higher than the floor of the canyon. Wooden steps led down from the porch. The newly arrived men were surprised to see Duff Pasko standing on the porch, looking down at them with a sly smile.

A few hollow-eyed slaves could be seen moving about the shacks and in and out of the mine. Their faces were drawn and their clothing was tattered. They cast dull glances at the new men, then went about their business. Two carts pulled by mules rolled out of the mine, gold ore piled high, and the men who guided the mules had the same vacant look in their eyes as those who moved among the shacks.

Emil Hadley looked up at Pasko and asked, "Shall I take the new ones and assign them to their shacks?"

"Later. I want to talk to 'em first. And after that, I want 'em to meet Max."

"Yeah, they need to get a gander at him." As he spoke,

Hadley mounted the steps and asked, "So was Morgan happy getting forty new slaves?"

A broad grin spread over Pasko's face. "Sure was. And since we've been gone, we've picked up some more new ones, too."

"Oh?"

"Take a look over there by the mouth of the mine."

Todd Blair and Lance Tracy had come up from the mine to take a short breather. They sat on the ground under the sharp eye of Ken Botham, who leaned against the granite mouth of the mine, talking to four men who had their backs toward the cabin.

"All I see are those two ranchers," Hadley said.

"No, look at those four Ken's talkin' to."

"Who are they?"

"Well, two of 'em are a rancher and his son Metz's guys picked up east of Denver. Morgan told me the other two—you ain't gonna believe this—the other two are deputy U.S. marshals."

"No kiddin'?"

"No kiddin'."

"How'd we get ahold of them?"

"They were snoopin' around up by the old burned-out cabin. Ken, Wayne, and Merv caught 'em."

"Well, I'll be switched! So we got a coupla federal boys gonna be slaves!" Hadley suddenly frowned. "Ain't Morgan afraid, messin' with government men?"

"Doesn't seem to be. But then, what could Ken and the boys do when they caught 'em snoopin'? Sure couldn't turn 'em loose."

"Well, you're right about that. But...what's Morgan gonna do if more federal men show up around here lookin' for these dudes?"

115

"Guess he'll cross that bridge if he comes to it, but he don't seem worried."

"Tough guy, isn't he?"

"I've never seen anybody tougher."

"Sure would like to meet him. There's a bunch of us in this canyon that would. We've worked hard for him. You'd think he'd appreciate it enough to let us see him face-to-face. I mean, nobody in this outfit has ever gotten to see him except you and Max...and the girl, of course."

"Mr. Morgan ain't comin' outta the cabin, Emil. He figures he pays you guys plenty good and doesn't owe you anythin' else. And nobody goes into that cabin unless Morgan does the invitin'. Just enjoy the money you're makin' and be satisfied."

10

WHILE DUFF PASKO AND EMIL HADLEY talked on the porch, the captives looked at the only window in the cabin's facade. Although the interior of the cabin was obscured by nearly opaque glass, they could see two shadowy figures observing them.

Clint Byers, standing by Moses Crowder, whispered, "You suppose one of them is Morgan?"

"Probably. But if one of them is Morgan, I wonder who the other one is?"

Pasko noticed that the new men were staring at the window. He smiled and looked down at the new men and said, "I want to point out a few things to you. By now, you all know—and I trust it's been explained to those who don't understand English—that you're in the custody of Mr. Morgan, the owner of the mine. There are some rules around here, and Mr. Morgan wants them made clear. First and foremost, we do not tolerate—"

"Excuse me, Pasko." George Matson stood with his men on the fringe of the prisoners. "But we'd like to collect our payment and be on our way. No sense in us hearin' these rules."

Pasko made a furtive hand signal that was picked up by the guards who stood nearby. "Oh. Guess I forgot to tell you, George. Mr. Morgan very much appreciates you pickin' up the forty new prisoners for him, but he figures a few more will be even better. You and your boys are prisoners, too."

The air was filled with the familiar sound of hammers being cocked. Before they could react, the Matson bunch found themselves facing a half-circle of threatening black muzzles.

"Drop your gunbelts!" Pasko said, looking down at them with piercing eyes.

"Hey, what is this?" Matson said. "Whattaya mean, we're prisoners?"

"Don't ask questions, George. Just do as I say."

"Now!" one of the guards snarled, aiming his weapon at Matson's face.

Matson looked around at his men. "Better do as they say, boys. I'll handle this."

Matson dropped his gunbelt and drew a slow, deep breath. His voice took on the biting edge of a man ready to explode. "Pasko, this is an outrage, you double-crosser!"

Pasko shrugged his wide shoulders. "I was only followin' orders, George. It was Mr. Morgan who double-crossed you."

Matson headed for the stairs of the porch. "Pasko, I want to see Morgan!"

One of the guards stepped in front of Matson and leveled his revolver at him. "Hold it right there!"

"You're in no position to demand anything, George!" Pasko said. "Now, just settle down."

"Settle down? We did a job for you and your boss in good faith. You promised us twenty thousand in gold. Now you tell us we're not gonna be paid, but we *are* gonna be slaves! Settle down? You're outta your mind, Pasko! We want our gold, and we want to leave!"

"It's outta my hands, George. Like I said, I'm just followin' my boss's orders. Besides, we can't let you boys go. You know where the mine is. There's no way Morgan's gonna let you go."

Matson's chest heaved. "This was the plan all along, wasn't it?"

Pasko grinned. "Yeah, Georgie. It was."

Matson glanced at the gun aimed at his head, then spit on the ground. "Pasko, I want to see Morgan, and I want to see him *now!*"

"No way."

Matson cursed vehemently. "Pasko, get this and get it straight! My men and I are not gonna be Morgan's slaves! We will not dig gold!"

"My boss has ways of makin' his slaves glad to work, George. Believe me, you don't want to irritate him."

"We will not be any man's slaves! No matter what your Mr. Morgan does, he can't make us work. I want those guns turned off us, and I want the gold you promised us. And if you won't do as I say, I want to talk to Morgan!"

Without a word, Duff Pasko turned and entered the cabin. A half minute later he emerged with a virtual giant of a man behind him. He was easily a head taller than Pasko and outweighed him by a hundred pounds. He had a full beard, and long, shaggy black hair hung almost to his jawline. A menacing scowl etched his face, and his black eyes had a fierce look under shaggy black brows. He was the hairiest, meanest-looking man George Matson had ever seen, and he had a bullwhip clutched in one hand.

Pasko looked at the captives and said, "Let me introduce you new boys to Max McGurskie. Any man who refuses to work will be turned over to Max for punishment. Very few slaves have lived through one of his whippings."

"This whole thing is uncalled for, Pasko!" Matson said. "Me and my men would never tell anybody the location of the mine.

All I want is a chance to talk to Morgan. I demand it, you hear me? I demand it!"

Again without a word, Pasko turned and entered the cabin.

Max McGurskie set his eyes on Matson and shook his head but said nothing.

Presently Duff Pasko reappeared, crossed the porch, and looked down at Matson. "Okay, George. Mr. Morgan says to bring you in."

The guards looked shocked. Matson's men grinned at each other.

Matson glanced contemptuously at the guard who held the gun on him and said, "You can put that thing away now, pal."

When Matson reached the porch, he looked up at the giant who blocked his path and said, "Pardon me, big boy. I have an appointment with Mr. Morgan." McGurskie shook his head and stepped aside. Matson looked at his men and smiled. "Hang on, boys. This whole nightmare will be over shortly."

Pasko opened the door, revealing only a shadowed interior, and gestured for Matson to enter.

There was no sound from inside the cabin for more than a minute, then Matson's voice cried in terror. "No! No! Please, don't—!"

His cry was cut off with the sound of a gunshot. A wordless wail followed, then two more shots rang out. A woman's scream pierced the air.

The door swung open and a cloud of blue-white smoke drifted out. Seconds later, Duff Pasko appeared, dragging Matson's body by the ankles. The dead man was on his back, his arms trailing above his head. Three bullet holes decorated his chest.

Everyone could hear a young woman weeping uncontrollably.

Then Max McGurskie stepped around Matson's body and

moved back inside. Just as the door was closing behind him, the prisoners heard the unmistakable sound of a slap followed by a shriek, then the young woman's weeping began to subside.

"Coupla you guards take this carcass and get rid of it," Pasko said.

Suddenly the cabin door opened again and Matson's hat sailed onto the porch before the door slammed shut again.

While a pair of guards carried Matson's body away, Pasko moved to the porch railing and looked at the wan faces of Matson's men and the rest of the prisoners. "Anybody else want to see Morgan?"

The only sounds were the rumble of the river and the faint hammer noises coming from inside the mine.

Pasko resumed speaking where he had left off, explaining Morgan's hard and fast rules. Then he ordered the prisoners taken to the shacks where they would bunk.

Clint Byers felt sick all over. Seeing the corpse of George Matson had made him think of Breanna Baylor's warning not to put off salvation. Death was always breathing down a person's neck, no matter who they were or what their station in life. As before, he shook off Breanna's words, telling himself he would consider turning to Christ soon.

When Chung Ho saw the guards dividing the men into a half-dozen groups, he approached the guard who seemed to be in charge. "Pardon me, sir."

"Yeah?"

"Please, mister—"

"Dutton."

"Please, Mr. Dutton, it is essential that my countrymen be in only three groups."

"And why's that?"

"Because only three of us can speak English." Pointing to Wan

Dun and Wing Loo, he said, "These are the other two. Our countrymen need us with them so they can understand what is happening at all times, and so they will be able to obey all commands."

Dutton nodded. "Makes sense. I'll go ask Duff if it's okay."

Moments later, Dutton returned, saying Pasko had given permission for the Chinese men to be divided into only three groups. Each of the men who spoke English would be with a group. Chung Ho politely thanked Dutton.

Clint Byers, Wally Wyman, Carl Lynch, and Moses and Malachi Crowder were grouped together. They would bunk with ten other men who were now working in the mine.

As the train slowed to enter Denver, Floyd Metz stood before a full-length mirror in his private coach, practicing facial expressions. He pretended he was entering Jonathan Squires's office, and he put on the proper smile. "Well, Mr. Squires, as I told you in my telegram from Cheyenne City, I had a productive trip to San Francisco."

"Yes, forty men hired to lay track!" he pictured Squires saying, with a happy look on his face.

"Forty, indeed, sir! I didn't go into detail in the telegram for obvious reasons, but I hired thirty-three Chinese men and seven others, including two husky Negroes."

"Metz, you're a good man," he imagined Squires saying. "I assume you were able to find places for all of them at the boarding houses until they start laying track."

Metz practiced batting his eyes and looking a bit befuddled. When he had it just right, he said, "Boarding houses, sir?"

"Why, yes. The boarding houses we made arrangements with before you left for California."

"But...but, sir, I figured you canceled those arrangements

when you set up the training camp in the foothills."

Glee bubbled up in Floyd as he imagined the frustrated look on the executive vice-president's face. "Training camp? What training camp?"

"Why, the one you spoke of in your telegram, sir. I thought at the time that it was an odd and sudden change in plans, but you are the boss, Mr. Squires."

"What telegram are you talking about?"

"Why, the one you had waiting for me at Fort Collins, Mr. Squires. The one that told me where to have the engineer stop the train outside of Denver so the trainees could be transported to the camp."

"Metz, I sent no telegram."

The mirror reflected Floyd's rounded jaw dropping. He had that shocked look down to perfection. "You *what?*" His hand dived into his coat pocket and removed George Matson's telegram. "But here it is, sir."

"Oh, that's good, Floyd," the fat man said with a laugh. "That's good! Ol' Squires will buy it. You really look shocked. Okay, you're ready for a star performance!"

The big engine chugged to a halt in Denver's Union Station with clanging bell and the usual hiss of steam.

As Breanna Baylor and Myrtle Henderson gathered their hand luggage and stood in line to leave the train, Breanna said, "Really, Myrtle, I can't impose on Mr. Clement. He's your neighbor and is only expecting to pick you up."

"Honey, I'm telling you he won't mind at all. Harold is a dear man and very congenial. We've been neighbors since before his wife died six years ago. I know him well. Believe me, he'll be honored to take you home."

"But I can hire a wagon."

"No need. It'll be all right."

When the two women stepped down from the coach, Harold Clement threaded his way through the crowd. As he drew up, he gave the women a big smile and said, "So how was the trip, Myrtle?"

"Very good, Harold. I'll tell you all about it when you come over for supper tonight."

Clement's face beamed. "Here, let me take your bag." As she handed it to him, he said, "Will you make me some of your famous fried chicken, mashed potatoes, and gravy?"

"Mm-hmm."

"And hot bread?"

"Of course. Harold, this is my friend, Breanna Baylor."

"Howdy, Miss Baylor." Clement touched his hat. "You're the traveling nurse who works out of Dr. Goodwin's office, aren't you?"

Breanna smiled and nodded.

"I've heard a lot about you from Myrtle and from many of your admirers. I've been a patient of Dr. Glen Wakeman's ever since he came to Denver, so I haven't ever been to Dr. Goodwin's office to meet you."

Breanna's mouth felt dry. She ran her tongue over the roof of her mouth and said, "I know Dr. Wakeman. He's a fine man and a good doctor."

"Harold," Myrtle said, "Breanna needs a ride home. She lives in a small cottage behind Dr. Goodwin's house. Would you mind taking her along with us?"

"Well, of course not."

"I have a heavy trunk and a suitcase, Mr. Clement," Breanna said. "Really, I can hire a wagon."

"Not with Harold Clement around, you won't. Any friend of

Myrtle's is a friend of mine. I'll be more than happy to take you and your luggage home."

As the wagon rolled through the streets of Denver, Breanna discreetly used a hanky to dab perspiration from her brow. But the move did not escape the older woman's eye. Myrtle was sitting next to Harold with Breanna to her right. She leaned so she could look into her young friend's face. "Honey, you really are peaked. Do you have a fever?"

"I'm just awfully tired, Myrtle. I'll be fine when I get home. I just need a few days' rest."

"Why would being tired cause you to perspire, honey?"

"Well, I—"

"I think we'd better take you right to Dr. Goodwin's office and let him look at you."

"No," said Breanna, shaking her head. "I'll be fine."

Floyd Metz entered the Union Pacific Railroad building within ten minutes after the train pulled in. His heart was pounding as he moved down the hall toward Jonathan Squires's office. He met fellow employees along the way, giving them brief answers about his trip.

He turned the doorknob of Squires's outer office and walked inside. Linna Bittner, the executive vice-president's secretary and receptionist, greeted him.

"Well, hello, Mr. Metz," Linna said in a friendly tone. "Glad to have you home."

"Thank you, Linna." He hoped she didn't notice his nervousness.

"Nice trip?"

"Yes, it was. Is Mr. Squires in?"

"Yes, but he's meeting with the engineers who'll be working

on the track-laying to Santa Fe. Should be through in about a half hour or so. Would you like to stay, or would you rather come back? I can tell him you're home."

"I'll...ah...just stay, Linna. Mr. Squires will want to know more about the men I hired."

"Of course. Did you hire many Chinese?"

"Yes. Thirty-three out of the forty are Chinese."

"That's about what you expected, isn't it?"

"Yes. I'm happy with the results."

"Mr. Squires will indeed be pleased. Just take a seat," she said, leaving the desk. "I'll let Mr. Squires know you're here."

Linna walked to the door of the inner office and tapped lightly. Squires's familiar voice responded. She opened the door, stuck her head in, and said something Floyd Metz could not make out. After a few seconds, she closed the door and headed back for her desk, where Metz had eased himself onto a straight-backed chair.

"Mr. Squires said he won't be much longer."

"Thank you," Metz said. He wiped sweaty palms on his pantlegs.

Nearly a half hour had passed before the engineers left the inner office. Jonathan Squires stood at the door, smiled at Floyd Metz, and said, "Come on in, Floyd. I'm pleased about the forty men. You did a good job."

"Thank you, sir."

"I'd like to have a look at them," Squires said, easing back in his chair.

"Certainly, sir." Metz waited for Squires to say something about the boarding houses, but the vice-president was waiting for Metz to tell him where he might view the men. "You'll probably enjoy the ride out to the camp, since it's in the foothills of the mountains."

"Pardon me?"

"The training camp, sir."

"What training camp? What are you talking about?"

"Why, the one you spoke of in your telegram. I thought at the time that it was odd and a sudden change in plans, but you are the boss, Mr. Squires."

The look on the executive vice-president's face was exactly as Floyd had imagined it. He laughed inside and almost mouthed Squires's next words.

"What telegram?"

"The one you had waiting for me at Fort Collins, sir, telling me where to have the engineer stop the train outside of Denver so the trainees could be transported to the camp."

"Floyd, I sent no telegram."

"You didn't? Then what's this?" Metz pulled out the bogus telegram and handed it to Squires.

The vice-president's eyes widened as he read the telegram, then his face lost all color. "Floyd, I did not send this telegram."

"But...but, sir. If you didn't, who did?"

Jonathan Squires ignored the question and leaned his elbows on the desk top. "Tell me what happened. Where are those men?"

"Well, sir, I—"

"You said something about the camp being in the foothills of the mountains."

"Yes. As you read in the telegram, I was instructed to have the engineer stop the train at a spot ten miles north of town where those two creeks intersect just west of the tracks. There were several men and four wagons waiting to take the men to the training camp."

"Did you recognize any of them?"

"No, sir. Talked to the man in charge. He knew me. Called

me by name when I left my coach to talk to him."

"Did he tell you his name?"

"No, I don't think so, sir. But I had no reason to distrust him. I had your telegram. At least, I thought it had come from you."

"But you'd know him if you saw him again?"

"Oh, sure. I'd know at least a couple of the others, too."

Squires raised his hands to his face, rubbed his eyes and said, "Floyd, I know what it is."

"Sir?"

"These kidnappings the past couple of months."

"You don't think—"

"What else could it be? Somehow, whoever is abducting all these men found out about you hiring those men in California. They sent that telegram and used it to trick you into letting them just drive away with our new employees. And it worked!"

Metz forced a worried look on his face. "Oh, how could I have been so stupid, Mr. Squires. I'm so sorry!"

"Don't blame yourself, Floyd. It certainly wasn't your fault. Like you said, since you thought the telegram had come from me, you had no choice but to obey it."

"Still, if I'd only double-checked it with you...since it seemed such an unusual request, I mean."

"Makes me sick to think of what might happen to those men, Floyd. It also makes me sick because we can't start laying track toward New Mexico until we come up with another crew."

"What should we do, sir?"

"First thing is to notify Sheriff Langan. He's got to find those men. Then we'll have to call an executive meeting to decide what to do next."

11

DEPUTY STEVE RIDGWAY WAS SWEEPING the office when he heard the train whistle. He paused to look at the clock on the wall and nodded. That would be the train from San Francisco due at eleven-thirty.

Just then he heard a wagon rattle up and stop in front of the office. He had the door open since the sun was shining from a clear sky and the late morning air was warm. He glanced through the door and saw Mae Trotter.

"All right, Ridgway! I want to know why Langan hasn't released 'em! Where is he?"

"In the mountains, searching for the kidnapped men," Ridgway said. "But—"

"How come he didn't let Harley and Cy out before he left? He was supposed to have a talk with 'em this mornin' and let 'em go."

"The sheriff's letting them go depended on their attitude, ma'am, but—"

"I know what their attitude was! It was good. Now, how come Langan didn't let 'em out?"

Ridgway sighed. "Mrs. Trotter, the sheriff released your husband and son more than four hours ago."

Mae gave him a skeptical look. "Then where are they?"

"You mean they didn't go home?"

"No! Where are they?"

"Well, ma'am, I have no idea. I—"

Mae charged to the cellblock door, shouting over her shoulder, "You're lyin', Ridgway! Harley and Cy are still locked up back here!"

The deputy leaned against the desk and folded his arms. He heard a furious string of profanities, then Mae returned to the office. "Where are they?" she half-screamed.

"I have no idea, Mrs. Trotter. Like I said, they've been gone for over four hours."

"That stinkin' sheriff has taken 'em somewhere else! What's he doin', torturin' 'em?"

"Ma'am, have you checked the saloons? Your husband and sons are known for hard drinking."

"I only got one son left, Ridgway, thanks to your no-good boss! But yeah, I checked every saloon in town. Nobody's seen 'em. Now, I want to know what Langan did with 'em!"

"The sheriff has done nothing but release them," Ridgway replied.

"You're a low-down liar, Ridgway! That murderin' sheriff wasn't satisfied to kill only half the men in my family, he had to kill Harley and Cy, too! Now, you either come clean or—"

"Excuse me!" Floyd Metz said as he plunged through the open door. "Where's the sheriff?"

Mae wheeled around and gave the railroad executive a cold look. "You just wait your turn, moneybags! I was here first."

"Mrs. Trotter," said the deputy, "I've told you all I can about your husband and son. If you choose to call me a liar, I can't help it. But I'm telling you the truth." He turned to Metz. "Sheriff Langan is out of town, sir."

"When will he be back?"

"About sundown. He's searching for the kidnapped men. Is there anything I can do for you?"

"It'll boil down to Sheriff Langan," Metz said, "but I'll explain it to you. We've got forty more men kidnapped."

"What?"

Metz quickly explained the situation, then said, "Mr. Squires wants something done about this immediately. I hired those men to lay track. We've got our engineers on the job already, expecting they would have a crew to start laying track tomorrow. The foreman is ready. The railroad needs—"

"Takes a lot of gall to come in here and butt in when I'm talkin' to the deputy!" Mae Trotter interrupted, her face flaming.

Ridgway gave her a steady look and said, "Mrs. Trotter, maybe Harley and Cy took a different route home for some reason and are there by now. Why don't you go home and see?"

"Lyin' snake," she muttered, heading for the door. "That sheriff has killed them. I just know it!"

Martha Goodwin was taking advantage of the exceptionally warm day by washing the windows of her large two-story house. Though her physician husband had repeatedly offered to hire her a maid, she wouldn't hear of it. "I'd get fat and lazy if I had a maid," she told him each time.

The sound of a wagon rattling down the street drew Martha's attention. When she saw the young woman riding next to the older couple, her heart leaped in her breast. Martha loved Breanna Baylor like a daughter. The Goodwins had never been able to have children of their own, and since Breanna had moved to Denver and taken up residence in the small guest cottage in their backyard, both Martha and the good doctor had "adopted" her as their daughter. Dr. Goodwin was proud to be the certified medical nurse's sponsoring physician.

Martha dropped her cleaning cloth on the porch swing and hurried down the steps.

"Welcome home, sweetie. It's been a long time!"

"Seems like a year," said Breanna, as she started to climb down.

"Wait a minute!" Harold Clement hurried around the rear of the wagon. "I'll help you down."

Martha knew Myrtle Henderson, who quickly introduced her to Clement. While he was assisting Breanna from the wagon, Martha spoke to Myrtle. "I heard you had gone to California to visit your son and his family. Did you have a nice time?"

"I enjoyed it thoroughly. But, of course, it's always good to get home."

"What about your trunk and luggage, Miss Breanna?" Clement asked.

"Oh. Well, would it be a problem to drive the wagon around back?"

"Not at all. You want them put inside your cottage?"

"That would be nice, if it's not too much bother."

Clement laughed as he climbed onto the seat. "I may not be a spring chicken anymore, Miss Breanna, but I can still handle most jobs. Is the door locked?"

"Not at the moment," Martha said. "I've got her windows open, airing out the cottage."

"Fine. Well, I know you two would like to have some time together, so Myrtle and I will say good-bye for now."

"Thank you so much for bringing me home, Mr. Clement," Breanna said.

"Yes! Thank you!" Martha added.

"Martha, you should have your husband look at Breanna," Myrtle said. "She's trying to cover it up, but she doesn't feel well.

132

I think I know what it is, but I'll let her tell you."

Martha turned to Breanna. "I thought you looked a little pale, honey. Are you all right?"

"We'll talk inside."

Myrtle waved as the wagon rounded the house, and Martha and Breanna waved back.

"It's time for our hug!"

Breanna took a backward step. "I'd love to, Martha, but I think I have scarlet fever. I sure don't want to give it to you."

"Scarlet fever! Honey, how—"

"Let's go inside and sit down. I'll tell you all about it."

Martha placed a tender hand on Breanna's cheek. "You're feverish, all right."

Martha led Breanna to an overstuffed couch in the parlor. Just before they sat down, she said, "I had scarlet fever as a girl. Now, how about that hug?"

After Breanna told Martha about caring for the men on the train, Martha stood up and said, "I'm putting you to bed, young lady. I'll have one of my neighbors go tell Lyle that you're sick. He'll want to check on you right away. You can stay in the room at the end of the hall upstairs."

"Oh, no," Breanna said, slowly rising to her feet. "I'll go on out to my house. And there's no need for you to bother Dr. Goodwin. I have some blue sage leaves in my medical kit. I'll get started on the sage tea, and Dr. Goodwin can look in on me when he comes home this evening."

Martha knew Breanna had a stubborn streak, and she did not try to dissuade her. Together they went to the cottage, and while Breanna laid down on her bed, Martha built a fire in the small stove and put the sage tea on to heat up. Though Breanna objected, Martha began unpacking the luggage. Breanna watched her from the bed.

"Martha, I've got some wonderful news."

"Oh?"

"John and I got together in Wyoming."

"Oh, honey, really?" Martha's eyes filled with tears. "Then everything has to be all right. I know John still loves you very much."

"Yes. He's so wonderful. I tried to make a big speech, explaining that being jilted by Frank Miller had made me fearful of trusting my heart to another man. John wouldn't even let me get it all out. He said what mattered was that I loved him and trusted him, and right then and there he said that one day—in God's time—he wants me to become his wife."

"Oh, Breanna, I'm so happy for you. Both of you. Lyle has told me of so many times when John would arrive in Denver and come to the office wanting to know where you were. The man truly loves you, dear."

"And I truly love him. More than anyone else in the whole world."

"Where is he now?"

"In Arizona. Chief Duvall sent him a wire at Placerville, California. You remember that I wired Dr. Goodwin from South Pass City, Wyoming—about the man who wanted to hire me to ride with the wagon train and care for his ailing wife?"

"Yes."

"Well, John stayed with the train all the way to Placerville, where Chief Duvall had left a message for him. The town marshal in Apache Junction was having problems with some kind of gang trying to take over the town. John left me at Placerville and headed for Arizona. He should come back to Denver when the situation there is settled."

Martha went to the stove to check on the tea. "Not hot enough yet." She returned to the trunk and continued to unpack it. "So you went to San Francisco, I understand."

"Yes." Breanna choked slightly and placed a hand to her throat. "And I have so much to tell you about Dottie."

"She and—what is his name?"

"Jerrod."

"She and Jerrod doing all right?"

"Jerrod's dead, Martha. I can hardly talk now. I'll tell you all about it when I'm better."

"Of course. I'm awfully sorry about Jerrod, though."

"Let me tell you this much. Jerrod died because of a mental illness brought on by the Civil War. But the future looks good for Dottie and the kids. You've heard of Dr. Matthew Carroll?"

"Who in the medical world hasn't?"

"Well, Dr. Carroll's wife died some time ago, and he has proposed to Dottie. He wants to adopt James and Molly Kate."

"Wonderful," said Martha, moving back to the bed. "Now, you shouldn't talk anymore. Let's get the sage tea into you. It'll help that sore throat, too."

Martha Goodwin and her husband pushed open the door of the cottage and peeked in. By the light of the low-burning lantern, they could see Breanna was asleep. They quietly backed out and closed the door.

As they headed back to their house, Dr. Goodwin said, "I'm glad you were here to care for her when she first got home. Tell me, does she have all the symptoms?"

"All of them. Her tongue was just getting the coating, and her throat's a raw red. I looked her over good. Red rash in all the usual places. I gave her a cold water enema about an hour ago, and she's had four cups of sage tea."

"Where'd you get the sage?"

"She had it in her medical kit. I'll explain over supper."

As they stepped onto their back porch, Dr. Goodwin paused and looked toward the cottage. "She's going to get the best of care from the two of us. We'll see her through it and have her up and about in a few days."

"Bless her heart," said Martha. "She's been such a help to so many people. It'll be a privilege to nurse her back to health."

At sundown, Sheriff Langan trotted his horse down Tremont Street and left it at the usual stable for the night. He paid the hostler an extra dollar to give the animal a good rubdown. It had been a hard day of riding with no results. As he headed for his office, Langan wondered if Dennis Coulter and Bob Lowery had returned. Steve would know.

Traffic on the street was diminishing as the business day came to a close. When he was within half a block of his office, the sheriff saw Floyd Metz leaning against the hitch rail. As he drew near, he could see anxiety on Metz's face.

Metz left the hitch rail and met the sheriff on the boardwalk. Just before Metz spoke, Langan recognized Sally Jayne's mare tied to the rail. His heart skipped a beat. She must be in the office with Steve.

"Sheriff, we've got real trouble!"

"Who's we, Floyd?"

"The railroad. We just had forty new employees kidnapped!"

"Forty?"

"Yes! I went to San Francisco and hired them for laying track on the new line from here to Santa Fe."

"Oh, yeah. Steve told me a few days ago that you were making a trip for that purpose."

"Yes. Well, let me explain what happened."

Metz told Langan the story of the telegram and the abduction. He finished by saying he and Jonathan Squires felt sure it was connected to all the other kidnappings of late.

"It has to be connected, Floyd," Langan said. "In the morning, if you'll take me out to the spot where the men were taken off the train, I'll see if I can track those wagons."

"I'll be glad to take you, Sheriff."

"Why don't you meet me here at eight-thirty tomorrow morning? I'm going to be at Chief Duvall's office when he gets there at eight. He's loaned me a couple of deputies to help search. Maybe he'll have one or two others he can spare to help me trail those wagons. If I find the place where they're taking all these men, I'll need some extra guns."

"I'm sure you will. I'll be here at eight-thirty in the morning."

"Good. See you then."

Langan watched Metz waddle down the boardwalk, then let his eyes stray to Sally Jayne's mare. His heart quickened as he turned the doorknob and opened the door.

Sally's back was toward the door, but when it opened, she turned and rose from the chair, her lips parted across white teeth.

"Hello, Sheriff!" she said.

"Hello, Miss Sally! It's nice to see you!"

She was dressed in a black riding outfit and white, frilly blouse. Her black, flat-crowned hat was tilted to one side, and beneath it, long auburn hair lay like silk. The lantern light showed the smooth ivory shading of her skin.

"I had some business to do in town for Daddy," Sally said, looking up at him with emerald eyes. "But I planned it a little late so I would be here at suppertime. Does that dinner offer still stand?"

"It sure does!"

"Good! Nick and Alf are making the rounds of the saloons

and will meet me here at the office later."

"You have honored me, Miss Sally. Have you eaten at the restaurant in the Diamond Palace Hotel?"

"No, but it sounds wonderful."

"Then that's where we'll eat. I've got to talk to my deputy here for a few minutes, then we'll be on our way. How's that sound?"

"Splendid," she replied warmly, then sat down.

Steve started to move from behind the desk. "Hey, stay where you are," Langan said, motioning with a hand. "I'll just sit here next to Miss Sally."

Deputy Ridgway tried to hide a grin.

"First thing, Steve, have Coulter and Lowery returned?"

"No, sir."

"They haven't? That worries me. They were supposed to come back by sundown today."

"Maybe they're onto something and can't leave the trail," Ridgway said.

"I hope you're right."

"I saw you talking to Floyd Metz out there. He's been on pins and needles wanting to tell you about the big kidnapping. What do you think of it?"

"I have no doubt it's part of this whole scheme."

"Big kidnapping?" Sally said. "Worse than the kidnappings you told me about, Sheriff?"

"Yes. Forty men all at the same time. Floyd Metz is a Union Pacific executive. He went to San Francisco to hire a crew of men to come here and lay track. Most of them were Chinese. The kidnappers tricked Metz with a phony telegram, and he had the train stop a few miles north of Denver under the impression that the newly hired men were to be taken to a special training camp in the foothills. The kidnappers now have them."

"What on earth could they want with all those men?"

"I don't know, but I'm going to see if I can track those wagons tomorrow. Metz is taking me out to the spot of the abduction in the morning."

"You don't mean you're going to follow those wagons all by yourself?"

"If I have to, yes. I'm going to see Chief U.S. Marshal Solomon Duvall first thing in the morning. He let me have those two deputies you heard me asking Steve about. I'm hoping he'll have some more he can send with me tomorrow."

"Please don't try it alone, Sheriff," Sally said. "You never know what you might run into. A man who would stoop to kidnapping won't bat an eye at killing a lawman."

"I appreciate your concern, Miss Sally. I hope I won't have to tackle this thing alone."

"Tell you what, Sheriff. I'll send Nick and Alf back in the morning. They're both good with a gun. That'll give you two men you can count on."

"But doesn't your father need them at the ranch?"

"He can spare them for a day or two. We have more cowhands. I'll feel better if they're riding with you."

"Well, Miss Sally, I really appreciate this. You're sure your father won't mind?"

"Not at all. If his little girl says the sheriff needs Nick and Alf for a while, he'll approve it without question."

"Good! The more the better."

"Say, why don't I come with Nick and Alf, too? I can ride and search as well as any man."

Curt shook his head. "No, Miss Sally. It's too dangerous. I don't doubt your riding ability, nor that you can follow wagon tracks. But this search could end in a gunfight. I don't want you in harm's way."

"How about if I just ride and search? If it looks like you're closing in, I'll find a safe place to hide while you men do the dangerous work. Really. I'd like to come along."

Langan rubbed his chin and looked at Ridgway. The deputy grinned.

"Well, if I have to split up my forces to take the search in more than one direction, I like to split in pairs. If it happens that way, Miss Sally, you'll ride with me."

"I won't argue with that."

"But the minute it looks dangerous, you'll have to find a place to hide."

"That I will do, Sheriff. I promise."

Deputy Ridgway chuckled.

"What are you laughing about?" Langan asked.

"You."

"What about me?"

"With Miss Sally along, your eyes won't be on the trail left by the wagons—they'll be on her!"

Sally put a hand over her mouth and laughed.

Langan couldn't help but laugh too. "Am I that obvious?" he asked.

"Quite."

"I'm sorry for my deputy's big mouth, Miss Sally. But I might as well admit it, I do have a hard time keeping my eyes off you. You're a very beautiful young lady."

Sally was nonplused.

Steve broke the momentary silence. "Sheriff, Mae Trotter was in here about noon."

"What for?"

"She said Harley and Cy didn't come home. She thought you were keeping them in the jail. When I told her you'd released them early this morning, she called me a liar and stormed back

140

to the cell block, expecting to find them still in the cell."

"Then what?"

"She was madder'n a wet hen. Said you had taken them somewhere to torture or kill them."

Langan sighed, shaking his head in amazement. "Those two sots probably found the first saloon that opened and got tanked up."

"She said she checked all the saloons. Nobody had seen them."

"Drinkers can always find a way to get their hands on a bottle. They probably drank themselves into a stupor and wandered off somewhere. I hope, though, they were home by the time she arrived back at the ranch." Turning to Sally, he said, "Well, Miss Jayne, if we leave now, we'll have time to walk down by the river before going to dinner."

"I'd like that."

As the couple headed out the door, Langan looked back at his deputy. Ridgway wiggled his eyebrows and winked. Langan gave him a mock scowl and closed the door.

12

SALLY JAYNE CARRIED HER JACKET to the door, but when she felt the nip in the air she decided to put it on.

"Here, let me." Curt helped her ease into the jacket, and she pulled it tightly around her.

"Guess winter's not too far away," she said.

"Not too far. If you're going to be out after the sun goes down from now till the first of May in this high country, it's best to have a heavier wrap."

"I'll remember that," she said.

Curt offered his arm and Sally slid her small hand into the crook of his elbow and gave him a warm look as they started down the street.

A few people were on the boardwalks, and there was light traffic along Tremont as twilight fell over Denver. An elderly lamplighter was doing his job just ahead of them. When they drew abreast of him, he recognized Langan and said, "Howdy, Sheriff. Who's that pretty lady you got there?"

"Josh Collins, this is Miss Sally Jayne. Her father owns a ranch in the mountains."

"Glad to meet you, ma'am," said Collins, touching the bill of his cap.

"Likewise, I'm sure."

"I s'pose you heard 'bout Miss Breanna, eh, Sheriff?"

"Breanna Baylor?"

"Yep."

"No. What about her?"

"Mighty sick li'l gal. Came down with scarlet fever."

"She's home?"

"Yep."

"I wasn't aware she was back. Scarlet fever. I'm sorry to hear about that. I suppose she was taking care of somebody who had it."

"Three of 'em, I hear."

"Oh?"

"Mm-hmm. Doc Goodwin and the missus are takin' care of her. Just thought if'n you didn't know, you'd want to...'specially since she saved your life."

"I have to leave town in the morning. Think I'll drop by and check on her yet this evening. Thanks for letting me know, Josh."

As Curt and Sally headed toward the South Platte River, Sally said, "I assume this Miss Breanna Baylor is a nurse."

"A visiting nurse. She's usually gone from Denver several weeks at a time. Dr. Lyle Goodwin is her sponsoring physician."

"You have to be a C.M.N. to work like that, don't you?"

"Yes. Breanna's really good. She could almost be a doctor, if you ask me."

"Mr. Collins said she saved your life."

"That's right. When I was deputy sheriff. Six months ago now. I broke up a saloon fight, and a friend of one of the combatants pulled a gun and shot me before I even saw him. I went down but managed to shoot him before he could fire at me a second time. He died on the spot. Then I passed out. The next thing I knew, I was lying on the operating table at Dr. Goodwin's

144

office. Breanna was preparing to dig the slug out of my chest with Dr. Goodwin's regular nurse at her side. The slug was quite close to my heart."

"Oh, my!"

"Breanna knew if the bullet wasn't removed immediately, I would die. So she did the surgery, and I owe her my life."

After a pause, he added, "Come to think of it, Breanna hasn't been home since I became sheriff. She'll take Sheriff Yates's death hard, but I know she'll be happy to know the people of Denver County gave me the job."

"I didn't realize this," Sally said. "This has been recent, then."

"Yes. Sheriff Yates was killed about two months ago."

They were approaching the bank of the river. "You call her *Breanna*. Is…is there something between you?"

"Oh, no. No. She's a beautiful and wonderful young lady, but nothing like that. We're just good friends."

Sally seemed satisfied. "Well," she quipped, "I guess since she saved your life, you ought to be good friends."

They sat down on a bench overlooking the South Platte and talked about Sally's past while they watched the last light of day fade behind jagged mountain peaks. Soon they returned to the wide, dusty streets and made their way to the Diamond Palace Hotel.

Sally was impressed by the elegance of the restaurant, and the two became better acquainted by candlelight while a violinist moved about the room playing romantic music.

Curt told Sally stories from his childhood, and when he threw in some funny experiences, she laughed heartily. He looked at her in the soft yellow light and told himself she was everything he had ever wanted in a woman. He liked the way she smiled at him and the way those emerald eyes clung to his face.

When dinner was over, they started back toward the office.

The night chill touched them, and Curt put his arm around Sally, saying, "You're getting cold, aren't you?"

"I was, but I'm not now."

"I don't want you riding all the way home without a better wrap. I'll loan you one of my mackinaws."

"That's sweet of you, Sheriff. I'll take you up on it."

When they reached the office, Alf and Nick were nowhere to be seen. "Let's go inside," Curt said, reaching in his pocket for the key. "Think they'll show up soon?"

"They will. Daddy would be very upset if we were late, and they know it."

Curt unlocked the door and pocketed the key. A lantern burned low inside. He turned toward Sally, meaning to tell her to step in ahead of him, but he froze when their eyes locked. He was about to take her in his arms and kiss her when he heard the soft clop of hooves.

"Sorry we're late, Miss Sally," Nick Beal said. "Poker game got interesting. You know."

Sally turned to look at them. "We'd better be moving, boys. But before we go, I want to explain something to you."

She took a brief moment to tell Alf and Nick about the forty men who had been kidnapped that day and said they would be coming back with her in the morning to ride with the sheriff and follow the wagons' tracks.

Langan further explained the danger involved, and that Sally had promised to find a hiding place if things got sticky. Both men were quite willing to help.

"Before you go," the sheriff said to Sally, "let me get my mackinaw."

Sally gave Curt's fingers a furtive squeeze as she settled in the saddle. "Thank you, Sheriff. And thank you for the lovely evening and the wonderful meal."

"You couldn't be more welcome. See you in the morning."

"You sure will," she said. "Goodnight."

"Goodnight."

Curt watched Sally ride away between the two cowhands. When darkness had swallowed them, he entered the office, snuffed the lantern, and headed up the street in the direction of Denver's wealthier section. Even as he walked, he knew he was going to have a hard time getting a good night's sleep.

"Good evening, Sheriff," said the silver-haired physician as he opened the front door. "To what do we owe this pleasure?"

Martha Goodwin stood beside her husband, looking at the lawman curiously.

"I learned about Breanna's illness a couple of hours ago, Doctor, and I wanted to find out how she's doing."

"Well, come on in."

Langan greeted Martha, removed his hat, and stepped inside.

Doctor Goodwin led the sheriff down the long hall to the library while Martha hurried to the kitchen for coffee. "I'm sure you know," Goodwin said, "about the forty railroad workers kidnapped off the San Francisco train earlier today."

"Yes. I'm starting a search in the morning. All my other searching has netted me nothing. I'm hoping this will be the break I've been looking for."

"Do you know about Breanna's having cared for three men on the trip who had scarlet fever?"

"I was told she cared for three people, but that's all I know."

"Well, those three Chinese men are part of the kidnapped group. It'll be a miracle if they don't have an epidemic of scarlet fever wherever they've taken them."

"Somehow I've got to find them before that happens. So tell me about Breanna. Is she going to be all right?"

"Oh, yes. Martha and I are giving her the best of care. She'll get sicker than she is right now until that fever breaks, but she'll be fine."

"Would it be possible to see her?"

"Have you had scarlet fever?"

"No, sir."

"Then, you can't go near her until she's on the mend and has no more fever."

"Even if I stood on the other side of the room?"

"Wouldn't help. You'd still breathe the germs."

"Oh. Well, I just wanted to see her and let her know I care."

"We'll tell her you were here. It'll mean a lot to her, I can tell you that."

Martha appeared with coffee, and they all sat down to chat awhile. When Langan got up to leave, he thanked them for taking care of the lady who had saved his life.

That night, as he pillowed his head, Curt's mind went to Sally Jayne. Just as he'd predicted, sleep eluded him. Finally, somewhere in the middle of the night, he drifted off to sleep.

Earlier in the evening, at the *Bar T Ranch,* Mae Trotter paced the kitchen floor, cursing the name of Sheriff Langan.

What had Langan done with Harley and Cy? "Probably took 'em out somewhere and shot 'em down like dogs," she said aloud. "Who knows? Maybe he'll even come out here and shoot me down, too!"

Mae opened the cupboard and took a whiskey bottle off the shelf. It was almost full. She popped the cork, put the bottle to her mouth, and took a long pull. She felt the whiskey burn all the way to her stomach. It made her eyes water. She blinked and stared at her reflection in a nearby mirror.

"Mae, you hit the bottle before, when your ma and pa died

in that fire…and again when Willie was murdered. Both times the stuff about did you in. Remember how sick you got? I mean, for better than a week both times! Put that bottle back in the cupboard."

She looked into the mirror for several more seconds, then cursed, put the bottle to her lips, and took several gulps.

Chief U.S. Marshal Solomon Duvall sat behind his desk and told Curt Langan he didn't have any more men to help with the search. Duvall stood up and walked around the desk. "Like you, I'm a little worried about Coulter and Lowery. If they don't show up today, I'm really going to be worried."

"Me too, sir."

"Curt, I sincerely hope you find those men. I'm glad you've got that rancher's daughter and the two cowhands to ride with you, at least."

"Me too, sir. And if Coulter and Lowery show up before I get back, make sure they report to Steve."

"I'll do it."

Curt rode his horse out of the stable and headed down Tremont Street. As he neared his office, he saw Sally Jayne, her two cowhands, and Floyd Metz standing by their horses at the hitch rail. Steve Ridgway was with them.

Sally smiled and held out the mackinaw he had loaned her. "Good morning, Sheriff."

"Good morning to you, Miss Sally."

He greeted the men, then accepted the mackinaw from Sally and handed it to his deputy. "Hang this up for me, will you, Steve?"

"Will do, boss. Sure wish I could go with you."

"It'd be a real help, my friend, but as they say, somebody's got to mind the store."

"Sure hope Coulter and Lowery show up today, Sheriff."

"Yeah, me too. I told Chief Duvall if they go there first to be sure and let you know they're back."

"Good. Be careful."

"I'll be fine with Nick and Alf along."

Steve stepped close to the sheriff's horse and said quietly, "I'm not talking about danger from the kidnappers. I'm talking about danger to your bachelorhood."

Langan snorted, slipped his foot from the stirrup, and kicked his deputy playfully. "Let me worry about that, you coot!"

Sally had been listening to something the cowhands were saying and caught the kick in her peripheral vision. Smiling, she asked, "What was that all about?"

"Nothing." Langan said. "My deputy just needs a good kick once in a while. Usually I kick him somewhere else on his no-good carcass."

Everybody laughed but Floyd Metz; he had his mind on other things. He was about to lead the sheriff to the very spot where the crime had been committed. *His* crime, actually. Duff Pasko had visited Metz at his home the night before. Duff had told him how smooth the whole thing went, and that Morgan had shot and killed George Matson.

Metz told Pasko that he would be taking the sheriff to the spot where the forty men had left the train, and that Langan was going to be following the tracks. Pasko assured Metz that he would take some men out at dawn and do what they could to obscure the trail, especially where the wagons pulled out of the creek.

Nevertheless, Floyd was uneasy. Curt Langan was a determined cuss. He wasn't going to stop searching until he found the kidnapped men. Metz knew from what Pasko had told him that Morgan was reluctant to have Langan killed. He feared that if the county's top lawman was murdered, the army would be brought in. If the soldiers should find the mine, Morgan's men could never fight off the United States Army.

"This is the place, Sheriff," Metz said as they drew up to the place where the train had stopped the day before. "You can see the wagon tracks right down there."

Langan left his saddle, as did Sally and her two companions. The wagon wheel tracks led westward toward the mountains.

"Okay, it looks like the kidnappers may have a place somewhere high in the Rockies."

"Or between the foothills and the high peaks," Alf Spaulding said.

"Well, we're about to find out," Langan said. "At least, I hope so."

"Me, too," Sally said. "Those poor men. What on earth could be the purpose of those kidnappings?"

"We'll find out if we find them."

"*When* we find them, Sheriff," Sally said. "Let's think positive. Those men are somewhere out there, and they must be found."

"That's right, ma'am," Metz said. "The railroad needs them real bad."

"I was thinking more of their personal welfare, and of their families."

"Oh. Well, yes, of course. Sheriff, I'll be going now. Plenty of work to do back at the office."

"All right, Floyd. Tell Mr. Squires I'm giving this everything I've got."

"I will."

As Metz rode away, Langan said, "Well, let's see where those tracks take us."

They rode a ways and soon came upon the place where the other riders had been waiting for the wagons. The sheriff leaned from his saddle and said, "Somebody met them right here. You can see straight ahead of us that they all left together."

"Quite a bunch of 'em, Sheriff," Alf said. "It's a big operation, whatever it is."

Langan rubbed his chin. "Especially when you take into consideration all the other men who've been kidnapped, plus more that we don't even know about."

"I just can't figure what it's all about." Sally adjusted her hat. "None of this makes sense."

"Maybe it will when we find them," Langan said.

The foursome followed the trail through the foothills, and by noon they were in the Rockies, climbing ever higher. They steadily wound upward into tall timber. After three hours of rough terrain, the trail angled a bit to the southwest. Soon they came over a sharp rise, broke out of the heavy timber, and dropped into a broad, sweeping valley.

They came to a grassy ravine with a shallow creek some twenty feet wide. Langan drew rein and studied the marks on the creek bank beneath him. Then he gazed at the opposite side. He rode across and scrutinized it carefully. "They didn't pull out over here."

"Then they're purposely trying to cover their trail," Nick said.

"No way to tell which way they went. Could be north. Could be south."

"Got a gut feeling?" Alf asked. "I've heard that lawmen have a sixth sense."

Langan grinned at him. "Well, I guess that's true. Only problem is, it doesn't always work. Right now, I don't feel north *or* south about it, but it has to be one or the other. All we can do is split up. You boys go south. Miss Sally and I will go north. If you find the place where they pulled out, one of you fire your gun three times in succession. We'll do the same and then converge on the spot."

"Sounds good to me," Nick said.

Langan pulled out his pocket watch. "Either of you have a watch?"

"We both do." Alf reached toward a small pocket beneath the beltline of his Levi's.

"Okay. It's now almost three. If we find nothing by four o'clock, we'll come back here and meet. It'll be almost five by then. You three can head for the *Circle J,* and I'll head for town."

"Certainly they didn't keep those wagons in the creek for more than an hour," Sally said.

"I wouldn't think so," Curt said. "One pair of us should find the place where they pulled out. We'll ride the center of the creek so we can see both banks. They might have pulled one on us and come back out on the east side."

"Good point," said Nick. "You lawmen think of everything."

"Well, not everything. If I could think of everything, I'd come up with where the kidnappers have taken their victims and what they're doing with them."

The pairs guided their mounts into the stream and rode in opposite directions. Sally and Curt went north, with Sally studying the east bank while Curt kept his eye on the west bank.

"You know, Steve was right," Curt said.

"Hmm?"

"He said I'd have a hard time keeping my eyes on the land with you along. I'd sure rather look at you than this creek bank."

Sally smiled. "Sheriff, you're good for a woman's ego."

Curt pulled rein and Sally followed suit. He nudged his mount close to hers and said, "Miss Sally, would you do me a favor?"

"Of course."

"How about calling me *Curt* instead of *Sheriff?*"

"I'll do it if you will drop the *Miss* and just call me *Sally.*"

"Okay, Sally."

"Okay, Curt."

Their eyes locked as they had the previous evening. Then they leaned toward each other and their lips met in a soft, lingering kiss.

At five o'clock the foursome met at the spot where they had entered the rippling waters. "This thing beats me," Langan said. "Certainly they didn't drive those wagons for miles before pulling out of the creek to go to their destination."

"Daddy said Nick and Alf could help again tomorrow if needed, Curt. He'll need them the next day, and several after that to help bring in hay from the fields for winter. I've got some things I have to do tomorrow, but if you want these two, they can come back and help."

"I sure do want them. We'll meet right here in the morning, fellas. How's eight o'clock?"

"Sounds good."

Curt Langan rode toward Denver, but as the animal beneath him covered the rugged ground at a gallop, he felt as if he were riding on clouds.

13

ON THE FOURTH MORNING after getting off the train, Breanna Baylor sat up in an overstuffed chair, watching Martha Goodwin change the sheets and pillowcases on her bed. Breanna's fever had broken during the night, and already she was feeling better.

The two women had been discussing Breanna's sister, Dottie, and the well-known physician and psychiatrist who had proposed marriage to her.

Martha tucked the bottom sheet under the mattress and asked, "So you have no doubt Dottie will accept Dr. Carroll's proposal?"

"None at all. Dottie will just need a little time. She was so in love with Jerrod, and so absolutely devoted to him. She proved that by staying with him when her life was almost a nightmare of terror and fear every day. If not always for herself, certainly for James and Molly Kate."

Martha spread the top sheet over the other one and began smoothing it out. "Has Lyle mentioned the hospital to you?"

"Hospital?"

"Mm-hmm."

"No. You...you mean one for Denver?"

"Yes."

"Oh, how wonderful! The way this town is growing, we needed one yesterday!"

"Well, you'll have to ask him about it. Plans are in the making. He and Denver's other two doctors have met five times to discuss it. I think they're close to coming up with enough money to build it. The next thing will be to look for people to staff it. Lyle has already contacted the medical school in Kansas City, and one of the other doctors is working on contacting that nurse's school connected to Women's Hospital in Philadelphia."

"Oh, this is exciting!" Breanna said.

"Let me tell you the best part. Lyle and the other doctors have discussed who they might try to get to run the hospital. They know it will have a mental ward."

"The best ones do."

"Well, this isn't for public knowledge yet, you understand...but they're thinking that since Dr. Carroll is both a medical doctor and a psychiatrist, he would be perfect as hospital administrator. He's head of staff at City Mental Asylum in San Francisco, I understand."

"Yes. And he's also on staff at City Hospital."

"Well, anyway, I think Dr. Carroll is going to be offered the job when this new hospital is built."

"Oh, wouldn't it be wonderful if Dottie does marry Dr. Carroll and they moved here?"

"Yes, it would. That's why I brought it up. I know Lyle would want you to know that it's at least a possibility. Depends on whether Dr. Carroll would want to leave his position in San Francisco for a higher one here."

"Well, now that I know about it, I can make it a matter of earnest prayer. Just think of it! Every time I came home I could see Dottie and those wonderful children. Dr. Carroll's going to make Dottie a wonderful husband...and he'll be a great father to

James and Molly Kate. Come to think of it, it will be really something to have such a prominent physician as my brother-in-law!"

"I assume Dottie will let you know when the wedding is to take place?"

"Oh, yes. Like I said, she'll need some time yet, but I have no doubt she'll become Mrs. Matthew Carroll."

Though Curt Langan and Sally Jayne's two ranchhands searched a second day, scouring the area where the wagon and hoof marks were last seen, they turned up nothing.

Morale was low at the federal office, for Dennis Coulter and Bob Lowery were on the official "missing" list. Chief Duvall pulled two deputies off other jobs and sent them to search in the territory where the deputies had gone under Sheriff Langan's orders.

A week passed, but neither Langan nor Duvall's men had turned up a thing. Langan and Duvall agreed that the deputies must have been spotted by the kidnappers and taken captive. They could only hope the two men were still alive.

At the close of a long, hard day of riding, Langan sat in Jonathan Squires's office, talking with Squires and Floyd Metz.

"Gentlemen," the sheriff said wearily, "I'm totally stumped. I was hoping the trail would lead me to the place your workers are being held, but I've come up with nothing. It's as if those men, horses, and wagons were lifted off the face of the earth at that creek bank."

Squires drew in a long breath and let it out in a gust. He stared into space for a long time without saying anything, then passed a hand over his drawn features. "Well, Sheriff, there's nothing more to say. You've done your best, and still the kidnappings remain a mystery. I don't suppose those two federal deputies have ever surfaced."

"No, sir."

To Metz, Squires said, "Floyd, we've got to hire forty new men or at least as close to that number as we can."

"Yes, sir. I'll come up with some kind of plan."

"I'm trusting you to do that."

"I'll do my best, sir."

The following day, Sheriff Langan was in his office, stoking up the fire in the potbellied stove before sitting down to work on a stack of mail only he could tend to. His deputy had kept up with the paperwork as much as possible, but the rest of it had to be handled by the man who wore the sheriff's badge. Since Steve had not had a day off in a long time, Langan told him to take the whole day and have a good time.

As he dropped the cast-iron lid on the stove, Langan looked toward the desk and noticed the Bible lying there. It had belonged to Sheriff Brad Yates and was usually in the bottom drawer of the desk. Steve must have been looking at it.

The clock on the wall struck nine as Langan crossed the room and sat down at the desk. He leaned over and opened the bottom drawer to put the Bible away. At the same time, the office door opened and Breanna Baylor walked in.

"Hello, Curt," she said, warming him with her smile.

"Well, hello, yourself!" He looked at the Bible in his hand, then at Breanna. Quickly he dropped it in the drawer, hoping she hadn't seen what it was.

As Breanna closed the door against the chilly air, Curt jumped from his chair and came toward her. "It's so good to see you up and about, dear lady! You must be feeling lots better. Here, come and sit down."

He grabbed a chair in front of the desk and spun it around.

"Thank you," she said, unbuttoning her coat. "I am feeling lots better."

"Here, let me take that."

After hanging up her coat, Curt said, "I hope the Goodwins told you I tried to see you several nights ago."

"Yes. I appreciate your coming by. Sorry I wasn't up to it, but since you've not had scarlet fever, it wouldn't have been wise to expose yourself."

"I'd have been back if I could, Breanna, but I've been run ragged trying to find all those kidnapped men. I guess you've been told about it."

"Dr. and Mrs. Goodwin have kept me up on the whole thing. Really strange, isn't it?"

"I've never seen or heard of anything like it."

"You know, I cared for three of those kidnapped men who had scarlet fever. I sure hope they're being treated humanely. They were very weak when they got off the train."

"Wish I knew what was being done to them," Langan said, with steel in his voice. "I've tried so hard to find them."

"Everyone in town knows that, Curt. No man could have done more."

"I feel like there's more I should have done, but I don't know what else it could be. It's like some unknown creature from the sky has swooped down and carried them all away, even the kidnappers, their wagons, and their animals."

"Curt, when I left here several weeks ago, you were the deputy and Brad Yates was the sheriff. I was stunned when the Goodwins told me he was shot down by Willie Trotter."

Curt nodded.

"Let me commend you for the way you handled it. From what I was told, you had no choice but to take Willie out."

"That's right."

"I was also told about you having to kill Chad. And that Harley and Cy gave you some trouble."

"I jailed them for a couple days. Then I gave them a good lecture and released them."

Breanna nodded. "Congratulations on becoming sheriff, Curt. Most men your age would have been bypassed for an older, more experienced man. That means the people have confidence in you. And so do I. If I'd been here, I would have voted for you."

"Thank you, Breanna. I...I hope my failure to find all those abducted men won't cause the people to lose faith in me."

"I haven't heard any talk like that. Everyone knows you've done everything you could."

"Well, I'm not giving up. I just had to stop working on it and catch up with the rest of my job."

"Good. That's what I like to hear."

He looked at her more closely and said, "You still look a little peaked. Are you sure you should be out like this?"

Breanna smiled. "I'm under doctor's orders to get out and breathe some of this fall air. I'll be fine, Curt." She let a few seconds pass, then said, "As I was coming in, I thought I saw a Bible in your hands."

Breanna had spoken to Curt on several occasions about his need for salvation. He had always been kind and courteous to her, but had shown no interest in the gospel.

The sheriff cleared his throat and said, "It's...ah...Sheriff Yates's Bible. My deputy, Steve Ridgway, looks at it now and then. He left it on top of the desk and I was just putting it back in the drawer."

"Have you ever read it?"

"No need. As I've told you before, I have my own ideas about heaven and hell."

"But your ideas don't count, Curt. Any more than my ideas, or those of any other mortal person. That Bible is the Word of God, the same God who created this universe. He gave you life, and He gave you a Book to tell you about your need of salvation."

"Breanna, it is my belief that as long as a person lives a decent life and is sincere in whatever he or she believes, that person will go to heaven when they die."

"We've been over this before, my friend. And you have yet to give me an answer as to why God sent His only Son to the cross if all we have to do is live a decent life and be sincere in what we believe."

As so many times before, Curt was at a loss for words.

"Curt, do you realize that if you are right, Jesus went to Calvary for nothing?"

Silence.

"God wouldn't have sent His Son to suffer, bleed, and die on the cross if good works and sincerity could get you to heaven."

"Breanna, are you telling me that all these people around the world are going to hell if they don't turn to Jesus Christ for salvation...even though they treat their neighbors right, serve mankind, and are sincere in their religion?"

"*I* am not telling you that, Curt, *God* is. Take the Bible out of the drawer and let me show you what He says."

Curt felt cornered, but there was nothing he could do. He deeply respected Breanna. She lived what she preached. He had never seen an ounce of hypocrisy in her, and he was convinced if there really existed a true Christian, it was Breanna Baylor. He opened the drawer, picked up the Bible, and handed it to her.

Breanna fanned pages in the Old Testament, found the forty-fifth chapter of Isaiah, and laid it on the desk in front of Curt. "There. Verses twenty-one to twenty-three. Please read them to me."

Langan cleared his throat and read aloud: "Tell ye, and bring them near; yea, let them take counsel together: who hath declared this from ancient time? Who hath told it from that time? Have not I the LORD? And there is no God else beside me; a just God and a Saviour; there is none beside me. Look unto me, and be ye saved, all the ends of the earth: for I am God, and there is none else. I have sworn by myself, the word is gone out of my mouth in righteousness, and shall not return, That unto me every knee shall bow, every tongue shall swear."

"Now think, Curt," Breanna said. "This is the Lord Jesus Christ in His pre-incarnate form speaking here. He's the only One who can save sinners unto all the ends of the earth. Do you see that?"

"That's what it says," came his weak reply.

"So no matter who the people are, or where they live on this earth, Jesus is the only One who can save them from the wrath of God and from hell. He says the day will come when every knee shall bow before Him. Does that include you?"

There was a pause. "Yes."

"Curt, you can bow before Jesus in eternity as a lost man and be cast into the lake of fire, or you can bow before Him now, acknowledge yourself as a helpless sinner, and ask Him to save you. The choice is yours."

Breanna, her heart burdened for Curt's soul, hurriedly flipped to the New Testament. "Here, Curt," she said, laying the Bible open before him again. "First Timothy 4:10. Paul is speaking of his work for the Lord and the persecution he was receiving for preaching Christ. Read it to me."

Langan wiped the back of his hand across his mouth and read: "For therefore we both labour and suffer reproach, because we trust in the living God, who is the Saviour of all men, specially of those that believe."

162

"This living God is the One who came into the world by the virgin birth, so as a sinless human being He could die and shed His blood for lost, sinful humans. He is the Saviour of *all* men. We have only one Person who can save us from sin and its penalty—Jesus Christ. He died for every human being that they might have salvation if they will accept it on His terms. Hebrews 2:9 says He tasted death for every man. This includes you, Curt. Jesus is the only One you can look to for salvation."

Curt ran a shaky palm over his brow. "Breanna, I've told you before that my grandparents raised me. Grandma believed just like you do. But Grandpa taught me that as long as a person leads a decent life and does what he can for his fellow man, he'll be okay."

"Curt, I mean no disrespect to your grandfather, but he was wrong. The devil will deceive you by false teaching if you let him. He's the enemy of your soul. He wants you to burn in the lake of fire with him. He hates the Word of God, and he will use anything or anybody he can to deceive you into believing a lie."

A sick smile curved the sheriff's lips. "Breanna, you know that I have the utmost respect for you. And I wouldn't do anything to insult you. But we just don't see eye to eye on this."

"I know. But your disagreement is not with me. It's with God."

"Breanna, I don't see it that way." He released a nervous chuckle. "What you believe is all right for you, but it's not all right for me. No devil can deceive me. I'm no fool. No man who's a fool can be the sheriff of Denver County. I don't mean to sound like a braggart, but I've got a grip on the handle of life. Satan's not going to pull the wool over my eyes."

"Curt, don't think you're above being fooled. Here, let me show you how Satan fooled Judas Iscariot into thinking—"

Suddenly the door of the office opened.

"Sally!" Curt exclaimed as he rose from his chair.

Breanna looked around and saw a beautiful woman clad in a dark brown riding outfit with hat and boots to match. Her frilly blouse was light tan, almost matching her heavy waist-length jacket.

Sally's eyes showed a spark of jealousy as she looked from Curt to Breanna and back to Curt. "I hope I'm not interrupting anything."

"Oh, no." Langan moved around the desk toward Sally. "Breanna and I were just having a friendly discussion."

Sally recognized the name and smiled. "So this is the nurse who dug the bullet out of you and saved your life!"

"Yes. Miss Sally Jayne, meet Miss Breanna Baylor."

Breanna was already out of her chair, having laid the Bible on the desk. She met Sally halfway, extending her hand. Sally gripped the strong fingers and said, "I'm so glad to meet you, Breanna. Curt speaks well of your medical expertise."

Breanna smiled and said, "He just talks that way because I saved his bacon."

Sally laughed, then said, "I understand you were down with scarlet fever. I'm glad to see that you're up again."

"Thank you."

"Curt was able to visit you when you were sick, I presume?"

"I tried that very night Josh Collins told me about it," Curt said. "But Breanna was too sick to see me. Besides, if I'd gone into her house, I would have been exposed to the fever."

"As a visiting nurse, I'm gone most of the time, Sally Jane," Breanna said. "How long ago did you move to town?"

"It's J-A-Y-N-E, Breanna. That's my last name."

"Oh, I'm sorry. I misunderstood—"

"Lots of people make the same mistake. Don't be sorry. Actually, I haven't moved to town. My father owns a ranch in the mountains. I only came here to live a short while ago. Curt and I have found that we have a lot in common."

"I think that's wonderful," Breanna said. "It's about time this young man showed some interest in a woman. In the time that I've known him, all he's thought about is being a lawman. I hope the two of you will find more in common all the time."

Sally smiled, feeling better.

"Well, I'd better be going," Breanna said. "Nice to have met you, Sally."

"Same here. See you again sometime."

"Glad you're better, Breanna," Langan said.

Breanna was at the door when she looked over her shoulder and gave the sheriff a friendly smile. "Think about it, Curt. Your eternal destiny is riding on it."

Sally glanced at the Bible on the desk, then blinked in puzzlement as Breanna stepped outside and closed the door.

14

SALLY STARED AT THE DOOR for a moment after Breanna closed it, then turned to Curt and asked, "What was that all about?"

"Breanna is very religious. She was using Sheriff Brad Yates's old Bible to show me some things. She's quite sincere in wanting other people to embrace her faith so they'll go to heaven when they die."

"Well, Breanna is certainly a charming and lovely person. Perfect personality for a nurse. Quite attractive, too. I can imagine that a lot of men almost enjoy sickness or injury when they have her to take care of them."

"I'm sure that's so," Curt agreed, stepping closer to her. "I'll tell you this much—if you were a nurse, I'd make myself sick if I knew you were the one who'd take care of me."

Sally giggled and cuffed him playfully on the chin. "You're so gallant, Curt."

"Gallant has nothing to do with it. You're the most wonderful woman I've ever met."

Sally tilted her head down. "Thank you." Then she looked up at him again and said, "Has your search netted anything since Alf and Nick rode with you?"

"Not a thing. But I'm not quitting. Sooner or later something will turn up that will break this case open. I'll stay after it till I hit pay dirt."

Sally stepped closer to Curt and brushed an imaginary piece of lint off his shirt. "If you have time, we could take a walk down by the river."

He took hold of her hand and squeezed it tenderly. "I'd love to, Sally, but I can't leave the office except for emergencies."

"Can't Steve watch the office for you? He's around somewhere, isn't he?"

"No. I gave him the day off. He hasn't had a break for weeks."

"Well, what about you? When does the sheriff get a break?"

"Not until those kidnappers have been found and pay the penalty to the full extent of the law."

"You are one persistent man, Curt. I admire you for it."

"It's just my nature."

"So you can't leave the office except for emergencies?"

"That's right."

Sally put a mock pout on her lips, stroked his cheek, and said, "But, darling, this *is* an emergency. I need to be with you where no one would bother us. That's why I thought if we could walk down by the river—"

"Did you say 'darling'?"

Sally smiled sweetly. "Sally always says what she means, and means what she says."

Curt folded her small frame in his arms and kissed her tenderly. They clung to each other for a long moment.

"I can hear your heart beating," she whispered.

The sheriff swallowed hard. "Sally, I…I might as well come out with it. I've fallen in love with you."

Sally looked up at him with misty eyes and said softly, "I might as well come out with it, too. I'm in love with you, Curt."

Their lips were about to touch again when the door burst

open. Both of them jumped, quickly separating, as a man charged into the office. "Sheriff! There's a fight goin' on at the Bullhorn Saloon! Zeke Jenkins and some cowboy are mixin' it up and about to tear the place apart!"

"That could be where Alf and Nick are," said Sally. "That's their favorite saloon. I'll go with you."

"Please stay here, Sally. You're a lady, and even if it should be Nick or Alf involved in the fight, I don't want you going into the saloon."

The sheriff ran as hard as he could for the Bullhorn Saloon. Curious, Sally stepped out of the office and followed at a distance.

Langan found Alf Spaulding sitting at one of the tables in the Bullhorn, holding a blood-soaked bar towel to his right cheek. Some of the customers were righting overturned tables and picking up chairs.

Nick Beal had a man down on the floor with a cocked revolver to his head.

"What's going on here?" Langan said.

"This hotheaded dude cut up my partner's face!" Nick said.

"Who started it?" demanded Langan, sure he knew the answer already. Zeke Jenkins's size was his downfall. He was always starting fights.

"He did," Nick said. "After he caught Alf with a sneak punch, he grabbed a beer bottle, broke it on the bar, and rammed it into Alf's face."

"It's the truth, Sheriff," spoke up the bartender, who was standing behind Alf Spaulding. "Zeke started it. When he used the broken bottle on Alf, Nick downed him with one punch, then put the gun on him."

Langan looked at Beal. "You're not planning on dropping that hammer, are you?"

"I will if he tries to get up before I tell him to."

The sheriff pulled handcuffs from his hip pocket and said, "Take the gun away from his head, Nick. Zeke, you roll over on your belly and put your hands behind your back."

Beal eased the hammer down and dropped the gun into its holster. Langan put the handcuffs on Jenkins then stood over him and said, "You stay right there on the floor, Zeke. I'm sure Mr. Spaulding will press charges. When he does, I'll escort you to the jail."

To Alf, who still held the bloody towel to his face, Langan said, "Pretty bad?"

"Enough that the cuts keep bleedin'."

"We need to get you to a doctor. Closest one is Dr. Lyle Goodwin. Can you walk?"

"I think so."

Nick Beal stepped up and helped Alf from the chair, putting a supporting arm around his waist.

Langan got on Alf's other side. To the man on the floor, he said, "Zeke, you stay put. I'll be back for you once I see how badly this man is hurt."

When they moved outside, Sally Jayne was waiting. "Oh, Alf! What happened?"

"We've got to get him to Dr. Goodwin's, Miss Sally," Nick said. "I'll explain on the way."

Sally fell in beside Curt and they headed up the street. "How bad is it, Alf?" she asked.

"I really can't tell you, Miss Sally. He got me pretty deep in a couple spots."

As they approached the doctor's office, Sally hurried ahead and opened the door. A woman dressed in white stood up from her desk, then hurried up to the three men and gently pulled the cloth away from Alf's face.

170

"I'm Dr. Goodwin's nurse, Letha Phillips. You seem to be bleeding quite a bit."

"Can the doctor see him right away?" Sally asked.

"Dr. Goodwin is at a ranch about twenty miles east. I don't know when he'll be back. Sheriff, you know that the next closest doctor is three blocks south."

Alf swayed a bit, and said, "Ma'am, could one of the other doctors in town come here and stitch me up?"

"Well, I— Tell you what. Nurse Baylor is back there in the clinic."

"She's as good as any doctor," Langan said. "If she's up to it, I know she can take care of Alf."

"She's far more qualified to stitch him up than I am," Letha said. "Come on. Let's get him to the clinic."

Breanna Baylor was sitting at a table in the clinic making bandages. She looked up when Letha came through the door. "Breanna, we need your help."

"This man is one of my father's ranchhands, Breanna," Sally said. "He got into a fight at the Bullhorn Saloon and got a broken beer bottle rammed into his face."

Breanna looked at Curt Langan. "Don't tell me. Let me guess. Zeke Jenkins."

"How did you know?"

"Maybe because I've patched up so many of his victims."

Letha spoke to Breanna. "Since Dr. Goodwin isn't here, I suggested that maybe you could stitch this man up."

Langan and Beal helped Spaulding onto the table, then stepped back. Breanna moved up to the table with Letha at her elbow and said, "Lie down flat, please. And what's your name, sir?"

"Alf Spaulding, ma'am."

She removed the towel and looked at the lacerations. "I need some cotton swabs right away, Letha. He's bleeding profusely from a couple of these cuts."

Letha quickly got the swabs. Breanna dabbed at the bleeding cuts, being careful not to touch his skin with her fingers.

"Alf, I've treated facial cuts like these before. From the looks of them, I would say that whether I do the work or a medical doctor does it, you're going to have a couple of pretty nasty scars."

"One thing I'm sure of, ma'am," Alf said. "You're a whole lot prettier than any doctor I ever saw. I'd rather it would be you to stitch me up."

"I'll wash my hands, and we'll get this job done as quickly as possible."

"I'm sure you would rather we left the room while you and Letha work," Sally said.

"Yes, please. Thank you."

"I've got to go arrest Zeke," Curt said. "Alf, as soon as you're able, I need you to come by the office and sign the necessary papers."

"I'm not pressir' any charges, Sheriff."

"The man disfigures your face, and you're not going to press charges?"

"I could have avoided the fight if I'd simply walked away, so it was partially my fault."

"Fists are one thing, but a beer bottle in the face is something else."

"Let's just say, Sheriff, that I want the town to have a good image of the *Circle J Ranch*. Maybe if I don't press charges, word will spread that those of us at the *Circle J* are a decent bunch."

"It'll spread, all right," Langan said. "I'll give the good news to Zeke. But while I'm at it, he's going to get a much-needed lecture. He's started fights in this town before, and he needs to learn better."

172

Sally, Curt, and Nick left the clinic and entered the waiting room. Curt turned to Sally and said, "I'll have to stay at the office. Please come by and let me know how it went."

"All right, darling. See you later."

"Darling?" Nick said, eyebrows arched.

Sally took hold of Curt's upper arm. "Are you going to tell me, Nick, that you haven't seen it coming?"

"Wouldn't say that. All you've talked about since you met the sheriff here is *him.*"

Curt gave her a smile. "Such pleasant words to my ears." He leaned down and kissed the top of Sally's nose. "Can't wait to see you again."

Just over an hour had passed when Breanna Baylor and Letha Phillips helped Alf Spaulding to a sitting position on the table. The entire left side of his face was covered with a bandage.

"Feel dizzy?" asked Breanna.

"A little."

"Well, just sit there till it passes. Big strong man like you will walk out of here on his own power."

"Yes, ma'am."

The nurses were busy cleaning up when Alf said, "I think I'm ready to go now."

Both women took up a position on either side of Alf. "Okay, let's see if you can stand up by yourself," Breanna said. "We're here to catch you if you start to go down."

Alf grinned. "I can make it." He rose to his feet and rolled his shoulders. "I'm fine, ma'am."

"Good."

"How much do I owe you?"

"Dr. Goodwin would charge five dollars, but since I'm only a nurse, we'll make it three—"

"Don't say it like that, ma'am." Alf reached into his pocket. "You did the job. You get paid as much as the doctor would. In fact, since you're so pretty, I'll add a little bonus." Alf placed a twenty-dollar gold piece in her hand.

"Oh, now, listen. You can't afford to—"

"If you hadn't gone right to work on me, Miss Baylor, I could've bled to death." Then he handed her an identical gold piece and said, "Give this to the doc so's he can pay Miss Letha and cover the cost of the medicine and bandages."

"You're very generous, Alf," Letha said. "Thank you."

"Now don't forget to come back in four days and let Dr. Goodwin change the bandages and examine the cuts," said Breanna, turning back to the table where she had been making bandages.

Alf assured her he would be back, and Letha walked him to the waiting room, closing the door behind her.

Sally and Nick were quickly on their feet, glad to see Alf able to walk. Letha explained that all went well and praised Breanna for doing a fine job.

"You sit down here, Alf," Nick said. "I'll go get the horses. You don't need to be walkin' that far."

As Alf eased onto a chair, Sally said, "Don't bother about my horse, Nick. Remember, we need to go to the sheriff's office before heading home, anyway. The mare is already at the hitch rail there. But first, I want to go back and thank Breanna for taking care of Alf."

Breanna looked up to see Sally enter the clinic. "Alf will be fine."

"Thanks to you. I just wanted to come back here and thank you for taking care of him."

"He paid me well."

"That's Alf."

"Sally…"

"Mm-hmm?"

"I've known Curt for some time now, and I've never seen him so happy. You've been good for him. Are you two serious about each other?"

"Yes, we are."

"You do make a nice-looking couple."

"Why, thank you."

"You understand that when you came into Curt's office this morning, the only reason I was sitting so close to him was because I was showing him some things from the Bible."

"Yes, Curt explained that. He said you were sharing some things with him about your faith."

"Ever since I came to know the Lord Jesus Christ, I've wanted others to know Him, too."

"That's nice."

"How about you, Sally? Are you a Christian?"

Sally felt her face flush. "I probably am, Breanna. My great-grandfather on my mother's side was some kind of a preacher."

"Honey," Breanna said, "a person is not a Christian because of what their ancestors were. You become a Christian by putting your faith in the Lord Jesus Christ to save you and wash away your sins in His blood. The whole reason He went to the cross—"

"Breanna," Letha said as she entered the clinic from the outer office, "we have a little boy here. He fell out of a tree, and I think his arm is broken."

A worried young mother hurried in behind Letha, carrying a small boy. The child's face was sheet-white, and he was trying not to cry.

Sally quickly headed for the door. "Thank you again, Breanna, for taking care of Alf."

"My pleasure," Breanna called after her, then turned her attention to the small boy.

Sheriff Langan was carrying firewood in from the back porch when the office door swung open.

"Hi," Sally Jayne said in a cheerful voice.

"Hi. How's Alf?"

"A little weak, but he's out there on his horse and ready to ride to the ranch."

"Breanna did a good job, then," he said, laying the chopped wood by the potbellied stove.

"Yes. Alf is very satisfied."

"Good. She's a great nurse...a real angel of mercy."

"She *is* adamant about her religion, isn't she?"

"She talk to you?"

"Yes. Or at least she tried to."

"Well, one thing you can say for her—she really believes what she believes, and she isn't afraid or ashamed to share it."

"Have to admire her for that. She certainly is a sweet person."

Curt took hold of Sally's hands and said, "Not as sweet as someone else I know."

A broad smile captured Sally's lips. "And who might that be?"

"Tell you what. I'll identify her with a kiss." He wrapped Sally in his arms and kissed her soundly. "Now do you know who she is?"

"I think so. Maybe if you kissed her again, I'd be sure."

When Curt had kissed her the second time, Sally smiled and said, "I knew who it was all the time."

"Oh, you did, did you?"

"Yes, Sheriff. I did. And I'm so glad. Well, I'm afraid I've got to go. See you soon."

"How soon?"

"Well-l-l, how about day after tomorrow?" she asked, moving out the door.

"A whole day in between without seeing you?"

"I do have things to tend to around the ranch house, darling. And Daddy needs me, too."

"Of course. I understand. Can you come late enough that I can take you to dinner?"

"Sure. If Alf isn't up to riding in, one of the other cowhands can take his place."

"Good. I'll look forward to it."

"Daddy's going to love you for feeding me these meals. Makes his food bill lower."

Curt laughed as he followed Sally to the hitch rail. He gave her his hand and she swung aboard the mare.

Curt looked at Alf. "Glad you're going to be all right, my friend. Sally tells me Breanna did a good job."

"She sure did." Alf managed a grin, though his color was a bit pale.

"Sally, I'd sure like to come to the ranch and meet your father," Curt said.

"Daddy's doing better, but he's not quite ready for company. Maybe in a few more days. I want him to meet you in the worst way, but I want things to be just right when it happens."

"I understand. That's the way I want it, too."

"It won't be long, darling, I'm sure. See you on Wednesday."

"Wednesday, it is. I love you."

"I love you, too."

Just before they rode out of sight, Sally turned and waved. Curt waved back, took a deep breath, and sighed, "I'm going to marry you, beautiful lady."

15

JUST AFTER BREAKFAST, Lance Tracy, Moses Crowder, Clint Byers, and five Chinese men found themselves swinging pickaxes deep in the bowels of the mountain, along with a few slaves who had been at the mine for some time.

Duff Pasko and two guards looked on by the glow of lanterns hanging from beams that braced the tunnel. Though most of the slaves were working the new vein in another section of the mine, Morgan had given orders for several areas in the old part to be worked until every nugget of gold was taken out.

The two guards standing with Pasko had overseen the work of the same group of slaves the previous day and had reported that gold in this location was about to play out. Morgan had told Pasko to check on it, and Pasko had just arrived on the scene. He was perturbed to find so little gold ore in the box-shaped car used to haul it out of the tunnel.

Pasko focused on Chung Ho, who was swinging his pick listlessly. "Hey, you!"

Every slave in the area turned to see who had earned the foreman's displeasure. Pasko towered over a blinking, fearful Chung Ho.

"That pick too heavy for you, little man?"

"No, sir."

Pasko yanked the pickax from Chung Ho's fingers and slapped him across the face, knocking him flat. The little man lay on the tunnel floor shaking his head.

A flame of anger bolted through Moses Crowder, and he rushed toward Pasko. The other two guards leaped in front of him.

"Back in your place!"

Crowder stared unwaveringly at Pasko. Tension ran high among the slaves.

"Move aside, boys!" Pasko said.

Both guards obeyed, leaving a path open between slave and foreman. They watched Crowder closely as he continued to glare at Pasko.

The big foreman's eyes widened as he poised himself, holding Chung Ho's pick like a weapon. "You have somethin' to say, blackie?"

"You had no call to hit him! He didn't do nothin' wrong!"

"He wasn't usin' his pick right. And I'm gonna show him how to use it. C'mere, you!" Pasko shoved Chung Ho to the wall and said, "Now, you watch."

Duff set the pickax between his feet, spit on his hands, then gripped the handle and began swinging. The walls of the mine rang with powerful blows. After a few minutes, Pasko shoved the pick into Chung Ho's hand and said, "That's the way you do it. Don't you slack off, even for a moment. You do, and these guards will report it to me. I'll turn you over to big Max. You understand?"

Chung Ho bowed. "Yes, sir."

"Good. Now all of you get back to work!"

Pasko then stepped in front of Moses Crowder, blocking his way. "You don't like me, do you, boy?"

"No, I don't. I've never liked a bully."

"You think you're man enough to put me down?"

The desire to do so was written all over Moses' face.

"Moses, don't push him," one of the veterans said.

"That's good advice he just gave you, boy," Pasko said. "Since you're new here, I'm gonna let your insolence pass just this once. But you'd better not smart-mouth me no more. You got that?"

Moses eyed him levelly and said, "You had no cause to hit him."

"I'll be the judge of that, blackie. And since you can't seem to keep your mouth shut, I'm gonna turn you over to Max. Maybe when you've felt his whip, you'll keep a civil tongue in your mouth!"

One of the guards said, "Duff, if Max whips him, he won't be able to work for at least a week. We need him swingin' a pick."

With an effort, Pasko breathed deeply, let it out slowly, and said, "You're right. We do need him swingin' a pick. You go on back to work with the rest of 'em, boy."

Crowder backed away three steps before bending to pick up his ax. To his back, Pasko said, "Black man, don't let there ever be a next time. 'Cause if there is, ain't nobody gonna talk me outta turnin' you over to Max."

Moses did not look around but gripped his pickax tightly and began swinging it. As if that was a signal to the others, they all went back to work.

Pasko raised his voice above the ringing blows and said to the guards, "I think you boys are right. This section is about played out. I got very little gold a moment ago."

"That's why we made the report. But we were noticin' before pickin' started this mornin' that—well, c'mere."

One of the guards stayed to keep an eye on the prisoners while the other led the foreman a few steps up the tunnel toward the cave's mouth. He held a lantern close to a natural crack about two feet from the outer edge of a thick vertical slab that had been picked clean.

"Look in there, Duff."

Pasko saw it immediately. "More gold!"

"Could be a whole lot back there."

"That'd sure make the boss happy. It'll have to be dynamited."

"That's what we figured."

"I'll go talk to Morgan about it."

A short time later, Duff Pasko emerged from the big cabin and approached a guard at the mouth of the mine. "I've got to do some dynamiting. Morgan's orders. Send a couple of guards into the mine and tell everybody to come out in half an hour. It'll take about that long to get the dynamite in place. I'll do an 'all clear' before settin' it off. As soon as the dust settles, the slaves can go back to work."

The guard moved quickly to obey Pasko's orders.

Pasko made his way through the mine's dark passage and soon came to the storage area near the back door of the cabin where the dynamite was stored. Although he had turned up the lantern's flame, he strained to see. He got out a reel of fuse, then reached into a wooden box and took out two heavy hammers and two chisels. He stuck the chisels in his hip pocket and rammed the handles of the hammers under his belt. He then took a box of dynamite from the top of the stack and set it in the light. He turned the wick back to its normal setting and hefted the box onto his shoulder.

Moments later, the two guards who had found the new vein of gold saw Pasko coming down the tunnel, carrying the dynamite and fuse. While one of the guards took the box from his shoulder, Pasko told the other to take the slaves outside.

Pasko and the guard went to work chipping holes in the thick slab of rock. Then they inserted the dynamite sticks and ran the fuses to a central wire. Pasko held the fuse reel, unrolling it as he backed out the tunnel. When he was within forty feet of the mine opening, he told the guard with him to go outside and make sure all was clear.

The prisoners sat on the ground in the open area between Morgan's cabin and the first line of shacks, glad to have a period of rest.

Max McGurskie stood on the cabin porch. Behind him and to his right was the shadowy figure.

Del Ashmore sat with two other prisoners, Chuck Hamm and Jim Weir, who had been there for over three months. As he looked toward the figure at the window, Jim whispered, "That's Morgan, I'm sure of it."

"You've never seen him?" Del whispered back.

"No. He never comes out of the cabin."

"What is he, a recluse of some kind? Or is he crippled or scarred in some way and doesn't want to be seen?"

"Your guess is as good as ours. None of the guards have ever seen him. The only ones in this canyon who know what Morgan looks like are Pasko, McGurskie, and the girl."

"I heard a girl weeping inside the cabin the day Morgan killed George Matson. Who is she?"

"She's Morgan's eighteen-year-old niece, Missy O'Day. Pretty girl. Sweet disposition. Her name is actually Melissa, but they call her Missy."

"She's as much a captive as the rest of us," Chuck said. "From what we've heard around the camp, the task of raising Missy fell on her Uncle Morgan several years ago. So he made a slave of her. She does all the cooking and housekeeping for Morgan, Pasko, and McGurskie."

"You say she's a pretty girl. You've seen her?"

"Once in a while she's allowed out of the cabin, but most of the time she has to stay on the porch. Morgan has only let her come down twice since Jim and I've been here."

"Like I told you," Jim said, "Missy's a sweet girl. She's shown compassion for the slaves. We've been told that she's suffered many beatings at Max's hands because of it, beatings ordered by her uncle. We saw her take a beating about three weeks ago. A couple of slaves tried to escape and were caught—nobody's ever made a successful escape from this place. Morgan's law condemns to death any slave who tries it. He ordered both of them shot. Missy tried to stop the execution, and her uncle ordered her to receive ten lashes from Max's bullwhip."

"The girl would try to escape," Chuck said, "but she knows if she were caught, she'd be shot too."

Del glanced toward the shadow at the window. "What kind of a beast is he, anyway? I can't imagine a human being so heinous and calloused!"

"He's a mystery to all of us," Jim said.

"He may be a mystery," Chuck said, "but one thing we know about him—he doesn't have an ounce of conscience. His greed for gold has made him absolutely heartless. Human suffering doesn't touch him at all. Another's death means nothing to him."

"Yeah," Jim said. "The dirty scum just stands up there at that window and watches his prisoners slowly waste away or die under Max's whip."

A queasy feeling washed over Del as the hopelessness of his situation came clear. "You mean, unless we can find a way to escape, the only way out of here is death?"

Both men nodded.

"And like I told you," said Jim, "nobody's ever escaped from here. We've learned of over a dozen who've tried. Every one of them was caught and executed."

Del's hands began to shake. "This Morgan. He must be something out of the dark regions of hell."

"That's putting it mildly," Chuck said. "All Morgan cares about is the gold we slaves are digging out of the mountain for him. Kidnapping new men to replace those who die from exhaustion so *they* can die from exhaustion doesn't bother him in the least."

A guard emerged from the mine, came over to the crowd of slaves and other guards, and called out, "Everybody present and accounted for?"

"Everybody but Duff!"

"He's on his way out," the first guard said.

Pasko appeared at the mouth of the mine. "All clear?" he yelled.

"All clear!"

Pasko nodded and disappeared again. A half minute later, he dashed from the mine.

The earth rocked when the explosion came. Seconds later, blue-gray billows of smoke gushed from the mouth of the mine, followed by clouds of brown dust.

Twenty minutes later, the guards ushered the slaves back to the mine. Pasko laughed with glee when he returned to the spot of the explosion and found more gold for the taking. He hurried back to the cabin to tell Morgan.

That night, after the slaves had been allowed to visit the privies and were locked in their shacks, Clint Byers and Moses Crowder sat on their bunks, talking to the other prisoners. The vague light of a harvest moon filtered through the small windows. The prisoners were not allowed to have lanterns or candles. Once the moon passed its high point in the sky, the deep canyon would become a black abyss.

In the shack were several thin, haggard-looking men who had been captives for over a year. Also there was Chuck Hamm, who had been there for better than three months, and Todd Blair, who was a more recent kidnap victim. All but one bunk had an occupant.

"You fellas know this Morgan's first name?" Clint Byers asked.

"No All we've ever heard is Morgan."

"He's heartless," another veteran said. "I think he'd slit his own mother's throat for a half-ounce of gold."

Moses rubbed his weary upper arms, looked at Chuck Hamm, and said, "Chuck, I was talkin' to Del Ashmore at supper. He said you told him ain't nobody ever escaped from this canyon. That every man who's tried has been caught and executed."

The sudden, unexpected sound of footsteps came from outside the door, followed by the rattling of a key in the lock. Every man's attention went to the door as it swung open and they saw guard Ken Botham in the moonlight.

"You guys have one bunk open, don't you?"

Several voices gave assent.

"Okay, lawman! Inside!"

Two other guards had a grip on Bob Lowery's arms and shoved him through the door. He stumbled and fell, and Moses left his bunk to help him up.

"Morgan's orderin' some changes," Botham said. "This is one of 'em "

The door slammed shut and the lock clicked.

Lowery thanked Moses for helping him up, then looked around at the obscure faces and said, "Hello, gentlemen."

"We heard there were two deputy marshals amongst us," one of the veterans said. "Just didn't know which ones you were."

"Morgan apparently wanted me and my partner separated," Lowery said. "Figures we might try something if we're bunking together."

Moses turned back to Chuck Hamm and asked again about his conversation earlier that day with Del Ashmore. The new men listened intently as Hamm told them of Morgan's intent that no prisoner ever leave the mine alive. His words were backed up by the veteran prisoners as they told of would-be escapees being executed, of men dying from overwork, and of Missy O'Day's whipping by Max McGurskie.

"So you're saying nobody's ever made a successful escape from here?" Todd Blair said.

"That's right. But don't despair, rancher. We're all hoping for some kind of a miracle. If we give up hope, that's when we're done for."

"That's right," Moses said. "I'm a born-again Christian, an' I have plenty of faith that the Lord is gonna do somethin' special to get us outta here." He turned to Todd. "You thinkin' 'bout a family back home?"

"Yes. I have a wonderful wife and three children. My oldest boy had his tenth birthday the very day Lance Tracy and I were captured. Poor Elaine and those kids must be out of their minds with worry."

"Well, don't you give up, my friend. I've been talkin' to Jesus plenty. He'll get us outta here."

"What do you think, deputy?" Chuck asked. "Will your fellow federal marshals try to find you and your partner?"

"I'm sure Chief Duvall will do everything in his power to find us. He's facing a real shortage of manpower, though. We've been stretched plenty thin, chasing outlaws of every description. We have to cover a vast amount of territory…from Denver, in every direction, an average of two hundred miles. The chief won't have many men to send on our trail. The sheriff in Denver's been working on this situation for months. We got caught trying to help him."

"So what if nobody comes to get us?" Wally Wyman asked.

"Then we'll die like those before us," said Chuck, in a quavering voice. "Morgan will work us to death. If you want to die faster, just try to escape."

Clint Byers sat in silence. His thoughts went to Breanna Baylor and her words from the Bible. He didn't want to die at all. But if it came, he knew he wasn't ready.

At the large bunkhouse where the guards spent their nights, Duff Pasko, Max McGurskie, and Emil Hadley were playing poker. The other guards were getting ready for bed. Some of them would have to rise in the middle of the night and relieve others now patrolling the canyon.

The bunkhouse door rattled and swung open. Ken Botham moved inside, leaving the door partially open. "Duff, I gotta talk to you."

"Close the door!" snapped Pasko. "That night air's cold!"

"Sorry," Botham said, hurrying to close the door. "Duff, we've got a problem. I think it might be a big one."

Pasko pulled the cigarillo from his mouth and laid his cards face-down. "What's the problem?"

"Four of those Chinese guys are sick."

"Sick?"

"Yeah. Two in one shack, and two in another."

"What kind of sick?"

"Their throats are sore, and they have bad headaches."

Pasko swore, adding, "That ain't so bad."

"But listen to this. Chung Ho and Wing Loo tell me the symptoms are the same as their three countrymen had before comin' down with the scarlet fever on the train. If that's what they've got, the whole camp could come down with it. Lots of times people die from it. And if they live, they're pretty sick for a long time."

Emil Hadley slammed a fist on the table. "If it's scarlet fever, it could spread to us, too!"

"Bring those two English-speakin' Chinamen to me right now," Pasko said. "I wanna talk to 'em."

When the two men were ushered into the bunkhouse, the poker chips and cards had been put away and Pasko and McGurskie were on their feet.

"You wanted to see us, Mr. Pasko?" Chung Ho said.

"Yeah. Ken tells me you got some sick ones."

"Yes, sir. Two in my shack and two in Wing Loo's."

"And you think it's scarlet fever?"

"The symptoms are the same as when our three friends became sick on the journey from San Francisco. And now, one of them in my shack is starting to show a fever."

"I heard there was a nurse on the train who treated 'em," Max said.

"Yes, sir."

"What did she do for 'em?"

"She gave them tea made from some kind of desert plant."

"What's the name of the plant?"

"I do not know, sir. The nurse spoke of it several times, but it escapes my memory."

To Wing Loo, Pasko said, "You remember what it was called?"

"No, sir. I don't think I ever heard its name."

"That all she did? Give 'em the tea?"

"She took them to the baggage car to keep them from the rest of us," Chung Ho said. "She was hoping to keep it from spreading through the train. Then she did some kind of flushing of their insides with cold water."

The other guards looked on with keen interest. One of them said, "Duff, we'd better tell Morgan about this. Things'll get real sticky around here if we get hit with an epidemic and have to stop diggin'."

"Okay, Max, you go with Ken and these little guys," Pasko said. "Take the sick ones to one of those unoccupied shacks close to the river. I want 'em isolated quick."

"But what if Ken and I get exposed?"

"Let Chung Ho and Wing Loo do the touchin' if it's necessary. You two just make sure they're locked up in one of them shacks alone. I'm gonna go tell Morgan about it right now. He ain't gonna take it good, but I'd rather tell him tonight than in the mornin'."

16

IT WAS NINE O'CLOCK the next morning when Sheriff Curt Langan and his deputy stood outside their office talking to Elaine Blair and Donna Tracy. The women had driven into town in Todd Blair's *T-Slash-B* wagon. Both showed signs of stress.

"I wish I could tell you I had a lead, ladies," the sheriff said, "but so far nothing. But don't you despair. I'm going to keep searching. Even the best criminals make a mistake sooner or later. I'm going to be there when it happens."

"We'll keep holding onto that, Sheriff," Donna said.

One of the horses bobbed its head and started to move forward. Elaine gave the reins a yank and said, "Hey, Big Ben! You stand still!" She looked at Langan and said, "I don't suppose you've come up with an idea as to what's being done with our husbands and all those other men?"

"No, ma'am, but I am optimistic that whatever it is, your husbands and the others are still alive. It's got to be something they need a lot of men to do together. Just kidnapping them to kill them would be senseless."

"Unless the whole gang is made up of psychotic killers," Donna said.

"Very unlikely," Steve Ridgway said. "Psychotic killers seldom work together."

"He's right," said Langan. "This thing's going to break open. You'll have your husbands back."

The two wives thanked the sheriff for his efforts to find their husbands and pulled away. When they reached the edge of town, they saw a wagon coming toward them and moving fast.

As the wagon drew nearer, Donna said, "It's Mae Trotter."

"Looks like she may finally be sober," Elaine said.

"You mean she's been on a binge again?"

"According to Sadie Patton—you know, the Trotters' closest neighbor."

"And?"

"Sadie told me Harley and Cy have been missing for several days. Mae's got it in for Sheriff Langan. Thinks he's killed them and buried them somewhere. Sadie said when she stopped by the Trotter place, Mae was so drunk she could hardly stand on her feet."

"I wonder if she's considered the possibility that the same thing that happened to our husbands has happened to Harley and Cy?"

"I don't know. Sadie didn't say."

Mae Trotter's bounding wagon came abreast of them without stopping. As the wagons met and passed, she gave no sign that she even saw the other women.

Mae snapped the reins, pushing the team as fast as they could go. On the seat beside her lay a loaded double-barreled shotgun.

Mae slowed the team when she reached the edge of town and then turned onto Tremont Street. She set the brake outside the sheriff's office and reached for the shotgun, but pulled her hand back when she saw Deputy Ridgway come out the door.

"Hello, Mrs. Trotter. I assume Harley and Cy finally came home?"

"They did not! I want to see the sheriff. He in?"

"No, ma'am. He left only moments ago. He's heading into the mountains again to look for the kidnapped men."

Mae swore under her breath. "So he'll be gone all day, I s'pose."

"Most likely. You have any idea what's happened to Harley and Cy?"

"Sure do." With that, the Trotter woman snapped the reins and put her horses to a trot.

"Deputy Ridgway," came a male voice behind Steve. He turned to see the familiar face of the reporter from the *Denver Sentinel*.

"Harold Bateman, Deputy. Remember me?"

"Sure. How are you?"

"Doing fine. Did you and Langan read the article I wrote about his adept handling of Harley and Cy Trotter?"

"No. And I doubt the sheriff did either. We haven't had time to read a newspaper lately. I'm sure if he had read it, he would have said something about it."

"Is he in, Deputy?"

"No. He left a few minutes ago to do some more searching for those kidnapped men."

"Well, maybe you can fill me in. Has he found any clues at all?"

"I think it would be best if you talk to Sheriff Langan, Mr. Bateman. It really isn't my place to comment on things like that."

"All right. Let me...ah, ask you this. Would you mind if I interview you for a human interest story?"

"What do you mean?"

"Firsthand, what's it like to be a deputy sheriff in a tough western town?"

Steve grinned. "Well, I guess I could handle that. Come on in. Let's sit down."

✦

Mae Trottler decided to pay a visit to Denver's largest feed and grain store and be back at the sheriff's office when he returned that afternoon. If she didn't catch him then, she knew where he lived. As Mae approached Dr. Lyle Goodwin's office she did a double-take. Sheriff Langan's horse was at the hitch rail right in front of the doctor's place.

Breanna Baylor smiled up at the sheriff. "You're entirely welcome. I was glad to stitch up Alf's face. Glad I was here so I could do it."

Dr. Goodwin and Nurse Letha Phillips were in the clinic, working on a patient.

"In my opinion, Breanna, you should be a doctor."

Breanna snorted. "Curt, you know that's next to impossible. Medical schools frown on the idea of women doctors."

"You said *next* to impossible. So it's not impossible, is it?"

"Well, there are a few women doctors in Europe, and I know of a couple women doctors back East. Maybe someday things will change. Anyway, thank you for the compliment, but I'm quite happy being a nurse."

"You're the best, I'll say that. Well, I've got to hit the saddle. Got another day's riding to do."

"Curt, when I talked to Sally the other day, she said things are serious between the two of you."

"Oh, she did, eh?" he said, giving Breanna a crooked smile.

"She did. And her eyes were dancing at the time."

"I'm glad to hear she told you that. Tell you a little secret. It's so serious with me that I'm going to ask Sally to marry me."

"That *is* serious! I hope it works out for you."

"Keep it under your hat, though, won't you? You're the only one I've told. Wouldn't want it to leak to Sally before I pop the question."

"My lips are sealed."

Curt grinned again and moved through the door.

Breanna started to sit down at the desk when she heard a female voice screaming at the sheriff and calling him vile names.

When the angry woman took a breath, Langan said, "Mae, this isn't going to settle anything!"

"Mae Trotter," Breanna told herself, shoving back her chair. She hurried to the door and saw people collecting on both sides of the street. The sheriff's back was to Breanna, and Mae was facing him, holding a double-barreled shotgun. Both hammers were cocked.

Breanna knew the Trotters well, especially Mae. Back in the spring, she had nursed the woman through a serious case of influenza at the Trotter ranch. Dr. Goodwin had made it plain that without the excellent care Breanna had given Mae, she would have died. Even Mae had told many of her neighbors that Breanna had saved her life.

Langan stood like a statue, knowing by the look on Mae's face and the sound of her voice that she meant business. His hands hung at his sides, and he didn't so much as twitch a finger as he said, "Mae, you've got it all wrong. I haven't seen Harley and Cy since—"

"Hah! Don't lie to me, Langan! First you took Willie from me, then you took Chad! Cut 'em both down in cold blood! And as sure as Monday follows Sunday, you took my poor husband and my only remainin' son somewhere outside of town, killed *them* in cold blood, and buried 'em in some remote spot!"

"Mae, that's absurd. I told you face-to-face that Willie and Chad gave me no choice but to take them out. And I've not seen

Harley and Cy since I let them go several days ago."

"Liar!" she screamed, shaking the shotgun menacingly. "You murdered 'em, and now you're gonna pay!"

"Mae, you know men have been kidnapped all over this area for the past three months. I think Harley and Cy have fallen victim to those kidnappers, too. If I'm right about that, I can bring them home to you. But not if you fill me with buckshot."

Mae's eyes showed no mercy. "You're a liar, a murderer, and a hypocrite, Langan! You oughtta be ashamed to wear that badge!" Shaking the shotgun, she added, "I'm gonna blow it right off your chest!"

"Mae!" came a breathless, fear-tinged voice. Mae watched Breanna move up beside the sheriff and stop. The shotgun remained steady in her hands. "Breanna, get away," she said in a tight voice.

"Do as she says, Breanna," Langan said. "I don't want you getting hurt."

Breanna gazed at the half-crazed woman with determined eyes. "Mae, get a grip on yourself. You're not thinking straight. Sheriff Langan is no murderer."

"You don't know, Breanna. He's got you fooled. He murdered Willie and Chad. All these people know that. And I know he murdered Harley and Cy, too!"

"You don't know that, Mae. Listen to me. If you pull that trigger, you are a cold-blooded murderer. You'll be as bad as you say he is. And you'll hang, too!"

"Get away from him, Breanna! He deserves to die! He killed my husband and my three sons. I don't care what happens to me. I have nothin' to live for now that my family's gone."

"You don't know that Harley and Cy are dead, Mae. Sheriff Langan just told you they're probably among the other kidnapped men. Let him do his job so he can bring Harley and Cy home to you. They're alive, Mae. You've got plenty to live for. Now put down the gun."

"No, he's gotta die! Get away from him!"

Breanna felt her pulse quicken as she slowly stepped in front of the sheriff. Mae blinked in astonishment, her mouth sagging open.

"Breanna, what do you think you're doing!" Curt whispered.

"Trust me," she whispered back. Then, raising her voice, she said, "Mae, put the shotgun down."

"Get outta the way, Breanna! It's him I'm after, not you!"

"In order to get him, you'll have to shoot me first," Breanna said, keeping her voice as steady as she could.

Langan wanted to grab Breanna and throw her out of the line of fire, but he feared the sudden move might cause Mae to squeeze the triggers.

"Put the gun down, Mae."

"No!"

By this time, Deputy Ridgway had been summoned to the scene and stood at the edge of the crowd with reporter Harold Bateman at his side. Bateman took out a pad and pencil and began writing. Ridgway wanted to rush in and seize the shotgun, but he knew if he attempted it and failed, he could get Breanna killed and possibly his boss, too.

Mae thought about how Breanna had labored at the Trotter ranch house last spring, going without sleep to save Mae's life. Because the Trotters were having a tough time financially, Breanna had even refused payment when the ordeal was over and Mae was on the mend.

Mae's eyes filled with tears. She lowered the gun and eased the hammers down.

Breanna rushed to Mae and took the weapon from her trembling fingers. There was a mixture of cheers and applause along the boardwalks. Deputy Ridgway was a few steps closer than Langan and got to the women first. Breanna handed him the shotgun, then wrapped both arms around Mae, who released a wordless cry of anguish from the depths of her soul.

Langan wiped his brow with a sleeve. "I've never known a woman with so much courage," he said to Ridgway.

The tightly knit crowd did not break up. They stayed, looking on, as if what they had just witnessed had been a nightmare shared by all.

While Breanna hugged Mae tightly, the older woman cried, "Oh, Breanna, you kept me from becoming a murderer! I couldn't shoot *you!* You saved my life!"

"Don't try to talk, honey," Breanna said. "Come on. Let's go into the clinic. I'll give you a sedative, then I'll take you home."

"No, wait," Mae said. "I've got to talk to the sheriff."

It was hard for Mae to look Curt Langan in the eye, but she straightened her back and finally said, "Sheriff, I was wrong to do what I did. I've been a thickheaded fool about your killin' Willie and Chad. And I should've known you didn't take Harley and Cy out somewhere and kill 'em. I'm...sorry for what I've done."

Langan glanced at Breanna as Dr. Goodwin and Letha Phillips walked up, then he turned back to Mae. "It's all right, ma'am. I'm glad you've come to your senses. Now I can get on with the job of bringing your husband and son home."

"Thank you, Sheriff," Mae said with quivering lips.

"Should I lock her up, Sheriff?" Ridgway asked.

"No, it's all over...thanks to Breanna. Mae's free to go home."

Mae couldn't seem to stop the flow of tears. "Thank you, Sheriff. After what I just put you through, I wouldn't blame you if you locked me up and threw away the key."

"Mrs. Trotter, let me take you into the clinic," Dr. Goodwin said. "You don't look well, and I want to make sure you're all right."

"I…don't have the money to pay you, Doctor."

"Don't concern yourself about that, okay? I just want to have a look at you before you head for home."

"Well, all right." Dr. Goodwin and his nurse started to lead Mae toward the office. She turned and said, "Breanna, you won't have to take me home. I'll be fine."

"We'll decide that after Dr. Goodwin examines you," Breanna said.

The crowd began to disperse, many of them praising Breanna for the brave thing she had done.

Harold Bateman cornered Sheriff Langan, asking if he could interview him and the woman who ended the ordeal.

"She's a nurse, I hear," Bateman said.

"Yes. The best. But before you talk to her, I want to see her alone for a few minutes."

Breanna heard the conversation and said, "I don't believe I know you, Mr.—"

"Bateman, ma'am. Harold Bateman. I'm new at the *Denver Sentinel.* I'm going to write up what I just saw and put it on the front page of tomorrow's edition. I'd just like to ask you a few questions."

"Really, Mr. Bateman, I'd rather you didn't make a big thing of this."

"But you're a heroine, Miss Baylor! People need to know what happened."

With a shrug, Breanna said, "I don't mind talking to you after I've talked with Sheriff Langan. Why don't you come back in half an hour or so?"

Bateman said it would be more like an hour, but he would be back.

"You want to step back inside?" Breanna asked Curt.

"Sure."

The door to the clinic was closed, and the voices of Dr. Goodwin and his nurse could be heard faintly from within. Breanna paused at the desk as Curt closed the outer door. He moved closer to her and said, "I just want to thank you for what you did, Breanna. You put your life on the line to save me."

She smiled. "I guess you might say that."

"Guess, nothing! That's exactly what you did. I know you're my friend, Breanna, but you went beyond the bounds of friendship out there. Why?"

Breanna looked him square in the eye. "Curt, I *am* your friend, and a friend will do things like that. But you're right. It did go beyond the bounds of friendship. I had to risk my life to save yours because if Mae had unleashed that shotgun on you, she'd have killed you...and you'd have gone to an eternity without God. If Mae had killed me instead, I would have gone to heaven."

Langan shook his head, looked away, then met her gaze again. "Why do I get that Breanna's-going-to-preach-to-me-again feeling?"

Breanna opened a closet door and pulled out a small Bible from her purse. "Because that's exactly what's going to happen, young man," she said with a smile.

"But I have to get going. I've got to search for those kidnapped men."

"They'll wait a few minutes. You come sit down over here."

17

THAT NIGHT, BREANNA WAS INVITED to eat supper with Dr. and Mrs. Goodwin. Martha had prepared a scrumptious meal, topped off with one of Breanna's favorite desserts, apple pie.

During the meal, Dr. Goodwin brought up the frightening moment when Breanna had gambled her life to save the sheriff's. Martha was deeply shaken as her husband told the story in detail. When he had finished, Martha reached across the table and took hold of Breanna's hand. "Breanna, you are truly a remarkable young woman. God most certainly has His hand on you."

"If He didn't, I'd have been out of this world a long time ago, Martha. I've had several close calls with death."

"Lyle," Martha said to her husband, "you didn't say if someone went home with Mae Trotter."

"Well, Breanna made her a firm offer, but Mae insisted she was all right and could drive herself home."

"Now that the poor woman has come to her senses, she at least has hope that Harley and Cy are still alive," Breanna said.

"Oh, I pray they are," Martha said. "Those people have had so much tragedy in their lives."

"Some of it the Trotters have brought on themselves, dear," put in the doctor.

"I know, but I hope they've learned some valuable lessons by now."

When the meal was over, the doctor went to his library and the two women did the dishes and cleaned up the kitchen, enjoying each other's company. Later they joined Dr. Goodwin, talking in front of the fire for the rest of the evening.

As the grandfather clock struck ten o'clock, Breanna covered a yawn and said, "Well, it's time for this visiting nurse to visit dreamland for a few hours."

The Goodwins walked Breanna to the back porch and stood there watching her walk away, rubbing their arms against the night chill.

Breanna turned and saw they were going to stay there until she reached her cottage. "Now you two get on back in the house. You'll catch your death. I'll be all right."

"Okay, dear," Martha said, and they moved back inside and closed the door.

Breanna had left lanterns burning in the cottage, and the windows were bright with yellow light. The night was dark around her as she made her way beneath the huge cottonwoods. Most of the leaves had fallen from the branches, and the wind moved the skeletal limbs with a sinister sway against a moonless sky.

Breanna was about halfway to the cottage when she thought she heard the crunch of dry leaves to her left. She paused and looked that way, then all around her, but she could see nothing in the darkness. She picked up her pace but couldn't shake the feeling that she was being watched.

"Oh, Breanna, get a grip on yourself. The house is only a few steps away."

She was almost to the porch when a dark figure came at her from the shadows to her left. She was about to scream when powerful arms seized her from behind and a hand clamped over her mouth. The man began dragging her into the shadows away from the light of her windows. A second dark figure followed.

The man's breath was hot on her ear. Speaking in a low, threatening tone, he said, "Don't fight us, lady! Just relax and listen to what we have to say."

Breanna's heart drummed her ribs and the blood pounded in her head as she made a tiny mew and nodded beneath the calloused hand clamped over her mouth.

The smaller man stepped close and said, "Your name's Breanna Baylor, isn't it?"

She nodded. She could barely see the man in the vague light.

"We know you took care of those sick Chinamen on the train," said the big man. "Well, we've got a bunch more sick men, Miss Baylor, and you're going to help make them well."

"We know you work for the doc," said the smaller man. "He got all the medicines you need at his office?"

"Mm-hmm."

"You got a key to the office?"

Breanna hesitated.

"I asked you a question, lady! You got a key to the doc's office? 'Cause if you don't, we're gonna have to involve the doc in this by bustin' into his house. He and his missus could get hurt."

Breanna made a high-pitched sound and shook her head.

"All right, then, lady. You have a key to the office?"

"Mm-hmm."

"Now, here's the way it'll be," said the one who held her. "We'll go into your house with you so's you can get the office key. Then we'll go to the office and get the stuff you need. You'll be comin' with us."

"Listen to me, lady," the smaller man said. "You give us trouble and we'll have to put a knot on your head. If we don't show up with you at the mine, our boss will have the sick men shot so's they don't spread the scarlet fever to any of the others. You got that?"

Breanna nodded.

"All right, lady," the man who held her said. "I'm gonna take my hand from your mouth. But if you try to call for help, I'll cold-cock you. Understand?"

"Mm-hmm."

Slowly, he relaxed the pressure against Breanna's mouth, then pulled his hand away.

"I'll need to pack my overnight bag and take along my medical kit."

"Okay. Inside."

"How far away is this mine?" Breanna asked while she packed her overnight bag with extra clothing and her Bible.

"We can be there by about three in the mornin' if we keep movin'," said the massive man. "You'll ride with Merv on his horse. We got the horses stashed in an alley across the street."

"Merv, huh?" Breanna said.

"Yeah. Merv Norden."

"You don't care if I know your name?"

"Don't hurt. My big friend here is Max McGurskie."

Breanna looked him up and down. "The name fits you."

"My mama thought so," he said with a chuckle. "I weighed seventeen pounds when I was born."

Breanna was tired and sleepy, feeling the effects of her own bout with scarlet fever by the time she was in the hidden canyon and standing before Duff Pasko. It was 3:30 A.M.

"Well, nursie," Pasko said, "I'm glad you were able to bring a healthy supply of those leaves to make the tea, and it looks like you must have quite a few water bottles."

"I brought all that Dr. Goodwin had at the clinic," she said.

"What's them leaves called you make the tea from?"

"Blue sage."

"Mm-hmm. Okay. Merv and Max will take you to the shack where the sick men are, and you can get started treatin' 'em."

Breanna nodded slowly.

"Now, nursie, let me explain somethin' to you," Pasko said, bending down to look her in the eye. "If you try to escape, you'll be shot down like a dog. Understand?"

"Yes," she replied, wondering what they would do with her once she had nursed the sick ones back to health.

Norden and McGurskie took Breanna to the shack where they now had five Chinese and four white men down with scarlet fever. She was pleasantly surprised to see Clint Byers with them, doing what he could to care for them. All of them were hot with fever, and he was bathing them in cold water from the river that flowed past the camp.

Breanna was glad to see that the shack had a small heating stove, though there was no fire in it. She asked Norden and McGurskie to build a fire so she could make the sage tea. She would need a pan to mix and heat it in, and tin cups.

Both men had been instructed by Pasko to give the nurse anything she needed to care for the sick slaves. Morgan wanted them up and able to dig gold as soon as possible.

Soon the fire was crackling and the heat felt good to Breanna, for the night air at that altitude was quite cold. Norden and McGurskie left, locking the door of the shack.

While Clint was still bathing men with icy water, Breanna had the tea heating, then took water bottles from a cloth sack. She thought of Dr. and Mrs. Goodwin. They would miss her at breakfast in the morning and wonder where she had gone.

When Dr. Goodwin went to the clinic, he would realize what had been taken and put two and two together. He would know that Breanna had been taken by force to treat an unknown number of scarlet fever victims.

While Breanna was giving the cold water enemas and Clint was administering blue sage tea to the sick men one at a time, he filled her in on the entire setup, explaining about the mysterious Mr. Morgan who only appeared as a shadow at the big cabin's window but controlled the camp with an iron hand. He told her of men who had died from overwork, of those who had been beaten to death by Max McGurskie, and those who had been shot for attempting to escape.

Clint also informed Breanna that in the cabin was an eighteen-year-old girl named Missy O'Day, who was Morgan's niece, but also a captive. He explained that he had not yet seen Missy, but he had heard her scream and weep and had heard Morgan slapping her.

"This Morgan has got to be the vilest creature to treat human beings the way you're telling me, Clint," said Breanna.

"Some of the men who have been here a while call him the devil incarnate." Clint went to the stove, poured another cup of the hot tea, then went to the next sick man and began giving him small sips of the tea. "Breanna, I guess I should tell you that the veterans here say that no one has ever escaped from this canyon. Morgan won't ever let any of us leave here. We would be a threat to his prosperous operation if we were allowed to leave. We could sic the law on him."

Breanna thought of Curt Langan, wishing she had a way to let him know how to find the mine.

Clint went on. "And Breanna, he'll kill us anyway when the gold plays out."

Breanna shuddered at such a thought. She was quiet a

moment, then said, "Clint, you say this Morgan is only seen as a shadow at the window of the cabin. You mean you've never actually seen his face?"

"Nobody in the canyon has. Not even the guards. The only two men who are allowed inside the cabin are Pasko and McGurskie."

"I wonder why Morgan is so secretive about himself."

"I don't know. Some of the men think he's been scarred in some horrible, repulsive way and doesn't want to be seen."

The hours passed slowly. Dawn was only a hint in the sky when every man had been given an enema and had swallowed his portion of the sage tea.

Clint and Breanna sat down beside each other on an unoccupied cot and rubbed their tired eyes.

Breanna knew Clint was in deep despair. Though she wasn't happy about the situation herself, she had already been asking the Lord to somehow deliver all of them from Morgan's clutches.

Breanna laid a firm hand on Clint's forearm. "Clint, I serve a wonderful and mighty God. I've been praying already for Him to get all of us out of here. Now, I wasn't abducted without the Lord allowing it. He let me be brought here for a purpose. Probably more than one purpose. You remember on the train, I talked to you about being saved."

"Yes'm." Clint stared at the floor.

"Have you taken care of that matter?"

"No, but I've sure thought a lot about it the last few days.'

"You need to do more than think about it. You need to *do* it. Life is too uncertain, no matter where we are, Clint." She gave his arm a squeeze. "But from what you tell me about the madman up there in the cabin, he just might decide to have you killed on a whim. You know where you'd go if he did."

"Yes'm." He lifted his head and looked at her. "And I don't want to go there, Breanna. I want to be saved."

"Right now?" she asked, her heart pounding.

"Yes. I've put Jesus off too long already. Would you help me?"

"Of course." Breanna felt pure joy and went to get her Bible in her overnight bag. With Bible in hand, she sat down beside Clint and said, "Let's go over it to make sure you understand."

While the sick men who were awake looked on, Breanna went over the gospel story, reading salvation verses to Clint Byers. When he convinced her he understood and that he believed Jesus Christ had shed His blood for *his* sins on the cross and had died and risen again so *he* could be saved, Breanna led Clint to Christ.

When Clint had finished calling on the Lord, tears were streaming down his cheeks. He rejoiced in his newfound faith and thanked Breanna for showing him the way.

Breanna smiled and said, "Clint, according to what we just read in the Scriptures, and according to what you just did, if you died right now, where would you go?"

Clint smiled, wiped away tears, and replied, "I'd go to heaven, Breanna! I'd go to heaven!"

"You'd go to heaven because you feel good inside now?"

"Oh, no. I'm going to heaven because God says so in His Word!"

"Right! You did what God says in His Word a person has to do to be saved. You came to Jesus in repentance and faith, believing on *Him* to save you. We don't go by feelings, we go by the Word. God cannot lie. *He* says you're saved."

And that's good enough for me!"

"Wonderful, Clint. Now, listen to me. You and I are both in the Lord's hands. He allowed both of us to be captured for a pur-

pose, maybe more than one. I can see one purpose already…
your salvation!"

There was a rattle at the door and guards brought in three
more sick men.

After eating breakfast with Morgan, McGurskie, and Missy
O'Day in the big cabin, Duff Pasko went outside and saw Ken
Botham and Wayne Decker waiting for him. Descending the
stairs, he asked, "What can I do for you, boys?"

"Want to tell you somethin'," said Botham. "Me, Wayne, and
Merv saw a lone rider three days ago, ridin' just south of the
canyon. He was clearly lookin' for somethin'."

"Yeah?"

"Yeah. He was far enough away that we couldn't make out if he
was anybody we know. But yesterday afternoon, me and Wayne
saw him again. We could tell by his horse it was the same guy."

So you got a better look yesterday?"

"Sure did. It's that tin star sheriff from Denver. Langan. We
know for sure because we saw the sun glint off his badge. We figured you'd want to tell Morgan. That dude's gettin' too close,
Duff."

"I'll tell him for sure. Morgan knows the kind of threat
Langan can be. He's had his eye on that stinkin' lawman. In fact,
he plans to kill the dude if he starts bein' a problem."

"Seems to me he's just about come to that place, Duff."

"Yep. If he was close enough for you boys to recognize him
from your lookout point on the rim, he's gettin' too close. When
Morgan hears this, he'll probably have some of you boys ambush
him. I'll go talk to him right now."

↑

At the same time Duff Pasko was reporting the news to Morgan, Sheriff Langan left his office and started down the street toward the livery stable. He would saddle up and ride into the mountains once more.

He was almost to the livery when he saw Dr. Goodwin coming toward him on the run.

"What is it, Doctor?"

"It's Breanna, Curt! She's been kidnapped!"

"What? When? From where?"

Goodwin explained that when Breanna did not come to breakfast, Martha had gone to the cottage to see if she was all right. Breanna was not there, nor were her overnight bag and her medical kit. Some of her clothes were missing.

On a hunch, Goodwin had gone to the clinic and found that all of his hot water bottles and supply of blue sage leaves had been taken. He was sure Breanna had been abducted by the same people who had kidnapped the forty men from the train. More scarlet fever had shown up among them, and they wanted Breanna to care for the victims.

Langan was visibly upset. "Doc, it's got to be that these kidnapped men are being used to do some kind of labor. Since no ransom has ever been required from the kidnappers, it's got to be that they're being used to work at something against their will."

"What do you think it is?"

"Well, since the wagons used to transport the men taken off the train have been tracked into the mountains, I tend to say it's a mine. Probably a gold mine."

Goodwin snapped his fingers. "Yes! That's it! The kidnapped men are coming down with scarlet fever, and they need Breanna to care for them! They can't dig for gold when they're sick with scarlet fever. You're on to it now, Curt."

"Now all I have to do is find the mine. It must be in some out-of-the-way place. With Breanna a captive, I've got to intensify my search. I'll take camping equipment and food and just stay in the mountains till I find it. Breanna's life is in danger, Doc. Whoever these vile men are, they'll never let her go when the scarlet fever is no longer a problem."

"Yes," said Goodwin, "I can see why. She could lead you right to them if they let her go."

"I'll not have time to put my camping equipment together today, so I'll be back late this afternoon. I'll let you know if I find anything."

The sun was setting when Curt returned to Denver after a day of intense searching. He stopped at the clinic to tell Dr. Goodwin he had found no sign of a trail to Breanna.

Moments later, the sheriff entered his office and found his deputy reading a copy of the *Denver Sentinel.*

Steve rose to his feet and said, "Boss, you gotta read this story about Breanna's saving your skin. Harold Bateman really did a good j—" Cocking his head, the deputy asked, "Something wrong?"

"I didn't have time to tell you this morning, Steve, but Breanna's been kidnapped."

Ridgway's face blanched. "Kidnapped! When?"

Langan told him the story and Steve agreed it had to be the same people who kidnapped the forty men. He also agreed that Langan's gold mine idea had to be correct.

"Yeah, and that's where all these other men have been taken, too," said Langan. "I'm sure of it. Some gold mining outfit is getting a lot of free labor."

"Dirty skunks," muttered Ridgway. "Oh. I went to see Chief Duvall like you asked me to do, Sheriff."

"And?"

"He just doesn't have any men to put on the search. In spite of the fact that two of his own men are missing, he still can't shake any loose. He wired the commandants of all four forts in this territory east of the Rockies to see if the army could help. Not one of them could spare a man. Their troops are up to their necks in Indian trouble."

Langan nodded solemnly.

"The chief did say he would give you some men just as soon as he can, though."

"Well, you go see him in the morning. Tell him I appreciate that. I'll be heading out at dawn—"

"Hello, Sheriff." The office door opened wide and in walked Sally Jayne.

"Well, boss," said Ridgway with a grin, "it's time for me to head for home. I hear my mother calling me. Lock the place up, will you?"

18

SALLY LAUGHED AS THE DEPUTY made his exit. She rushed to Curt's arms. They embraced and kissed tenderly. Sally laid her head against his chest, and said, "Darling, I just couldn't stay away any longer. I had to come to town to see you. I knew you'd be searching the mountains all day, so I waited till late this afternoon to ride in."

Curt kissed the top of her head and said softly, "Sweetheart, I wish we could be together every night."

Sally looked up into his eyes. "Me, too. Though we've only known each other a short time, the love I have for you is as strong as it would be if I'd been in love with you for years."

"It did kind of happen to us fast, didn't it?" he said, his voice full of emotion.

"That's the way it was with Daddy and Mother, too," she said.

"Really?"

"Mm-hmm. It was love at first sight for both of them."

Curt's blood was pumping hard. He could feel it pulse in the sides of his neck. *Why not now?*

"Sally…"

She drew back and looked into his face. "Yes?"

"Since...since we're doing things fast...I can't hold back any longer."

"About what?"

"Sally, will you marry me?"

Her eyes opened wide and she stared at the tall handsome man, trying to find her voice.

When she didn't answer right away, Curt's countenance fell. "*Too* fast?"

Sally blinked, shook her head, and forced the words out. "No. Oh, no! I just didn't expect—"

"Will you?"

Sally's eyes moistened. "Yes! Yes, darling! I'll marry you!"

Curt kissed her, then held her close and said, "Oh, Sally, you've made me the happiest man in the world!"

She stroked his cheek tenderly. "And you've made me the happiest woman in the world."

"I'll buy you an engagement ring as soon as I can. But since we're officially engaged, anyway, let's go to the Diamond Palace and celebrate. I'll buy you the most expensive dinner on the menu!"

Sally hugged him tight, and said, "I'll take you up on it, Sheriff Langan."

"Great, Sally Langan...almost."

"Sally Langan," she echoed. "That sounds wonderful!"

"We won't wait too long to tie the knot, will we?"

"I guess not," she laughed. "Not the way you and I do things!"

A smile bloomed on Curt's face. "Wonderful! How's month's engagement sound?"

"Sounds fine to me."

As the happy couple walked toward the Diamond Palace Hotel, Sally held onto her future husband's arm.

"Sally …"

"Yes?"

"During your rides between town and your father's ranch, have you seen anything unusual at all?"

"You mean that would give a clue as to who is involved in the kidnappings, or where they might be holed up?"

"Yes."

"Not a thing, darling. I would let you know if I had."

"Of course. Why did I even ask?"

Noting a hint of worry in Curt's eyes, Sally said, "Something's wrong, Curt. What is it?"

"I hate to put a damper on this joyous moment of ours, but, well, Breanna's been kidnapped."

"Oh, Curt! When did that happen?"

"Last night. She lives in a cottage behind Dr. Goodwin's home. Someone forced her to open up the doctor's clinic and take materials and medicine that are used to treat scarlet fever. What I figure is that those Chinese men who were taken off the train have come down with scarlet fever. They were all exposed to it. I think all these kidnappings have been to make slaves of the victims and force them to work in a gold mine somewhere in the mountains."

Astonishment showed on Sally's face. She asked how Curt came to that conclusion, and he explained it to her in detail.

After they ordered their meal, Sally said, "Curt, I really like Breanna. She may be extreme with her religion, but she's really a very nice person. I want her found as soon as possible. Is there anything I can do?"

"No, not that I can think of. But I'll tell you what; I'm going to catch the dirty criminals who kidnapped her. And when I do, they're going to wish they'd never been born."

Sally noted the iron in his voice and said, "I'm glad I'm on *your* side, Sheriff Langan. I sure wouldn't want you breathing down the back of my neck!"

Curt chuckled. "Tell you what, beautiful — if I breathe down the back of your neck, it'll be to kiss it."

As they walked back to the sheriff's office after dinner, Sally clung to his arm and said, "I told Daddy I've found the man I plan to marry."

"Oh, you did, eh?"

"Mm-hmm."

'So you were scheming all the time."

She giggled. "You found me out!"

"So how did Daddy take the news?"

"Quite well. Sort of surprised me, but he wants to meet you as soon as possible."

"Really?"

"Yes! When can you come to the ranch?"

"How about tomorrow?"

"Tomorrow? Wonderful!"

They were at the office door. Alf and Nick had not yet arrived. As they stepped inside, Curt asked, "Would you like me to build a fire?"

"No need. My bodyguards will be here any minute. Now, about tomorrow. Can you really spare the time? When you're so involved in searching for this illicit mine, I mean."

Curt explained that he was planning on carrying food and a bedroll to stay in the mountains, rather than keep riding back to Denver each day. The snows would come soon, and he wanted to find the mine before that happened. By staying in the mountains he could cover more ground each day and talk to more ranchers to see if they had seen anything that could give him a clue as to where the mine might be.

"If you will give me directions to the *Circle J*," he said, "I'll make it a point to come by and meet your father first thing in the morning, if that's all right."

"Of course," Sally smiled. "Oh, I can't wait for you two to meet! If you have a slip of paper, I'll draw you a map."

Curt produced the paper from a drawer and gave her a pencil. Sally hastily drew the map, asking, "Do you know where Eagle Rock is?"

"Sure do."

"Well, as you can see here," she said, indicating Eagle Rock on her map, "I've used it as an identifying landmark. The trail I've marked out here will run you right by Eagle Rock. Then you just follow this dotted line I'm making and you'll come to the *Circle J*. It's some five or six miles southwest of Eagle Rock on a trail leading into a rich, grassy valley.

As she made three "X" marks, she said, "You'll pass three ranches, here, here, and here. The next one is the *Circle J*. You can't miss it. Daddy had a big arch built at the gate with the name of the ranch on a bold-lettered sign."

"All right," he said. "I assume it's all right for me to ask your father for your hand in marriage tomorrow?"

"Of course."

"Good. Then we'll set the wedding date after he's agreed to put his blessing on our marriage. And Sally, if your father still needs someone to care for him after we're married, we'll hire a woman to live in and do so."

Sally wrapped her arms around his neck and planted a kiss on his lips. "Oh, Curt, you're wonderful! I appreciate that more than I can tell you!"

Nick and Alf pulled up outside and one of them called her name.

"Well, here are my escorts," she said and sighed.

"I'll get an early start in the morning, so I should be at the ranch by about nine o'clock."

"I'll be watching for you, darling."

The sheriff pillowed his head that night, concerned about Breanna Baylor's safety, but thrilled beyond anything he had ever imagined to have the most beautiful and wonderful woman in the world in love with him and now about to become his wife.

Breanna's first morning in the hidden canyon proved to be quite difficult. She had been given nothing to eat, and having lost a night's sleep, and still not fully recovered from her bout with scarlet fever, she was extremely weary.

The guards had come and taken Clint Byers away at breakfast time, making it clear that Clint would be working in the mine. This left Breanna with a dozen feverish men to care for. She had to make more sage tea and start the round of enemas again.

By ten-thirty, the guards had brought five more men out of the mine with scarlet fever symptoms and placed them in the shack with the others. Two of the three were Deputy U.S. Marshals Dennis Coulter and Bob Lowery.

The white men with scarlet fever now outnumbered the Chinese. The shack had nine cots running along each side wall, making the capacity eighteen. There was now only one unoccupied cot.

Coulter and Lowery told Breanna who they were and how they got caught. Silently she prayed that the Lord would let Curt Langan find the old burned-down cabin and the sheds atop the canyon.

Just before eleven o'clock, Breanna heard the lock rattle in the door. From where she knelt beside a cot she could see Duff Pasko helping a pale-faced Emil Hadley into the shack. Rising wearily, she waited for Pasko to speak.

"Ma'am, this is Emil Hadley. He's my right-hand man around here. He's got a sore throat and a headache, and he's already runnin' a fever."

"Those are the symptoms," Breanna said blandly, pointing to the last unoccupied cot. "Over there, Mr. Hadley."

When Emil was stretched out on the cot, Breanna said, "Mr. Pasko, as you can see, this shack is up to capacity. If you bring me any more infected men, I'll have to have another shack."

"We've got more," he assured her. "Anything else you need?"

"Yes. Like most people, I'm accustomed to eating periodically. I wonder if I could have some food."

Pasko grinned. "I'll have Missy fix you up some grub.

"Missy is Morgan's niece, I understand."

"Yeah."

"Do you know if she's had scarlet fever?"

"Don't know. Why?"

"I need help, here, Mr. Pasko."

"Oh. Well, I doubt she'd be allowed to come help you, even if she's had it."

"Then, how about letting me have Clint Byers? I can't properly care for all these men by myself. Clint knows what to do and can be a real asset in speeding up their recovery."

"Okay. I'll bring Byers to you."

"Bring some more firewood while you're at it, too, will you? It's running low, and I need to have plenty of tea hot at all times."

"Will do."

Just as Pasko opened the door to leave, loud voices were heard, coming from the mouth of the mine. Breanna rushed to the door, looked past the foreman, and saw Max McGurskie dragging a Chinese man out by his shirt collar. She recognized Chung Ho following on McGurskie's heels. He was begging

Pasko not to hurt his countryman.

The guards were ushering all the other men out of the mine behind them. McGurskie ignored Chung Ho's pleas and dragged the man to the front of the cabin, throwing him to the ground.

As the slaves gathered on the open spot before the cabin, Breanna recognized Harley and Cy Trotter, though both had lost some weight. Her eyes fell on Clint Byers in the crowd. She pointed to him and said, "There's Clint, Mr. Pasko."

"Later, lady. Right now, *everybody* except these sick men have to gather in front of the cabin."

"Why? What's going on?"

"We've got an insubordinate slave, that's what's goin' on. He's gonna get himself a good whippin' by big Max. It's Morgan's rule that when a slave is disciplined in the camp, *everybody* has to witness it."

"Me, too?"

"Yep. Morgan wants every prisoner here to see what happens to those who get outta line. Preventative measure, if you know what I mean."

Breanna looked around at her patients, most of whom were asleep.

"They'll be all right," Pasko said. "Let's go."

Pasko locked the door behind them and led Breanna to the spot where the slaves and guards were gathering. As they drew up to the edge of the crowd, Clint Byers looked their way and Pasko motioned him to come. Clint quickly threaded his way amongst the men.

As Clint was heading for Pasko, Max left a trembling Ling Mang in the hands of two guards and mounted the steps of the cabin. Chung Ho pleaded on Ling Mang's behalf, but McGurskie ignored him. He reached the porch level and disappeared inside.

When Clint reached them, Pasko said, "Byers, you're to be the nurse's assistant until further notice. Got it?"

"Yes, sir," said Clint, smiling at Breanna.

Breanna was pleased to see the change on Clint's countenance. Jesus had already made a big difference in him, despite present circumstances.

Breanna let her eyes stray to the canyon wall behind the cabin, all the way to the top. She could make out a shed near the rim. Clint saw what she was looking at and said, "It was probably too dark for you to see the buildings up there when they brought you into the canyon last night. The remains of a burned-out cabin are up there, along with some sheds. What you're seeing is the largest shed."

Breanna nodded, realizing it was up there that deputies Coulter and Lowery had been captured. Suddenly she saw a movement at the large window to the left of the cabin door. A figure appeared as a shadow behind the smoky glass.

Morgan!

Breanna was studying the mysterious master of the mine when Max emerged from the cabin with the bullwhip coiled in his hand.

Ling Mang was on his feet now, held fast by the guards. As Max started down the stairs, Ling Mang focused on the whip and whimpered.

Clint leaned close to Breanna and whispered, "I'm told that few men survive Max's whippings. He's a heartless beast!"

Breanna clenched her teeth. "The *real* beast is the man in that cabin!" Her eyes were fixed on the obscure figure behind the glass, then she ran her gaze to Pasko as he reached Ling Mang. Chung Ho stood close by, his face pinched with fear for his Chinese brother.

Suddenly Breanna saw Moses and Malachi Crowder standing at

the front of the crowd. When her eyes met theirs, they nodded and tried to smile. She nodded back.

Pasko ran his gaze over the faces of the slaves and said loudly, "You men who have been here for a while know that rebellion is not tolerated in this camp! You newcomers have been told to stay in line and obey our commands, but it seems that there's always some dude who comes in here and thinks he don't have to obey when spoken to."

"That's right!" spoke up guard Ken Botham, who stood near the Crowder brothers.

"This here is Ling Mang. For some reason, he thinks he can sass-mouth the guards and get away with it! Well, let me tell you somethin'! Ain't none of you lowly slaves gonna sass-mouth us without payin' for it!"

"That's right!" Botham said again.

The foreman went on. "Ling Mang, here, disobeyed Mr. Botham down in the mine! When Mr. Botham told him to do a certain thing, he jabbered somethin' insolent at him in Chinese. Well, this kind of rebellion will get him nothin' but the bite of Max's wh—"

"Mr. Pasko!" Chung Ho said. "Please, sir! Ling Mang does not understand English. There was no one there at the moment to interpret what Mr. Botham was saying. Ling Mang was frightened and was trying to explain that he was not understanding Mr. Botham's commands. His words seemed to be insolent, they were words of fear and confusion. He was trying to get Mr. Botham to understand that he did not know what he was telling him to do."

"You shut up!" Pasko snarled. "Your pal *was* bein' insolent! Mr. Botham said so!"

"No!" cried Chung Ho. "You do not understand! Please do not inflict punishment on Ling Mang! He did nothing wrong!"

One of the guards rushed up behind Chung Ho and cracked him on the head with the butt of his rifle. Chung Ho collapsed and lay still.

Breanna gasped, putting a hand to her mouth. She started to head that direction but was stopped as Clint seized her by the arm.

"No, Breanna!" he half whispered. "If you go to Chung Ho, you're liable to get the same thing he did! Morgan will take it that you're interfering, and you'll pay for it!"

Breanna nodded that she understood and glanced at the dark figure in the cabin window. *What kind of inhuman, unfeeling beast can Morgan be?*

Duff Pasko looked at Max and asked, "You ready?"

The huge man nodded.

There were eight heavy posts that held up the porch.

Pasko told the guards, "Strip off his shirt and tie him to that end post."

Chung Ho was beginning to stir.

While the guards roughly removed Ling Mang's shirt and used it to bind his wrists to the thick wooden post, Max uncoiled the whip in a dramatic manner, drew his arm back, and cracked it so loud it sounded like the report of a rifle.

Breanna's hand went to her mouth. "What kind of animals are these, Clint?"

"The *bad* kind," he answered in a low tone.

"Oh, Clint, this has got to be stopped!"

"There's nothing we can do. We're totally helpless against these beasts."

Every eye was fastened on Max as the two guards stepped away, leaving the small Chinese man tied to the post, stripped to the waist. Max grinned evilly and cracked the whip again. It's loud pop echoed along the walls of the canyon.

Chung Ho was shaking his head to clear it and rising to his

knees. Breanna noticed blood in his hair and on the back of his neck.

Pasko climbed the steps and stood in his lofty position on the porch. He glanced at the obscure figure in the window, nodded, then looked down at Max and said, "Get on with it."

The huge man gave the whip one more pop, then let it lie on the ground like a lifeless serpent. He looked at the crowd of slaves and roared, "This is what happens to rebels!"

The whip suddenly came to life, cut the thin mountain air in a deadly hiss, and laid an ugly red welt across Ling Mang's back. The small man let out a painful cry.

McGurskie drew the whip back to unleash it again. Chung Ho sprang to his feet, crying, "No!" and seized the huge man's muscular arm. "No! Don't hit him again! He has done nothing wrong!"

Max shook him off like he would a fly, then backhanded him and sent him rolling. Some of the Chinese men hurried to Chung Ho and spoke in their native language.

Everyone, including the guards, cringed as the big whip laid another burning welt across Ling Mang's back.

Suddenly the door of the cabin burst open and a pretty blond girl appeared, heading for the steps. "Stop it, Max! Stop it!"

Duff Pasko was taken by surprise and made a lunge for Missy O'Day. She avoided him and darted down the stairs, repeating her cry for Max to stop. The door stood open, and the inside of the cabin was dark and obscure, but the shadowy figure still stood at the window.

Missy rushed to Ling Mang, wrapped her arms around him, and placed herself between him and Max McGurskie. "No!" she screamed. "Don't hit him again, you heartless beast! This little man didn't understand what Botham was telling him to do! If Morgan won't have mercy, Max, at least you can!"

Breanna's nerves were wire-tight. She wanted to go and stand with Missy. Clint saw her chewing on her lips, her eyes fixed on the scene, and whispered, "No, Breanna! He'll whip you, too, and Ling Mang will still take his punishment!"

"But the girl—"

"You can't help her!"

Max looked up at Duff, not knowing whether to lash Missy with the whip or not.

Duff wheeled, poked his head inside the cabin for a few seconds, then closed the door and turned around. Looking down at Missy, he bawled, "Get away from him, girl, or feel the whip yourself!"

Missy broke into tears. "He didn't do anything wrong! Don't whip him! Please don't whip him!"

"Get away from him!" roared Max. He raised the whip. With a sob, Missy ducked her head but clung to Ling Mang.

The whip hissed and tore Missy's dress, leaving a red stripe on one arm.

Breanna saw Clint stiffen. His face went beet-red and his eyes were bulging. "I can't stand this!" he said, and bolted for McGurskie.

Breanna's mouth formed a word to call him back, but he was too fast.

McGurskie's back was to the crowd. Clint moved so quickly that before any of the guards could react or call out, he hit McGurskie from behind. The impact shot streamers of pain through Max's body. His knees buckled, and he fell to the ground.

Instantly, Clint was on top of him, pounding him with his fists. The two guards who had held Chung Ho threw themselves on Clint and rolled him off McGurskie, pinning him to the ground. Four more guards closed in, including Ken Botham. Together, they picked Clint up and slammed him against another post that held up the porch. He tried to fight them off, but they pinned his arms and held him tight.

"You dirty devil!" Clint screamed at McGurskie. "How could you hit the girl like that? Have you no decency in that soul of yours?"

Max rubbed his back, gritting his teeth from the pain Clint had inflicted. To the guards who held Clint, he said, "Get away from him. I'm gonna beat him to death!"

This time it was Breanna who lost all control. She ran amongst the slaves, crying, "No! Don't you touch him, you animal!"

At the same time, Missy O'Day let go of Ling Mang, screaming at McGurskie. In obedience to Max, the guards had backed away, leaving Clint vulnerable to the whip. Both women converged where Clint stood and placed themselves in front of him, facing McGurskie.

"Don't you hit him, Max!" Missy wailed. "He was only trying to protect me!"

Breanna started to say something to Max, but Clint cut her off. "Ladies, I don't want you hurt. Please. Get away before he unleashes that whip on you!"

Missy looked up at Pasko and said, "Please, Duff! Stop this horrible brutality!"

Pasko hunched his shoulders. "I got orders from your uncle."

Breanna took a step away from the edge of the porch floor, looked toward the dark form behind the window and cried, "Mr. Morgan! How can you let such inhuman, unfeeling brutality take place here? It's bad enough to make slaves of these men, but this kind of barbaric conduct is outrageous!"

The figure behind the window shifted positions, but the door remained closed and silence prevailed.

Breanna drew a deep breath and called loudly, "You heard it,

Mr. Morgan! Ling Mang doesn't understand English, like most of these Chinese men. It was all a mistake! It wouldn't have happened if Ling Mang had understood the guard's order. Please! In the name of common decency, stop this horror!"

Silence.

Duff Pasko was looking toward the window. Every eye in the crowd saw the dark figure make a hand signal.

Pasko opened the door, stuck his head inside the cabin, nodded, then closed the door. Turning back, he looked down at Breanna and said, "Mr. Morgan says you need a good lesson, nursie. For your insolence, you will feel the whip!"

A loud protest came from the crowd of slaves.

Pasko and McGurskie cursed them, but their voices could hardly be heard above the tumult. The guards cocked the hammers of their guns, ready to start shooting if the men got out of hand.

Suddenly Moses Crowder darted to the front and stood beside Breanna. The crowd went quiet. Max started toward Moses, but the black man raised a palm and said, "Just a minute, Max! Lemme talk to your boss!"

Max looked up to Duff, who nodded.

Moses set his gaze on the form behind the window and shouted, "Mister Morgan! Please don't let him whip Miss Breanna! If there must be punishment here, let Max whip *me* in her place!"

"Moses, no!" gasped Breanna.

"How about it, Mister Morgan?"

"No, Moses!" said Breanna. "I can't let you do it!"

Pasko barked, "Both of you shut up! Let me talk to the boss."

Again the foreman stuck his head inside the cabin. After a few seconds, he returned to the porch railing and said so all could hear, "Mr. Morgan has ruled that if the black man takes the whippin' this whole thing will be over."

"No!" cried Breanna. "Moses, you can't do this!"

Crowder stepped close to her and said, "Miss Breanna, this is the only way to keep you an' this little gal an' Ling Mang from being whipped. Better that one person should be whipped than the three of you."

"All right," Pasko said. "Guards, release Ling Mang and the nurse. Missy, you get up here and go inside!"

Missy's face took on a pallor as she started toward the steps. She looked back with fear evident in her eyes. "Thank you, Miss Breanna." Then to Moses, "Thank you, dear man." Then she climbed the stairs and went inside.

A series of muffled blows could be heard, but were identifiable as open-handed slaps to the face.

Moses relinquished himself to the guards and peeled off his own shirt. While they were tying him to the post, Breanna backed up to the front line of the slaves. Clint moved next to her, his face ashen.

Breanna bit hard on her forefinger and tears coursed down her cheeks as Max popped the bullwhip for effect then took his stance to lay stripes on Moses Crowder's back.

19

ELMA DUVALL OPENED THE DOOR to Curt Langan with a smile. "Good morning, Sheriff."

Langan touched his hatbrim and said, "I'm sorry to bother you so early in the morning, Mrs. Duvall, but I need to see the chief if possible."

"Of course. Come in. Sol is shaving at the moment, Sheriff," said the silver-haired woman. "I'll go upstairs and tell him you're here."

Curt watched her mount the stairs and thought of how Sally might look when she reached her late fifties. Mrs. Duvall still had her beauty in spite of some wrinkles and the silver hair. He knew Sally would still be beautiful when she reached that age.

His heart warmed as he thought of their upcoming wedding. He couldn't wait to meet Sally's father.

The lanky, silver-haired lawman appeared at the head of the stairs and started down. Before Duvall reached bottom, Langan said, "Good morning, Chief. Sorry to intrude like this, but I have to head for the mountains right away, and I wanted to leave something with you." As he spoke, he pulled a folded slip of paper from a shirt pocket.

"No intrusion, Curt. What is it?"

Langan explained that he was going to the *Circle J Ranch* to meet the father of a young woman he was interested in, then would be resuming his search for the kidnapped men. He shared his idea with Duvall that it might be a gold mine operation using the kidnapped men for free labor.

Langan showed the paper to Duvall, telling him that the young woman had drawn him a map so he could find the ranch. This was a copy for Duvall. He pointed out Eagle Rock and told the chief that he was going to be staying in the mountains for however long it took him to find the illicit mine. If Duvall had any men who could come and help, they were to go to Eagle Rock and wait for him. Every night he would camp by the well-known landmark, so if any deputies could come, they were to meet him at Eagle Rock early in the morning or in the evening.

Solomon Duvall thanked the sheriff for the map and the instructions, saying he hoped he would have some men free to help very soon. He wanted deputies Coulter and Lowery back.

Curt Langan traveled at a steady trot and soon reached the high country. As he rode among towering peaks and through brush-covered ravines and thick forests, it struck him that in the level open country that lay ahead of him was a massive camp of the Arapaho Indians. Chief Hawk Wing headed up that part of the Arapaho Nation and had shown himself tolerant of white men. Hawk Wing and his warriors would not bother whites if they did not bother his people.

Langan lashed himself for not thinking of the Arapaho before. Hawk Wing and his people knew every square foot of the area. They roamed all over that part of the Rockies. No wagons or riders could come and go as much as the men who had been doing the kidnapping, and not be seen by the Indians.

When he was deputy sheriff, Langan had met Hawk Wing on two occasions and the chief had been friendly to him.

Langan decided that when he left the *Circle J* this morning, he would ride to the Arapaho village and talk to Hawk Wing. Maybe the chief could lead him straight to the mine—or whatever else the operation might be.

Langan was suddenly very encouraged. His contact with Hawk Wing would be the ticket to ending this kidnapping situation and delivering the captives back to their homes and families.

Soon he was riding on the edge of familiar territory. Just north was the valley he had crossed several times of late as he followed the trail of the wagons that had kidnapped forty railroad employees.

He veered slightly south, and soon Eagle Rock came into view. It was situated at the top of a gradual rise before the land dipped into the valley southward, where according to Sally's map, the *Circle J* was situated.

As he drew closer to the rock, Curt marveled at how its craggy crest, which stood some forty feet from the ground, resembled the majestic head of an eagle.

His eyes were fixed on the rock when suddenly he saw three riders come from its back side. They reined in, looking in his direction. He wondered if—

Another fifty yards confirmed it. Sally and her two bodyguards had ridden to Eagle Rock to meet him. There was a moderate breeze, and it was blowing her long auburn hair under a flat-crowned hat as she sat her horse between Spaulding and Beal.

Langan was only about two hundred yards away when Sally rose up in the stirrups and waved at him. He lifted his hat, waving back, and put his horse to a gallop.

Suddenly six riders appeared from a nearby ravine, wielding

revolvers. They quickly encircled Sally and her companions, disarmed Beal and Spaulding, then forced them to head northwest at a gallop.

Panic rose in Curt. He veered his mount, angling toward the nine galloping riders, and used his spurs for greater speed. Were these six men part of the kidnapping gang? Could the mine be hidden somewhere back in the dense forests to the north of the valley?

Within seconds, Sally, Nick, and Alf and their abductors disappeared into the deep woods. By the time Langan slowed his horse and entered the shadowed forest, the riders were nowhere in sight. This was familiar territory, however, and he felt sure they would head for the shallow creek where he and Sally had ridden side by side while following the trail of the wagons. Somewhere along the banks of that creek was the path that would lead him to the kidnapped men.

Just as Curt reached the south tip of the ravine, he caught a glimpse of the nine riders. He was right! They were headed straight for the creek.

They vanished from sight again, but he was not more than two hundred yards behind them. The horse's hooves made little sound on the thick carpet of pine needles as Curt guided him among the towering pines. Within minutes, he reached the creek and caught sight of the riders just before they disappeared around a bend upstream. They were riding the middle of the creek.

He must not let them emerge from the creek before he could get close enough to watch where they came out.

After rounding two bends in the stream, Langan saw them again, just as they were pulling out. He jerked the reins to the left, guiding his mount to dry ground. Once on the bank, he spurred the animal hard, heading for the spot where the kidnappers had emerged from the water.

There was a path leading away from the stream into more dense forest. Curt followed the path, which took him almost due north. The trees were thick and the path was narrow. It weaved through tall timber, slowing him somewhat. He kept peering ahead, trying to catch another glimpse of the riders, but to no avail. After a while, the forest was so thick the horse slowed to a walk.

Soon the sheriff's ears picked up the distant sound of a waterfall, and the further he rode, the more distinct the waterfall's roar became. Presently he saw a clearing ahead. He could make out some old unpainted buildings. As he drew near, he could see the blackened remains of what had once been a cabin. There was a barn with a corral and some sheds.

The roar of the waterfall filled the air as he cautiously rode into the clearing. The wind was picking up and whining through the treetops. There was no sign of the nine riders, but he was sure they had come into the clearing. There were hoofprints leading into it, and they looked fresh.

He slid from the saddle and pulled his gun, letting his eyes scan the area. He moved past the largest shed and spotted more fresh tracks leading to the edge of the clearing. When he reached it, he saw a winding path that led down into a deep, rock-walled chasm.

Curt stood on the rim of a rocky precipice and peered into the canyon. Though he couldn't see the waterfall, the air below him was heavy with water spray.

Curt moved several paces to his right, trying to get a better view of the trail. Suddenly he saw men milling about at the very bottom of the canyon. A little further, he saw a mule-drawn ore cart leave the mouth of a large opening in the side of a mountain. It was a gold mine, just as he had thought!

Movement caught his eye about halfway down the trail. It

was the gunmen and their captives, leading their horses and picking their way toward the bottom of the canyon. They were in an open area for a few seconds, then vanished from view.

Curt shook his head. It was bad enough that the despicable beasts who ran the mine would kidnap men and force them to dig out their gold, but now they had two women, Sally and Breanna!

The sheriff's first impulse was to ride back to Denver and form a posse. Certainly he could get many volunteers now that he had actually found the mine. He ran back toward his horse, the wind plucking at his hatbrim. He would have to ride hard. He was about to vault into the saddle when suddenly he stopped.

He spun around and looked back toward the canyon. What had those despicable men done to Breanna by now? Maybe she would escape their evil desires because she was needed to care for the sick men in the mine. But Sally—she was in real danger. Men who were so degenerate that they thought nothing of stealing husbands and fathers away from their families and making slaves of them would also think nothing of violating a beautiful, helpless young woman.

By the time he rode to Denver and returned with his posse—

No! He could not leave Sally in their wicked hands! He must go down there right now and rescue her! That bunch of filthy vermin would—

But he was only one man. How could he hope to invade that canyon alone and rescue her?

He vacillated between his two options, growing angrier by the second toward the mine owner and his men. Wrath overwhelmed fear, and finally the die was cast. There really was no choice. Somehow he had to find a way to rescue both women.

He glanced at the barn, thinking he would hide his horse in there, but changed his mind when he saw fairly new horse droppings in the corral. Apparently the gang in the canyon used the barn.

The large shed! His horse would be better hidden in there.

Quickly he led the horse to the shed, flipped the rusty old latch, and swung one of the double doors open. He saw a dust-covered old wagon with rocks in it standing on a wavy wooden floor.

The stiff wind swung the old door back and forth on its creaky hinges while Langan led his horse inside. He patted the horse's neck and said, "Hopefully, I won't be long, ol' boy."

He was heading for the door when a whistling sound caught his attention. He followed the sound that seemed to be coming out of the floor. It was a wind whistle.

Curt knelt down, running his hands over the floor. He felt the pressure of the wind on his palms. It was whistling through a tiny crack that squared off perfectly. A trapdoor!

Further search revealed special grooves where his fingers slipped in, giving them a grip. The door was heavy, but he lifted it a few inches. The gust of wind that came out of the dark shaft below was strong. Above the wind, he heard the faint sound of male voices and the unmistakable chinking of pickaxes on rock.

Curt could see the rungs of a ladder. He leaned the door against the wall of the shed and peered into the shaft. There was a soft yellow glow at the bottom, which came no doubt from a lantern.

The sheriff's first thought was to climb down the ladder and enter the mine that way. But he quickly changed his mind. It would be too dangerous. The best thing to do was to sneak down the trail, reach the bottom of the canyon in daylight, and make his next move from there.

He lowered the trapdoor and stood up. The whistling started up again. As he stared at the trapdoor, he decided to block it so no one could open it. If he was able to get the upper hand when he reached the bottom of the canyon, he didn't want anyone making a run for it and escaping through the shaft.

The wagon. The load of rocks in the wagon bed weighed at least a thousand pounds.

He grasped the dusty old wagon tongue and worked the wagon back and forth until he had maneuvered a rear wheel on top of the trapdoor. Patting the horse's neck again, he said, "See you soon, ol' boy."

Clint Byers was giving blue sage tea to four more men who had begun to show signs of scarlet fever. They were bedded down on cots in a second isolation shack. When he got a sufficient amount of tea in them, he would begin bathing them with cold water as instructed by Breanna Baylor. When their fever went higher, they would be given the cold water enemas.

Byers heard footsteps on the porch, then the lock rattled and the door came open. Guard Wayne Decker held a bucket in each hand. "Here's the water you wanted," he said.

Clint was on his knees beside a cot. Looking over his shoulder, he said, "Okay. Thanks."

"Don't mention it." Decker set the buckets on the porch. "You come and get 'em. I ain't goin' in there."

Clint retrieved the buckets of river water and moved back inside. Decker started to close the door, but checked himself when he saw Duff Pasko approaching with Missy O'Day at his side.

"Hold it, Wayne, Missy's goin' in there," Duff said.

"What for?"

"Morgan's gettin' worried with all these dudes comin' down with the fever. The nurse has got her hands full takin' care of the ones in the other shack. And right now, she's tendin' to Crowder and Chung Ho in their shack. The nurse asked for someone to help Byers, so Morgan decided since Missy had scarlet fever when she was ten, she should come and help him take care of these."

Missy quietly stepped inside the shack and smiled at Clint.

"I'll check on you later," Pasko told her, and closed the door.

The key made its familiar metallic sound in the lock, and Pasko and Decker could be heard talking to each other as they walked away.

The shack had four small windows, which allowed moderate light inside. Missy looked at the men on the cots, then at Clint, and said, "I wanted to go into the shack where Miss Breanna is caring for Moses to thank him for taking the beating for the three of us, but Duff wouldn't let me. He said I can do it later. I really am eager to tell Moses what his unselfish deed means to me."

"He's some kind of man," Clint agreed. "I was able to express my appreciation to him shortly after they carried him to the shack."

"Duff called Miss Breanna onto the porch and told her that my uncle said I was to get instructions from her. She said you would tell me what to do."

Clint gave her a lopsided grin. "I'm glad you're here."

"Miss Breanna told me your name is Clint Byers. And you know I'm Missy O'Day."

"Yes. I want to thank you for jumping in there with Breanna to try to protect me."

"First thanks should be mine," she said. "You were in trouble because you went after Max to protect *me*. That was a brave thing to do."

Clint's features tinted slightly. "I just couldn't stand it when that big bully turned the whip on you. I had to do what I could to stop him."

Missy smiled. "You hurt him when you butted him, I could see that." She paused, then asked, "What can I do to help here?"

"Well, let's see, why don't I let you administer the hot tea to these men while I build up the fire in the stove?"

"All right. Who's first?"

Clint pointed out who had received tea and who had not. While Missy went to work with the tea, Clint mixed more and stoked up the fire. He then began bathing the feverish men with the cold water.

While the two of them worked, Missy studied Clint, admiring him. "You know, Clint, what Moses did for you and Miss Breanna and me was a little bit like what the Lord Jesus Christ did for all sinners."

Clint's eyes lit up. "You're right, Missy! Jesus took the punishment that should have been ours when he went to the cross. You're a Christian, aren't you?"

"I sure am," she smiled. "And, well, I have a feeling you are, too. It just seemed that the Holy Spirit was telling me that you are."

"Amazing," Clint said .

"You really think so?"

"Well, for me it is. I've only been saved a few hours."

"What?"

"Mm-hmm. Breanna led me to the Lord about…ah…four o'clock this morning. We first met on the train coming from San Francisco."

"I know about her being on the train."

"Well, she talked to me real straight about being saved during the trip, but I was sorta stubborn. The Lord had to let me get into this situation before I was willing to open my heart to Jesus. But, thank God I'm saved now!"

"Wonderful! I've had that kind of feeling about Miss Breanna, too, but I haven't had that much opportunity to talk to ner. I took her some food earlier this morning and talked to her on the porch of Moses' shack, but that's all."

"She's a real, gen-u-ine Christian," Clint said with conviction. "She lives what she professes. And speaking of Christians, Moses and his brother, Malachi, are Christians, too."

Missy smiled from ear to ear. "Oh, Clint, I'm so glad to hear that!"

In the shack that Moses Crowder and Chung Ho shared with several other slaves, Moses lay face-down on his cot while Breanna knelt beside him, preparing to wash the bloody stripes on his back.

Chung Ho lay on his cot a few feet away, his head wrapped in a heavy bandage. Since the gash on the back of his head was bleeding profusely, Breanna had tended to him first. She had given him powders to ease the pain, then stitched up the gash. He was drowsy now and almost asleep.

Breanna had heated a pail of water on the small stove in the shack, and as she dipped a cloth into the water, she said, "Moses, there's no way I can keep this from stinging."

"That's all right, Miss Breanna. They've gotta be washed up."

Breanna gently laid a cloth on his back. Moses flinched, sucking air through his teeth.

"I'm sorry," she said. "I wish I didn't have to hurt you."

Breanna had just finished washing Moses when Ken Botham stuck his head in the door and said, "Lady, we got a guard in pain out here. Come out and look at him."

Breanna stood up and said, "Moses, try to lie perfectly still. I have salve in my medical kit. I'll put it on your stripes when I come back."

"Yes'm."

Better than an hour had passed when she returned. Moses hadn't moved and Chung Ho was still asleep.

"You've pretty well stopped bleeding, Moses. How's the pain?"

"Not hurtin' so bad, Miss Breanna. What was wrong with the guard?"

"One of the mules kicked him in the leg. Cut the flesh. I had to put in a few stitches."

Breanna reached in the kit for a jar of salve and said, "I hope you won't think ill of me for saying this, Moses, but I feel like pinning a medal on the mule."

Breanna's comment made Moses chuckle, and the movement shot pain over his lacerated back. He moaned, sucked air, and forced himself to lie still.

"I'm sorry," Breanna said. "I didn't mean to cause you more pain."

"That's all right, Miss Breanna. I don't think ill of you. I agree with you!"

Breanna unscrewed the lid on the jar. "And what's more, I'd like to turn that blessed mule loose on McGurskie for what he did to you, and on Morgan for letting it happen. Nobody should have had to take that whip."

"You're right. But since somebody had to take it, I'm glad I could be the one."

Tears welled up in Breanna's eyes. She was about to speak when the door came open and Missy entered.

Missy closed the door behind her, noting that Breanna was wiping tears from her eyes. "You all right, Miss Breanna?" she asked.

"I'm all right. I'm just overwhelmed by what Moses did for us. He took that whipping so we wouldn't have to."

"Yes," Missy said softly, moving closer to the cot. "Clint and I were talking about it. What Moses did for us is like what Jesus did for a world of sinners, including us."

Moses moved his head at Missy's words and looked up at her, but it was Breanna who spoke.

"Missy! You're a Christian?"

"Yes, ma'am. I was so pleased to learn that you and Moses are, and that you led Clint to the Lord in the wee hours this morning."

"Did Clint tell you my brother, Malachi, is saved, too, Missy?" asked Moses.

"He sure did. I have mixed emotions about all this."

"What do you mean, honey?" Breanna asked.

"Well, I'm sorry you dear people have been captured by these wicked men and brought to this awful place. But it sure is nice to have some Christians here."

"How long have you been saved?" asked Breanna.

"For ten years. Both my parents were Christians. We were in a good Bible-believing church. I was saved during a revival meeting when I was eight years old."

Breanna dipped a cloth into the salve, and before applying it, she said, "Missy, it must be hard for you to live with such a wicked man as your uncle. How long have you been with him?"

Missy's face lost color. Fear leaped into her eyes. "I...I'm forbidden to discuss it, Miss Breanna. I have strict orders never to talk about it to anyone. I...I'm sorry."

Breanna laid the cloth down and rose to her feet. "Oh, Missy, please forgive me for asking. I—"

Tears filled Missy's eyes. "There's nothing to forgive, Miss Breanna. There's no way you could have known about my restrictions."

Breanna folded the girl in her arms and held her close. "You poor, sweet thing. One way or another, you're going to get out of here."

"Nobody can get away from Morgan," Missy choked, clinging to Breanna. "If we tried to escape, we wouldn't make it. We'd be killed for attempting it."

Breanna squeezed her hard and said, "Missy, the same God who delivered the people of Israel out of wicked Pharaoh's hands can deliver us from the wicked hands of your uncle. He can set captives free today as well as then. I've been praying that way, and I know Moses and Malachi have."

"Yes, ma'am," Missy said, falteringly.

"You must pray the same way, honey, and believe that our God is going to deliver us. Do you remember the song that Moses and the children of Israel sang when they were on the victory side of the Red Sea?"

"I don't remember the exact words, but I know they were sure praising the Lord."

"I can't quote the entire song," said Breanna, "but it started out, 'I will sing unto the LORD, for he hath triumphed gloriously!' and a few lines later, they sang, 'Thy right hand, O LORD, is become glorious in power: thy right hand, O LORD, hath dashed in pieces the enemy.... Who is like unto thee, O LORD, among the gods?'"

"Those are powerful words!" Moses said, wincing as he spoke.

"They sure are," said Breanna. "And powerful truth! The Lord's right hand is going to dash our captors in pieces and set us free, too. And when He does, they'll know there is no god like our God among the false gods of this world!"

"Amen," Moses said. "There is no God like our God! He will set us free, Missy. You wait an' see!"

Breanna gave Missy another squeeze and said, "You just trust Him to deliver us, honey."

Missy closed her eyes, took a deep breath, and said, "I will.

You two and Clint have been such a strength to me."

Breanna knelt beside Moses and said, "All right, Moses. Brace yourself. I've got to get this salve on your stripes."

Moses gritted his teeth as Breanna began spreading the salve.

"I almost forgot what I came in here for," said Missy. "I wanted to thank you, Moses, for taking those stripes for me. You are a wonderful man."

"I ain't nothin'," Moses said quietly. "Just give the praise to Jesus. He's the One that gave me the courage to take the whippin' for you and Miss Breanna, and for Clint."

Missy's eyes were wet with tears again. "Miss Breanna, will he be all right?"

"He will," Breanna assured her. "It's just going to take time for these cuts to heal."

"I'll pray that the Lord will hasten the healing."

"You do that," said Moses. "I'll appreciate it very much."

Missy looked down at the nurse and said, "Miss Breanna, did you know about Clint being jilted by a girl in California?"

"Yes. He told me about it."

"He's such a fine young man. How could that girl have done such a thing?"

"Well, maybe the Lord had His hand in it," Breanna said. "If Clint had married her, he and I would have never met. I never would have been able to give him the gospel. I believe God let it happen so he would be on the train where I could witness to him. Now that Clint is saved, and the Lord is going to get all of us out of here, no doubt the Lord has a very special young lady picked out for him. A *Christian* young lady."

Missy took it all in, nodding. "You have a lot of wisdom, Miss Breanna. So you really believe the Lord has picked out a certain young woman for Clint?"

"Yes, I do."

Missy smiled. "Then you must believe the Lord has a certain young man picked out for me."

Breanna paused in her work to look up at the girl. "God has a plan for our lives, Missy. Sometime I'll tell you how He worked out His plan for my life. I was engaged to marry a man in Kansas, but he jilted me."

"Really?"

"Mm-hmm. And I was devastated. But in time, the Lord sent the man into my life He had chosen for me. He's a wonderful man, and one day—in God's time—we will marry."

"Oh, that's wonderful! Well, I'd better get back to Clint. He's looking in on the men in the first isolation shack. He may need me."

When the girl was gone, Moses said, "Miss Breanna, I think maybe that li'l gal has eyes for Clint."

A smile curved Breanna's lips. "And it wouldn't surprise me if he feels the same way about her."

20

LESS THAN TWO HOURS AFTER CURT LANGAN had ridden away from his house that morning, Chief Marshal Solomon Duvall entered the sheriff's office.

Deputy Ridgway was just coming in through the alley door with a wastebasket in his hand. "Morning, Chief Duvall," he said. "What can I do for you?"

"Nothing, my friend. I just thought you might like to know that I have one man on his way into the mountains to catch up with your boss. He came in from an assignment early this morning and stopped by my house to tell me he was back. When I told him about the kidnappings, and that Sheriff Langan needed help in his search, he volunteered to go. I told him the sheriff had ridden west only a half hour earlier. He said he would stock up on saddlebag supplies and leave right away. Curt gave me a map of the area where he's going. Said he was going to visit a woman he was interested in, then resume the search."

"He's interested in her all right. Her name's Sally Jayne. Her dad owns a ranch up there somewhere."

"Yes. Just southwest of Eagle Rock, according to the map. My man is well acquainted with the area. I gave him the map. He said he'd ride hard. If he didn't catch up to Curt before he reached the *Circle J Ranch*, he'd meet him when he headed back toward Eagle Rock."

"Great, Chief!" Ridgway said, grinning broadly. "My boss will be glad for even *one* man to help him in the search."

Gun in hand, Curt slowly picked his way down the steep trail that led to the mine. It took him through thick brush and dense aspen trees and around massive boulders.

As he descended the twisting path, the roar of the waterfall increased in volume and the spray moistened the air around him, even collecting lightly on his face and clothing. The determined lawman continued down the trail, his wary eyes watching for any sign of movement below. The roar of the unseen waterfall was almost deafening.

Suddenly the wind gusted up from the canyon below, swirling the spray in every direction just as Langan rounded a massive boulder and the waterfall came into view. The wind-driven moisture was heavy enough that it pelted his face and filled his eyes. For a moment, he was blinded. He stopped to thumb away the moisture and when his vision cleared, his heart lurched as he saw two men standing in front of him with guns leveled at his chest.

"Drop the gun, Sheriff!" shouted the one to Langan's left.

"Now!" came a sharp voice from behind.

Reluctantly, the sheriff let his revolver slip from his fingers.

The one behind him laughed and said above the roar of the waterfall, "Well, whattaya know, Ken…Wayne! We got us Denver County's hotshot sheriff!"

"Yeah, Merv! Morgan's liable to reward us real good for this!"

Curt was guided along a narrow, rocky ledge toward the waterfall with Botham and Norden behind him and Decker in the lead.

The roar of the waterfall was deafening as they passed behind it on the ledge. When they reached the other side, they followed the river for some five hundred yards, descending deeper into the vast shadowed canyon. At the bottom, Langan was ushered to a large open area where he saw the big cabin socketed in the side of the mountain and the bunkhouse, tool shed, barn, corral, and shacks and sheds of various sizes and descriptions. Directly ahead of him was the gaping mouth of the mine. The roar of the waterfall was only a distant sound now, but the swift current of the river that ran through the canyon could be heard clearly.

As his captors led him to the front of the cabin, Curt's eyes darted about, looking for some sign of Sally and her bodyguards. "Where is she?" he demanded.

"Shut up!" Botham said. "You'll speak only when spoken to!"

"Now look, you! Sally Jayne was brought in here, along with two cowhands from her father's ranch! I want to know what you've done with them!"

Botham's fist lashed out, catching Langan on the jaw and knocking him off his feet. His head spun as he rolled to his knees.

"I told you to shut up, Sheriff! You'll speak when spoken to, y'hear? Now, get up!"

While Curt staggered to his feet, Max McGurskie emerged from inside the cabin. When he saw Langan from the lofty porch, he laughed and said, "Well, lookee who we've got here! That badge on your chest says you're the sheriff of Denver County, fella! Curt Langan. That right?"

"Yes."

"Ken," said the huge man, "you stay here and keep your gun on the mighty sheriff. Wayne, you and Merv go round up everybody in the camp except the sick ones, of course. Morgan's gonna want to celebrate this with every able-bodied person lookin' on!" With that, McGurskie reentered the cabin.

Langan saw men filing out of the mine under the guns of Morgan's guards. Others were coming from the shacks. The weary-looking, emaciated men assembled forty feet from the porch, staring at him with vacant eyes. Their despair was evident. Suddenly the sheriff recognized Harley and Cy Trotter, though both were noticeably thinner than they were when he had last seen them. Father and son met his gaze and nodded solemnly.

Langan nodded back just as solemnly. Suddenly he caught sight of two blond women on either side of a young man. The one on his left looked familiar. Breanna!

No one knew why they were to assemble, only that they were to gather in front of the cabin immediately.

Suddenly Breanna saw Curt. "Oh, no! They've got Sheriff Langan!"

"*Denver's* sheriff?" Missy said.

"Yes. I was so hoping that—"

"That he would rescue us?" asked Clint.

"Well, I know he was searching diligently for the kidnappers' operation. I figured the Lord would probably let him find the canyon then bring an army of men with him." She paused, then said, "But the Lord is not limited to what we figure. He will still deliver us."

Missy wished she was as sure about it as Breanna was. Clint was having some doubts, too.

Breanna caught Curt's eye as they gathered with the crowd of men. He gave her a discouraged look but tried to force a smile. She nodded back, her expressive eyes telling him she was sorry he was in the hands of Morgan and his men.

Under her breath, Breanna said, "Lord, I'm trusting You to

248

deliver us from these vile men even though Curt is now a prisoner, too."

Curt wondered if Breanna knew where they were keeping Sally, Alf, and Nick. His attention was drawn back to the cabin when the door opened and Duff Pasko came out.

The man's face was familiar but he couldn't place it. Where had he seen him before?

Then he saw a shadowed figure appear at the window to the left of the cabin door. At first he thought it was the huge man he had seen moments before, but as he focused on the vague form, he could tell the person was not nearly as large.

Curt's eyes swung back to Pasko, who was shouting for stragglers to hurry up and get with the rest of the slaves.

Suddenly Curt remembered this was the man he had seen talking to Floyd Metz at Denver's Union Station the day Metz left for California to hire men to lay track.

So this is Morgan!

Pasko's voice boomed over the crowd of slaves and guards as he pointed at Curt. "I'd like to announce that we've got us a special prisoner! This is the rough-and-ready sheriff of Denver County! I guess he came in here to rescue all of you. Took you a long time to find us, tin star. Pretty stupid, I'd say, to come in here alone."

"I came in alone because I saw six of your henchmen kidnap my fiancée and her two escorts. Where are they, Morgan?"

Pasko jutted his jaw. "I'm not Morgan! Name's Duff Pasko. Not that it matters as far as you're concerned, since Morgan's gonna have you executed shortly for trespassin' ."

The lone rider reached Eagle Rock when the sun was not yet midway in the morning sky. He took out the map Chief Duvall had given him, studied it for a moment, then set his gaze south-westward. He noted the scattered ranches in that direction, then dismounted.

He began pacing back and forth at the foot of the giant rock, keeping his eyes to the southwest, the direction the map indicated the *Circle J Ranch* was located. He expected that at any moment he would catch sight of Sheriff Curt Langan riding toward him.

When nearly a half hour had passed, Chief Duvall's man decided he might have arrived after Langan had already left the *Circle J*. The best thing to do was to ride to the ranch and find out. If Langan was already gone, he would need to ride hard to catch up with him. Swinging aboard his mount, he put it to a gallop.

Fifteen minutes later, the lone rider had his horse running at top speed as he raced across the rolling terrain. He passed Eagle Rock, then swerved due west.

At the hidden canyon, Breanna Baylor stood in the crowd and sucked in a short sharp breath when Duff Pasko told Sheriff Langan that Morgan was going to execute him. Oh, no! Lord, You can't let them kill him!

Missy saw the look on Breanna's face and laid a hand on her shoulder. Breanna responded by touching the hand with her own and squeezing it.

Curt said, "Look, Pasko, if I don't show up back in Denver by sundown, there'll be a whole passel of U.S. marshals on your necks! I want to know where Sally is, and I want to talk to this Morgan guy! Now!"

Pasko guffawed while descending the stairs. "A whole passel of federal lawmen, eh, Sheriff? C'mon, now. If this passel of government men knew where the mine was, they'd have been here a long time ago. You just played the fool and got yourself caught. You've already seen your last sunset, tin star!"

"You think they won't find this place if I turn up missing?"

Pasko threw his head back and laughed. "Well, we've had two of their own for several days. How come they ain't come to rescue *them?*"

"What have you done with Deputies Coulter and Lowery? If you've killed them—"

"They ain't dead!" Pasko said. "We got a scarlet fever epidemic goin' on, here. Both of 'em are down with it, along with a bunch of others, includin' one of our guards."

"I figured you had the epidemic. That's why you kidnapped Miss Baylor."

"So you figured that out, eh?"

"Wasn't hard. Now, I want to know where Sally is!"

Moving closer, Duff put his nose a hand's breadth from Langan's and said with a sneer, "I'll tell you where your little redhead is. She's inside the cabin, right where Morgan wants her."

The thought that this Morgan may have violated Sally made Curt crazy. "I want her out of there right now, Pasko! You hear me? *Right now!*"

Pasko grinned, looked around at the crowd, and chuckled, "My, my! Do you hear that, boys and girls? The big tough sheriff is givin' me orders. That's not allowed here in the Morgan camp. Somebody talks like that, they usually get to taste Max's whip! However, this time, I'll administer the punishment."

Even as he spoke, Pasko unleashed a hissing fist at Curt's jaw. Curt ducked it and countered with a powerful punch to Pasko's nose that sent the bigger man staggering backward. Before Pasko could clear his vision, Clint landed another solid punch to Pasko's nose. Blood spurted as the stunned Pasko swung blindly.

Suddenly Curt was tackled from behind by Ken Botham. Four more guards dashed in. Curt elbowed one on the mouth, splitting his upper lip, and managed to clip one with a stinging blow to the jaw before they smothered him, pinning his arms and legs to the ground.

Pasko ran his hand under his nose. When he saw the bright crimson smear, he stood over Langan and growled, "You just made the biggest mistake of your life, Sheriff! Get him on his feet, boys!"

The guards yanked Langan to a standing position.

"Couple of you hold him. I'm gonna teach him a lesson!"

Curt pulled tight against the hands that gripped him and riveted Pasko with blazing eyes. "So you aren't man enough to take on a man thirty pounds lighter than you huh, Pasko? You've got to have your pals hold him for you!"

Tension swept like an ocean wave over the crowd of prisoners. Breanna stiffened at Langan's challenge, knowing that if these men so desired, they could beat him to death. And the wicked Morgan, who stood at the window, would let them do it.

Pasko ran his hand under his nose another time and stomped up to Curt. He slapped him savagely across the face. The sheriff's head whipped to the side, and Pasko slapped him again, calling him all kinds of vile names. The guards still held him tight.

Curt suddenly swung both of his feet up and kicked Pasko in the face. The blow sent the man reeling backward, and he fell flat on his back. He lay there stunned, moaning and shaking his head.

The guards moved in and began pounding Curt. When Breanna saw it she bolted toward them. Missy ran behind her. Both women tugged at the arms of Merv Norden and Ken Botham, begging them to stop.

Missy screamed toward the window where the dark figure

stood. "Morgan! Stop this horrible thing! They'll beat him to death!"

The cabin door came open and Max McGurskie appeared. He moved to the railing and shouted for the guards to stop. Botham and Norden obeyed and looked up at Max.

"We weren't gonna kill him, Max," Botham said. "We were just gonna beat him to such a pulp he would *wish* he could die."

Duff Pasko—who was now on his feet—roared, "Ain't nobody gonna kill him but me!"

As Pasko staggered toward Curt, McGurskie's voice boomed like a cannon. "No, Duff! Morgan wants him inside the cabin!"

Missy's eyes bulged. "Miss Breanna, nobody but Duff, Max, and me can go in there and come back out alive!"

"Oh, dear God," Breanna said. "Don't let them kill him!"

As the guards hoisted Curt to his feet, Ken Botham glared at him and said, "Well, you wanted to see Morgan, pal. Believe me, you're gonna wish you hadn't!"

Curt blinked to clear his vision and licked blood from his lips. He gave Botham a steely look but did not reply. The guards released Curt as Pasko took him by the arm and guided him toward the porch stairs.

McGurskie looked down at the women and said, "Missy, Morgan wants you and the nurse in there, too!"

Missy gasped, took hold of Breanna's arm, and said, "Pray hard, Miss Breanna! This isn't good. I don't want you killed!"

The cabin door stood open, revealing a murky interior. Pasko held Curt at the threshold, waiting for the women to reach the porch. Curt peered inside but could make out only part of a table and a couple of straight-backed wooden chairs. The shadowed figure had vanished from the window.

As the women reached the top of the stairs, Pasko said, "Okay, Sheriff! Inside!" He gave him a shove through the door, then waited for Missy and Breanna to go in ahead of him.

When they were all inside, Pasko pushed the door shut.

The room was so dark it took a few seconds for their eyes to adjust as Pasko moved to the table, struck a match, and lit the wick of a lantern. As he turned up the flame, the yellow glow revealed Sally Jayne seated on a straight-backed chair in a corner. Alf Spaulding stood on one side of her and Nick Beal on the other.

Curt dashed to Sally. "Are you all right? If any of these wicked animals have harmed you, I'll—"

Sally rose to her feet. Her face was grim. "I'm all right," she said.

Curt wrapped his arms around her, holding her tight, then looked over his shoulder at Pasko and snapped, "Where's Morgan?"

Curt felt Sally stiffen in his arms as Pasko said, "Sheriff, you're holdin' Morgan."

21

BREANNA'S HEART CONSTRICTED and she stood transfixed. She struggled to take a breath. The look on Sally's face told her what Pasko had just said was true.

Missy stood like a statue next to Breanna, her mouth dry and her eyes fixed on the sheriff.

As Duff Pasko's words slowly registered in Curt's mind, he eased his hold on Sally but kept his arms around her and looked into her eyes, hoping what he saw there would refute this terrible lie. He looked at Alf and Nick, and his gaze fell on their gun-belts. They both had their guns again.

Sally remained stiff within his grasp, and the awful truth clawed its way into the sheriff's brain. Sally pushed herself free of his arms, staring at him with passionless eyes. His entire body had gone numb.

As Sally moved between Max and Duff, Curt stammered in disbelief, "Sally...*you* are Morgan?"

"Yes. I'm Morgan."

"But I thought your father...the *Circle J*..."

Curt felt nauseous, even as his heart pumped madly and his fists clenched into hard knots. The cabin was warm, but he felt an icy chill around him.

His eyes flicked to Breanna, whose face was devoid of color, then to the woman who had given him the shock of his life.

"But Sally...you...you said you loved me. We were going to marry. I thought you were the sweetest thing I'd ever seen in my life. How could you? It's like you've ripped my heart out by the roots!"

Max McGurskie laughed, "Boy, you sure put one over on this tin star, didn't you, Morgan?"

Morgan looked at Curt and Breanna and gestured toward the table. "Sit down. Both of you. You ought to see yourselves! You look like you've seen a ghost. Go on, sit down! I might as well fill you in on the whole story. I'll enjoy telling you about it. Missy, you take a seat at the table, too.

"Max, send the slaves back to work—there won't be a show for them right now—then come back here. Alf, you go tell Clint Byers to get back to the sick men; see that he gets anything he needs. I want those men well so they can produce gold! Nick, go do something worthwhile. Duff, you stay."

As the men filed out the door like obedient little boys, Sally sat down at the head of the table and Pasko sat at the other end.

Sally fluffed her long auburn hair and gazed from Breanna to Curt. "To begin with, my name isn't Sally. My name is Morgan Jayne Montgomery. Jayne was my mother's maiden name. For my little masquerade in town, I took the name *Sally*, and merely used my middle name as my surname."

"But why the masquerade?" Curt asked.

"I had to get close to you. You were on our trail ever since we started kidnapping men around here. The best way to keep track of your investigation was to get close to you and bring about your demise if you started closing in on us."

Curt's head bobbed at the thought that this woman he had fallen in love with could so coldly talk about killing him.

Breanna fervently talked to the Lord while she studied Morgan Jayne Montgomery and shook her head.

Morgan noticed the motion and snapped. "And you, Miss Goody-Goody! I took a real disliking to you the moment I found out you were one of those Bible-spouting fanatics like Missy, who by the way, isn't my niece. She's my cousin."

Breanna spoke up. "How did Missy have the misfortune to fall into your clutches?"

"You'd best keep a civil tongue in your head!" Morgan said.

Breanna just gave her a level stare.

"Missy's mother was my aunt. She and Missy's father were killed when Missy was thirteen. My parents took her in. When my mother died two years later, my father kept my little cousin in his home."

"When Morgan's father died, she took me in," Missy said.

"I wasn't going to at first," said Morgan, giving the girl a bland glance, "but then I figured she'd make a good housekeeper. Why not keep her around and save myself a lot of work?"

Curt's heart was bleeding. How could he have been so easily taken in by this woman? "So how did you become the boss around here?" he asked.

"Simple. My father inherited this mine from an old friend who died. He was going to sell it. We were living in Silver City, New Mexico, at the time." She looked straight at Breanna as she said, "I didn't want the old boy to sell it. We'd come and taken a look at it, and I saw the potential for real riches here."

Breanna saw Missy grimace in anticipation of what was coming next.

"So," said Morgan, "sweet Daddy had an 'accident.'"

"You…you murdered your own father?" Curt gasped.

Morgan laughed. At that moment, Max entered the cabin. "Every able-bodied slave is back at work, Morgan," he said.

"Good. Take a seat. I'm just filling our guests in on how I became boss of this outfit."

"I'll sit here by the window," said Max, picking up a chair and carrying it to where Morgan had been seen so many times as just a shadow. The glass had been treated with a special chemical to make it slightly opaque.

Morgan shifted her gaze from Max to Curt. "Any more questions?"

"Yes," Curt said. "Couldn't you have kept an eye on my investigation by simply making friends with me? Why did you have to lure me into your web, then pretend you had fallen in love with me?"

"Because a man in love is easier to manipulate. You were the only real threat to this operation. Sooner or later, you would have found this place on your own."

Curt shook his head sadly. "And it worked," he said.

Duff Pasko chuckled. "You really went for it hook, line, and sinker, pal. Morgan had you in her grasp from the first day the two of you met, and now you're still her captive. Your investigation is officially over, and now you're gonna die."

Missy gave out a tiny, high-pitched whine, shaking her head in protest.

"Shut up!" Pasko said. "Don't start that kind of stuff again!"

Missy made a defiant leap at Morgan. "You can't do this! You can't murder these two people! God says in His Word you'll reap what you sow. Your sin will find you out!"

Morgan glowered at the girl. "Sit down and shut your mouth! I don't want to hear any of that Bible stuff!"

"Do you think because you choose to ignore God that you won't have to face Him?" Missy said.

"I told you to shut up!" screamed Morgan, jumping out of her chair. "Come over here."

Missy swallowed hard. Her hands trembled. "No, Morgan. Please don't—"

"I said come over here!"

Sniffling with fear, Missy obeyed. When she stood directly in front of Morgan, she said, "Please don't hit me, Morgan. Please!"

Morgan stung her with a violent openhanded slap across the face. Missy shrieked and backed away, but Morgan followed and slapped her repeatedly, driving her against the wall.

Curt leaped to his feet, but was instantly faced with both Duff Pasko and Max McGurskie and their revolvers.

"Don't even think about it, Langan," Pasko said.

The sheriff dropped back onto his chair and watched the merciless redhead, thinking how she had seemed so sweet and feminine. Now she showed none of those qualities. She might as well have been a stranger.

Missy slid down the wall to the floor, using her arms to ward off the blows. Finally Morgan, her wrath spent, stepped back and looked down at her cousin. "Let that be a lesson to you, kid. You keep your mouth shut, and don't you speak unless spoken to. You got that?"

Missy nodded, her lips quivering. Her face was blotchy red where Morgan's hand had struck her.

"Get up and sit on your chair," Morgan said.

When Missy was seated once again, Morgan looked at Breanna and Curt. "Now back to the story. Duff...Max...put your guns away and sit down."

"With the inheritance of this mine," Morgan proceeded, "I came up with the idea of slave labor. I could pay my guards well and keep more gold for myself that way. Duff and Max were already employed at the mine as foreman and assistant foreman. I had Duff fire everybody else so we could start over with the slave idea. Duff hired the guards, many of them old prison mates of his when he did time at the Colorado Territorial Prison at Canon City."

"Correct me if I'm wrong, but doesn't Floyd Metz figure in here somewhere?" Curt asked.

Surprise showed on Morgan's face.

"I saw him talking to Pasko at the railroad station the day he left for San Francisco," Curt said.

"Sharp eye," Morgan said. "I was about to get to Metz, anyway. While in prison, Duff learned that the supposedly respectable Mr. Metz—although an executive with the Union Pacific Railroad—was known by the criminal element as a shady dealer. Duff approached him about setting up a kidnapping scheme to provide slaves for the mine. When Floyd learned what kind of money the mysterious Mr. Morgan would pay him for it, he joined up.

"When I came to the mine and took on the role of Mr. Morgan, I brought Missy with me. She does a good job as cook and housekeeper. Her only problems are her Bible-spouting mouth and her periodic complaints when she sees slaves being disciplined around this place."

"You can't fault her for having compassion toward human suffering," Breanna said. "A normal person has that. Because Missy is a Christian, she has even more."

Morgan gave Breanna a petulant glance, then said, "This operation has been a big success, Curt. And one of the primary reasons is that I've kept the slaves intimidated by concealing myself from them, letting them believe that Morgan is a monstrous, brutal man."

She chuckled. "Even the guards think they're working for some hard-nosed outlaw. I've shrouded Morgan in mystery, keeping all but a few in this canyon off balance. Works like a charm."

Curt eyed her levelly and asked, "How many slaves have you killed?"

"Always thinking like a lawman, aren't you? I haven't kept count. Some have died from exhaustion, and some have been beaten to death by Max for insubordination. Others got themselves killed when they tried to escape. By the way, nobody's ever made a successful escape from here."

Curt glared at her. "This operation isn't going to last forever, you know."

"Of course I know it," she said. "All mines play out sooner or later. But when this one does, I will have accumulated enough wealth to last me the rest of my life. At that time, the remaining slaves will be disposed of. I'll give my foreman and assistant foreman huge bonuses, and I'll see that the guards are well paid. Then little Morgan will head for San Francisco to live like a queen."

Curt glanced at Missy, whose head hung low. Then he looked at Breanna, wishing there was a way he could take both women out of there to freedom.

Sick at heart, he let his gaze drift to the finely sculptured features of Morgan Montgomery. What a fool he had been! She had deceived him completely.

Suddenly Breanna's words about Satan's power to deceive came home to his heart. He could see it all now. Just like Morgan, the devil had blinded him. The truth and the light of the gospel were now crystal clear.

"Well, that's the story, Langan," said Morgan.

Pasko turned to his boss and said, "So when do we publicly hang the sheriff?"

"Just a minute, Duff," Morgan said. "There's something I haven't told you or any of the boys. There may not be a hanging."

"What're you talkin' about?" Pasko asked. "Before you ever made yourself known to this tin star, you said when he got too close to the operation, we'd bring him here and hang him!"

"Well, something happened that I didn't anticipate."

"Like what?"

Morgan turned her eyes on the sheriff and said, "Little ol' Sally Jayne found herself not having to pretend that she had feelings about this man."

Max swore. "Morgan, what're you sayin'?"

She reached across the table and took hold of Curt's hand. "I'm saying that if the sheriff will throw in with me, he and I will be partners in love and in the gold mining business. When the mine plays out, he and I can go to San Francisco and live like royalty for the rest of our lives. How about it, Curt? You want to toss that badge in the river and throw in with me?"

For a moment Curt couldn't speak. While Morgan waited for him, she said to her men, "Since nursie, here, brought plenty of sage leaves and water bottles, and has taught Clint Byers and Missy how to care for the infected men, we don't need her anymore."

Breanna's face blanched. Lord, she said in her heart, if it's Your time for me to die, I can face it. But if it's not, I'm looking to You to put a stop to this.

Morgan rose from her chair and looked down at Langan. "I really do have tender feelings for you," she said. "We could have a wonderful life together."

Curt knew death would be his fate if he refused. He could almost feel himself standing on the brink of hell.

Breanna silently prayed, Lord, Curt is going to do the right thing. I know it. But please don't let him die lost!

Curt shoved his chair back, stood up, and looked Morgan square in the eye. "I want no part of you or your operation."

Morgan stepped to a desk, yanked open a drawer, and pulled out a Colt .45. As she cocked the hammer, she hissed, "Max! Duff! These two have to die right now! We'll forget the sheriff's necktie party. Let's take them out the back way. They're going to slip and fall down one of the dark mine shafts where they'll never be found."

Both men were instantly on their feet with guns drawn. Max moved up to Langan and rammed the gun's muzzle into his back. "Okay, hotshot lawman, let's go out the back way. You too, nursie."

Missy broke into tears. "No, Morgan! No! Don't do this awful thing!"

Morgan used her free hand to slap the girl again and said, "I told you not to speak until spoken to!"

Suddenly, rapid gunfire exploded outside, punctuated by the whooping and screeching of Indians.

"Max, see what's going on!" Morgan said.

The huge man glanced out the window. "I can't tell anything from here!"

"Well, go out and take a look!"

"Come on, Sheriff. You go out ahead of me. If somebody's waitin' out there to shoot the first person who goes through the door, I'd rather it be you than me."

Morgan pointed her revolver at Curt's head. "Go on. If you don't, I'll drop you where you stand."

Curt gave Breanna a worried look as he passed her and whispered, "Pray for me."

The gunfire continued outside, mingled with the shouts and whoops of Indians. Max carefully opened the door a couple of inches and peered out. He motioned to Curt. "Okay, Sheriff, out the door. I'll get a good look from here."

Curt stepped out on the porch and saw the entire camp alive

with Indians blasting away at Morgan's guards. The guards were firing back from inside the mine, from behind shacks, and from the windows of the bunkhouses. Some already lay dead.

When no bullets came at Langan, Max stuck his head out the door. "We got a whole lot of redskins out here, Morgan! Too many for our men to handle!"

Suddenly a strong hand shoved Curt out of the way and seized Max by the shirt, throwing him hard across the porch. McGurskie plowed into the rail, shattering it, and pitched head-long to the ground ten feet below.

Curt recognized the man on the porch and smiled.

The man said, "Go down there and make sure the big guy's out of commission, Curt. Use his gun to help the Indians."

"Will do. Boy, am I glad to see you! Chief Duvall told me he was sending a man, but he didn't tell me it was you!"

As Curt dashed down the stairs, he saw Arapaho Chief Hawk Wing near the mouth of the cave, leading his men in the fight.

Inside the cabin, Duff Pasko shot at the door, splintering wood from the frame, and took Morgan by the hand. "Let's get outta here!"

Morgan also fired at the door to keep the man out there at bay. "Out the back door!" she said to Pasko.

Breanna and Missy were bending low over the table, still in their chairs, when a strong voice called loudly, "Breanna! Hit the floor!"

Breanna shoved her chair back and grabbed Missy, taking them both to the floor.

As Morgan and Pasko bolted for the rear of the cabin, a Colt .45 unleashed four shots in succession, filling the room with gunsmoke. The slugs chewed into the back wall, but the fleeing pair were already past a sheltering corner.

Pasko pushed the back door open and let Morgan pass into

the dim tunnel, then plunged through. There were brackets anchored into the heavy door frame so it could be barred from the tunnel side. A steel bar leaned against the wall next to the frame.

Pasko slammed the door and quickly dropped the steel rod into the brackets, blocking the cabin door shut. In his haste, he stumbled against the lantern that was always kept burning just outside the door. It dropped off the nail and hit the rock floor, its glass bowl shattering. Kerosene spread out in a pool, and hungry flames spread with it.

Morgan saw the flames race down the slightly slanted tunnel floor toward the dynamite. "Duff!" she gasped. "The flames will set off the dynamite! We'll be blown to pieces or buried alive! We can't go out the tunnel's mouth, bullets are flying everywhere! We don't have time to climb the secret shaft!"

"Yes, we do!" Duff said. "The flames won't reach the boxes for another couple of minutes, and it'll take another couple minutes for it to burn through the wood. C'mon! We can make it!"

Inside the cabin, Breanna looked up from her prone position and saw a tall, wide-shouldered figure step inside. The smoke was thick, and she couldn't make out his face.

The tall man raced to the rear of the cabin, tried to open the door, but found it barred from the outside. He turned back toward Breanna, who was on her feet and helping Missy up.

"*John!*" Breanna gasped. "Oh, John, darling! The Lord answered my prayer! You're here!"

While Breanna rushed into the arms of John Stranger, Missy's attention was drawn to the rear of the room. The gunsmoke was flattening against the ceiling, but there was more smoke coming from the back.

"There's a fire in the tunnel," Missy yelled, "and there's dynamite in storage back there! We've got to get out of here!"

Duff Pasko scurried up the ladder with Morgan Montgomery on his heels. When he reached the top of the ladder, he pressed one hand against the trapdoor and gave it a push. This time it didn't budge.

"Hurry up, Duff!" Morgan said.

"Somethin's wrong." He braced himself on the ladder and used both hands. "The thing's stuck!"

"Well unstick it!" she cried, fear evident in her voice. "That dynamite's going to go off any second!"

Pasko climbed a couple of rungs so he could get his back against the trapdoor. He strained with all his might, but to no avail.

"Hurry, Duff! Hurry!" cried Morgan, on the verge of panic.

Missy's words came back to her. "God says in His Word you'll reap what you sow! Your sin will find you out! Do you think because you choose to ignore God that you won't have to face Him?"

Stark terror clawed at Morgan's stomach.

Pasko's back bowed against the trapdoor.

"I can't budge it! It won't move!"

22

THE GUN BATTLE ENDED shortly before Missy, Breanna, and John Stranger plunged through the door of the cabin and bounded down the steps.

The bodies of some of Morgan's guards lay about the grounds. Those still alive were disarmed and being herded by the Arapahoes to a spot near the bunkhouse. All the slaves who were not in the shacks with scarlet fever were with them.

John took both women by the hand, almost dragging them as he ran, shouting, "Everybody get down! Get down! The mine's going to blow!"

Curt was on the outer perimeter of the crowd of men. As John Stranger and the two women dropped to the earth beside him, he said, "John, the big guy you threw off the porch—Max McGurskie—is dead. He landed on his head when he hit the ground. Must've broken his neck."

Stranger nodded.

"Sheriff," Missy asked, "did Morgan and Duff come out the mouth of the mine?"

"No. I'd have seen them if they had."

"Then they got away through the secret shaft behind the cabin!"

"You mean the one that comes out in the floor of the biggest shed up on top?"

"Yes!"

"Well, then, they did not get away. I put my horse in that shack and then discovered the trapdoor. You know that old wagon with the rocks in its bed?"

"Yes."

"One of its wheels is sitting on top of the trapdoor."

Clint Byers darted out of one of the isolation shacks and headed straight toward Missy. He threw himself on the ground beside her and asked, "You all right, Missy?"

Suddenly the earth shook and a roar rumbled through the mine. John Stranger threw his body over Breanna's. Clint blinked at what he saw, then did the same thing for Missy.

The entire canyon rocked as more explosives went off in a series of rapid, ear-splitting concussions. Smoke, dirt, rocks, and dust vomited out of the mine's mouth.

There was a strange belching sound, and suddenly the big cabin disintegrated in a huge ball of flame and smoke. Broken glass, shattered pieces of furniture, and various chunks and pieces of matter blew a hundred feet into the air.

Curt looked up to see the shack atop the canyon's rim blow to bits from the force of the explosions below. He lamented the loss of a good horse, but was glad to be alive.

What was left of Morgan's cabin began to come back down. Fortunately the heavy pieces hit the ground near where the cabin had stood. Only the lighter materials rained down on them.

As the air cleared, they could see that the tunnel behind the cabin had collapsed on itself, choked with tons of rock and debris.

Curt was first on his feet as John and Clint helped the women up. He looked around and asked, "Everybody all right?"

There was a general affirmative reply.

Curt then stepped close to the five guards who were still alive. "It's all over for you guys," he said flatly. "Morgan, Pasko, and McGurskie are dead. You'll be going to Denver to face murder charges. For now, you'll be locked up in one of the shacks."

The sheriff then turned to the slaves. "I'll be heading to Denver in a little while, but I'll be back in the morning with enough wagons to take you all to town. You men with families will be reunited with them tomorrow. You Chinese and the others who were hired to lay track for the railroad will finally get the chance to go to your jobs."

Wing Loo translated the sheriff's words for his countrymen.

"We'll be taking the sick men to town, too, where they can be cared for under the proper conditions."

"Sheriff..." Harley Trotter said.

"Yes, Harley?"

"Cy and I owe you an apology. We did you wrong, accusin' you of murderin' Willie and Chad. They brought their deaths on themselves. Can you find it in your heart to forgive us?"

"You're forgiven," Langan said with a grin. "Mae's waiting for you at home."

Father and son smiled, nodding.

Langan turned to see John Stranger holding Breanna in his arms and Clint holding Missy.

The sheriff looked at Stranger with a slight frown and said, "I didn't know you two knew each other."

"Oh, we do," said the tall, dark man with twin scars on his right cheek.

"We'll tell you about it sometime," said Breanna with a smile.

"I'd like to hear it. John, I'm sure glad you showed up with Chief Hawk Wing and his men."

"Amen!" said Breanna. "And just in the nick of time! How did this come about, John?"

269

"It's a long story."

"We want to hear it, don't we, everybody?"

Everyone agreed and gathered round.

"Well, I'll make it the short version," said Stranger. "I've been down in Arizona on a special assignment for Chief U.S. Marshal Solomon Duvall. I arrived in town early this morning and went to Duvall's home to let him know how it went in Arizona. He told me of all the kidnappings…of the scarlet fever on the train from San Francisco, and that my Breanna, here, had been abducted to care for men among the kidnapped who had come down with the scarlet fever.

"He told me that Sheriff Langan had ridden out for the mountains about a half hour before I arrived. Said he was going to a ranch to see a woman, then would resume his search for the spot of the illicit operation. He had left a map with Duvall, showing where he was going, and where any deputy U.S. marshals could meet him if they were able to come and help him in the search.

"When the sheriff didn't show up at Eagle Rock, I followed the map to what was supposed to be the woman's ranch. It turned out the ranch did not exist. I realized I was quite close to the Arapaho camp where my friend Hawk Wing is chief. I was sure Hawk Wing would know if there had been any unusual traffic in that area of the mountains, such as hauling men in wagons from the east. When I explained the situation to Hawk Wing, he knew exactly where to bring me."

"We owe a great deal to Hawk Wing and his men," said Langan.

The ex-slaves lifted a rousing cheer for the Arapahoes while the guards stood with downcast countenances.

Hawk Wing and his braves nodded at the group, a pleasant look on their faces. The chief then went to Stranger, saying he and his men would now be leaving. As they headed up the narrow trail, they were given another rousing cheer.

Curt turned back to the two couples and said, "Breanna, can you stay until I come back with the wagons in the morning? Those sick men will need you."

"Of course," she said.

"Clint and I will be happy to help her," put in Missy.

"You want to ride back to town with me, John?" asked Langan.

"Today, you mean?"

"Yes."

"I'll be staying here tonight, Curt," said Stranger. "I want to be near Breanna."

The nurse looked up at him with adoring eyes.

"I understand," said Langan. "We'll empty this place out tomorrow and all ride back to Denver together. When I get back to town late this afternoon, I've got to make a stop at the Union Pacific offices. I've got a big surprise for a certain crooked railroad executive named Floyd Metz."

"Metz?" said Stranger. "I know him. Does he figure into this situation?"

"He sure does. I'll let Breanna explain it to you."

Breanna stepped close to Curt while John, Clint, and Missy looked on.

"Curt," Breanna said softly, "I'm sorry you had to suffer such a bitter disappointment. I know Sally—Morgan—broke your heart."

Langan's features stiffened. "She really pulled one over on yours truly, Breanna. Boy, was I blind!" He paused, scrubbed a nervous hand over his face and said, "Breanna, could I talk to you in private?"

"Of course." Breanna's heart quickened. To John she said,

"Darling, Curt and I need a few minutes alone. Do you mind?"

"Of course not," Stranger said with a grin.

"How about the tool shed, Curt?" she asked.

"Sure."

As Breanna and Curt headed there, Stranger struck up a conversation with Clint and Missy, planning to give them the gospel. He was delighted to learn they both knew the Lord. Clint happily told him how Breanna had witnessed to him on the train and had led him to Christ there in the canyon.

Curt stopped just inside the tool shed door and said, "Breanna, I can never thank you enough for the way you tried to convince me Satan had me deceived about how a person gets to heaven. Your words went deep into my heart. It took this experience with Sal—Morgan—to show me how easily I could be deceived. You heard me say over and over that nobody could deceive me, not the devil nor anyone else."

"Yes."

"Well, I've finally seen the light. Satan has been doing the same thing to me that Morgan did. I want to be saved. Will you help me? I want to be sure I do this thing right."

Curt and Breanna had been gone about ten minutes when John, Clint, and Missy saw them emerge from the tool shed. Breanna was smiling, and the sheriff's face was beaming.

As they walked up, Breanna said to the trio, "Curt has something he wants to tell you!"

Still beaming, Langan said, "I just got saved! This dear lady has been on my case, trying to tell me that Satan was holding me captive. I wouldn't believe it. Well, she's been praying that the Lord would open my eyes to it, and He did! I became captive of a wicked woman, and was totally blinded to it. It stunned me when I learned the truth. It took that to open my eyes to the way Satan also had me in his grasp. Well, Jesus saved me, and you're looking at a captive set free!"

The trio rejoiced with the new convert, then Breanna said, "Missy, I have a cozy little cottage in Denver. I would love to have you come and live with me. You can stay till you figure out what you want to do with your life."

"I already know what I want to do with my life, Miss Breanna."

"Oh?"

"Mm-hmm. I want to be a nurse like you!"

"Well, wonderful! I'll do whatever I can to help you. I think I might even be able to talk Dr. Goodwin into letting you train under him."

Missy was elated. "Oh, Miss Breanna, I'd love that!"

"Would you like to live in my house while you're training? I'm gone most of the time, but you're welcome to move in."

"I'll take you up on it!"

Clint took Missy's hand and said, "I'll be laying track for the railroad, but I'll be in Denver often. Could...could I come and see you when I'm in town?"

"Oh, yes! I want you to come and see me as much as possible!"

At that moment, Todd Blair and Lance Tracy stepped up to their sheriff, expressing appreciation that he had worked so hard to find the mine and free them. They also thanked John Stranger for bringing their captivity to an end and making it possible to return to their families.

"Well, I'd better start for Denver now," said Curt to John and Breanna. "I'll see both of you tomorrow."

They watched the sheriff head for the corral, then John took Breanna by the hand and said, "Darlin', I know you need to look in on your patients, but could we take a short walk over there by the river, first?"

"Take your time, Breanna," Clint said. "Missy and I will see to your patients."

Breanna thanked them with a radiant smile, then said, "I haven't seen Malachi Crowder anywhere."

"He's in the shack with Moses," said Clint.

"Good. You tell them I'll be there to check on Moses in a little while."

"Will do. Let's go, Missy."

Breanna watched them walk away together, then took John's arm and they strolled toward the gurgling river.

"Chalk up another time you saved my life, John. Morgan was going to kill Curt and me. I was praying so hard the Lord would deliver us, and somehow I knew He would."

John folded Breanna in his arms, kissed her tenderly, then said, "The Lord timed it perfectly, sweetheart. He let me arrive in Denver this morning at just the right moment. He knows I need you in this world with me, and He wanted to save Curt from going to hell, too. What a magnificent God we have!"

"Oh, yes! John, I was talking to Missy this morning, trying to encourage her about this whole horrible thing. I reminded her of the song that Moses and the children of Israel sang when they were delivered from Egyptian bondage. Remember they sang, 'I will sing unto the LORD, for he hath triumphed gloriously.' And a few lines later, they sang, 'Thy right hand, O LORD, is become glorious in power: thy right hand, O LORD, hath dashed in pieces the enemy...Who is like unto thee, O LORD, among the gods?' "

"I sure do remember it. And the Lord did exactly that. He literally dashed our enemies into pieces. Must have been a terrifying experience for Morgan and her cohort inside that mountain when the dynamite went off."

"Yes," said Breanna, shuddering.

"I love those words: 'Who is like unto thee, O LORD, among the gods?'"

Breanna smiled at him and said, "Truly there is no god like *our* God!"

OTHER COMPELLING STORIES BY
AL LACY

Books in the Battles of Destiny series:

☛ *A Promise Unbroken*

Two couples battle jealousy and racial hatred amidst a war that would cripple America. From a prosperous Virginia plantation to a grim jail cell outside Lynchburg, follow the dramatic story of a love that could not be destroyed.

☛ *A Heart Divided*

Ryan McGraw—leader of the Confederate Sharpshooters—is nursed back to health by beautiful army nurse Dixie Quade. Their romance would survive the perils of war, but can it withstand the reappearance of a past love?

☛ *Beloved Enemy*

Young Jenny Jordan covers for her father's Confederate spy missions. But as she grows closer to Union soldier Buck Brownell, Jenny finds herself torn between devotion to the South and her feelings for the man she is forbidden to love.

☛ *Shadowed Memories*

Critically wounded on the field of battle and haunted by amnesia, one man struggles to regain his strength and the memories that have slipped away from him.

☛ *Joy from Ashes*

Major Layne Dalton made it through the horrors of the battle of Fredericksburg, but can he rise above his hatred toward the Heglund brothers who brutalized his wife and killed his unborn son?

☛ *Season of Valor*

Captain Shane Donovan was heroic in battle. Can he summon the courage to face the dark tragedy unfolding back home in Maine?

Books in the Journeys of the Stranger series:

☞ *Legacy*

Can John Stranger, a mysterious hero who brings truth, honor, and justice to the Old West, bring Clay Austin back to the right side of the law...and restore the code of honor shared by the woman he loves?

☞ *Silent Abduction*

The mysterious man in black fights to defend a small town targeted by cattle rustlers and to rescue a young woman and child held captive by a local Indian tribe.

☞ *Blizzard*

When three murderers slated for hanging escape from the Colorado Territorial Prison, young U.S. Marshal Ridge Holloway and the mysterious John Stranger join together to track down the infamous convicts.

☞ *Tears of the Sun*

When John Stranger arrives in Apache Junction, Arizona, he finds himself caught up in a bitter war between sworn enemies: the Tonto Apaches and the Arizona Zunis.

Books in the Angel of Mercy series:

☞ *A Promise for Breanna*

The man who broke Breanna's heart is back. But this time, he's after her life.

☞ *Faithful Heart*

Breanna and her sister Dottie find themselves in a desperate struggle to save a man they love, but can no longer trust. Is young Dottie Harper destined to a life of fear, or can peace and happiness come again to her faithful heart?

Available at your local Christian bookstore